Sally Hawkins was born in Rotherham, South Yorkshire, and now lives in Surrey with her husband and four dogs. She has two grown up children and works as a volunteer for an international dog rescue group, fostering, rehabilitating and rehoming abused and neglected dogs.

Dedication

To Carrie, Jim, Steve and Fabienne, for your unfailing
support and enthusiasm.

Sally Hawkins

ELISE

AUSTIN MACAULEY PUBLISHERS™

LONDON * CAMBRIDGE * NEW YORK * SHARJAH

A CIP catalogue record for this title is available from the British Library.

ISBN 9781787102286 (Paperback)
ISBN 9781787102293 (E-Book)

www.austinmacauley.com

First Published (2018)
Austin Macauley Publishers Ltd.
25 Canada Square
Canary Wharf
London
E14 5LQ

Chapter One

Elise was extremely nervous, but she forced herself to smile, in an effort to bolster her self-confidence in preparation for the day ahead. She had only been away for four weeks, but it seemed like a lifetime. She parked her car in front of the huge glass-fronted office block and got out. Having quickly checked her face in the wing mirror and smoothed out her skirt, she ran up the steps and into reception.

"Morning, Sam," she said, as she walked across the lobby. "Long time no see." The security guard hardly glanced up from his paper; he had recognised her car and didn't feel the need to be sociable. "Morning, Elise."

"Hope they haven't changed the door code." Sam grudgingly checked his computer screen. "Nope, still the same. Did you have a nice holiday?" With his attention firmly back on a particularly tricky anagram, Elise decided that it was hardly necessary to answer, but well-mannered as always, she responded, "Yes, it was lovely, nice to be back here, though." With that Elise headed briskly up the stairs.

Sam was right, nothing appeared to have changed. Elise punched the code into the panel and entered the office. She checked her watch; she should have enough time to get organised before the others arrived. She made for the ladies' and locked herself into the end cubicle. She felt jittery and her stomach was playing its old trick of tying itself in knots. "Just breathe deeply," she told herself. Suddenly, she heard a clatter of heels and the sound of voices. Elise went from trying to breathe deeply to trying not to breathe at all and carefully lifted her feet from the floor.

Elise, perched precariously on the loo with her arms around her knees, closed her eyes tight. Of all the people she could have done without, Alice, her arch nemesis, was at the top of her list. Their mutual dislike was only surpassed by Alice's ability to crush Elise with her vile scathing insults. Where Alice went, everyone followed, and she had swept the other girls along in her tirade against Elise. No one had even tried to defend her and egged on by Alice, they had eventually joined in the campaign of hate.

"Oh God, the Frog is coming back today." Elise froze. She knew only too well the drawling tones of Alice.

"You need to chill, Alice, you should be thanking your lucky stars that she sorted out that bloody mess or we would all be seriously fucked." Elise recognised Kate's breathless comments, and felt slightly mollified. "Not all bad then," she thought.

"Oh, well, at least we won't have to put up with Kelly getting the bloody coffees mixed up any more, and I swear I would have died if Gerry hadn't bought that bloody dishwasher. I have to admit she did keep me amused; especially her outfits. I used to piss myself every day, waiting to see what she had dragged out of the rag basket." Alice laughed loudly. "And I won't have to put up with any more of that French shit now she's back."

"No, and at least the reps won't be screaming about you being rude to their clients, fucking up their diaries and not getting their expenses cleared! Anyway, don't be too hasty. Remember she's been in Paris, they might have posher charity shops there," Kate added with a nervous giggle.

Elise cringed, and felt her cheeks starting to flush. She could live with the 'clothes' insults, but who on earth would have let Alice loose on her clients?

"Eric will be happy to get back to his proper job. I don't think he liked being stuck in the office all day. I was thinking of telling Gerry that I would take over permanently as his account administrator. You know, he calls me 'Peevy'. He told me it was Russian for beautiful."

Elise, despite her predicament, had to muffle a giggle. Trust Arek!

"Alice, you know I love you, and I really did want to tell you before, you know… it's just I didn't want to hurt your feelings, but well, all the reps call you P.V. He's the only one who says it to your face. It's not really Russian."

"Oh, must be Polish then? Eric's really got a thing for me, hasn't he?"

'Peevy' was a new one on Elise; she had never heard any of the reps call Alice anything other than 'Dumb'. Maybe things had changed since she had been away.

"Alice, it's not Polish. It's… well, it's English." Kate sounded as if she was about to have an asthma attack. "It's just initials, not really a word."

"Kate, for fuck's sake, don't tell me you're jealous of Eric and me. Anyway, I'm only playing him along. As if I'd be seen dead with a rep! To be honest, you're welcome to him, I just get the impression he doesn't like girls with big arses."

"I'm not jealous. Jesus, Alice, they are initials, short for "Pretty Vacant.""

Elise almost lost her grip on the loo seat.

Alice giggled loudly. "Don't be silly, Kate, I told you it's Russian. You really are jealous, aren't you!"

"It's not fucking Russian. They all take the piss out of you, and if you didn't always have your head up your arse, you might have figured it out for yourself."

Elise couldn't believe it; little Kate daring to have a go at Alice! Maybe things had changed!

Alice was apparently steaming. Elise wondered if she could lean forward enough to spy through the keyhole without losing her grip, then she realised that there wasn't one and sat back feeling slightly disappointed.

"You two-faced bitch, I thought you were my best friend," screeched Alice.

"Look, Alice, please, there's no need to be so nasty. I just don't want to see you get hurt. Arek had a thing for Elise for years. Everyone knows about it; well, apart from you." Kate's voice drained away.

Elise was stunned by the revelation about Arek. She had no idea of a 'thing' between them; they were just good friends, who worked well together.

Screams and the sound of splashing water filled the air, followed by the noise of someone choking and lots of coughing.

"Alice, get off me, I was just trying... oh my God, look what you've done to my fucking hair." Elise could still hear a bit of a scuffle going on; this was definitely turning into an exciting morning.

"Don't worry Kate; no one is going to take any notice of your barnet now the scarecrow is back in town."

Kate's voice had adopted a more desperate tone, "Please, Alice! Elise is harmless, just leave her alone, don't stir up any more shit. Gerry swore you were on your last warning after what you did to her."

"Oh, fucking 'Elise' is it now? Gerry can fuck off if he thinks I'm going to kowtow to him or that stupid Elsie, and why the hell does he think he has to go arse-licking to 'Miss Dress to Depress'? Uncle Mike would kill him if he says two words to me about that miserable cow, and that fucking rep is history."

"Your Uncle Mike really hasn't been that impressed with your efforts to take over Elise's job. Gerry's going nuts 'cos you've fucked up royally on everything whilst she's been away," muttered Kate.

"You mean the fact that Gerry can't do shit without Lanky Elsie holding his hand; he's just trying to dump on everybody else."

"Uncle Mike is just a money grabber, that's all; shitting himself at the thought of his profits going down. If he thought I was going to rush around like that idiot, he must be mad.

Anyway, I don't give a shit. My mum would kill him if he ever tried to say shit to me."

Elise, still balancing herself on the loo seat, remembered her first meeting with Mike. He had been sitting in what was now Gerry's office, when she had nervously poked her head round the door.

It was Elise's first ever job interview. Elise had felt terribly guilty about not fulfilling her grandmother's dreams for her to go to university. School had finished, Elise's A-level results were better than she had even dreamed of, but now she was not really sure what she was going to do. Mother had dismissed any notion of Elise studying for a degree. "What's the point in spending all that money, why can't she just get a job and earn her keep like I did?" Grandmere's face had taken on a shade of dark red that Elise had never seen before. She was incandescent with rage, but Elise's mother didn't appear to notice and wandered out of the room. Elise was relieved; the thought of going away to university terrified her. She realised that for the first time she could remember, she had sided with her mother against her beloved Grandmere.

Grandmere wasn't one for giving up without a fight and had tried again the following day: "But it's such a waste, you are such a clever girl."

"She's not clever, she's just never had anything better to do than stick her nose in stupid books. Anyway, I told you it costs a fortune, and who is going to pay for that?"

Grandmere had shaken her head. "Well, I can't fight both of you," she said.

Three days later, Grandmere had handed her a piece of paper whilst they were eating breakfast.

"I want you to give this man a call. He is a friend of Alex Forbes, and is looking for help to run his wine importing business. They got talking at the golf club and Alex kindly mentioned your name and Mr Fenton is interested in meeting you."

Elise wasn't sure how her grandmother's solicitor even knew her name, but feeling terribly guilty over refusing to go to university, she took the piece of paper. 'Mike Fenton, First Blush Wine Importers'. The address was in Clapham, which wasn't too scary.

"He's opening up a new office. They have parking spaces, so you'll be able to drive," added her grandmother. "He's going to be there tomorrow afternoon and will be expecting you."

Mike Fenton was surprisingly nice, and very complimentary. "Well, you are an extremely accomplished young lady. You did your French A level at fourteen?" Elise had resisted the urge to apologise.

"My grandmother is French, so I'm bilingual."

"Yes, yes, of course, Alex mentioned that." Mike nodded his head. "Excellent. Just what we are looking for, and I hear that you are a budding wine connoisseur to boot!"

This time Elise did turn a shade of rose. "Well, my grandmother paid for me to attend wine tasting and appreciation courses as birthday presents."

"And you still had time for IT, business and maths?" At that point, Gerry had stuck his head around the door. Mike stood up.

"Elise, I'd like to introduce you to Gerry. He's going to be my Sales and Accounts Manager. We are a very small operation, so everyone's going to be doing a bit of everything. Gerry, come in and say hello to our new Office Administrator." Mike headed for the door. "I've managed to bag those two reps, both fantastic guys," he said to Gerry as he was leaving. "They'll be coming in tomorrow, to meet with you and go over the details."

Mike nodded again at Elise. "Thank you for coming in. Do you think you could start tomorrow and help Gerry get everything up and running? I'm usually out in the field, so Gerry's going to need your help." Elise had conjured up an image of Mike wearing wellies, and leaning on a spade. She nodded vigorously. "Yes, of course I can, and thank you."

"Gerry, can you take it from here and sort out the salary, etc. I think this young lady is going to be worth her weight in champagne!" Mike had left in a rush, leaving Gerry frowning in his wake.

Gerry strode into the office. He was extremely tall, with an elaborately-styled shock of impressively black hair and expertly-manicured designer stubble. He was wearing what appeared to Elise to be a very loud suit with black lapels accessorised with a pale pink shirt.

"Hi, Elise, is it?" he asked, in an accent that would have put royalty to shame. Elise offered a shy smile in response. "Excellent!" he exclaimed. "I'm Gerald-Christian Thompson-Bartlett, but you may call me Gerry." Elise smiled again, not really sure what to say.

Gerry swung himself into a chair and casually picked up Elise's certificates. He glanced at Elise and then quickly read down her C.V. "Oh good, you speak French, and you know about spreadsheets and the like? That's what we're going to need here. You won't mind being stuck in the office all day? Excellent, of course, when things take off, I'm going to be literally snowed under, so I will be funnelling all the boring stuff down to you, so that I can deal with all the big fish."

That bit was music to Elise's ears, and her head nodded vigorously. Gerry handed the sheaf of certificates back to Elise, with a dismissive look on his face. She felt the little bit of confidence that Mike had given her ebbing away, and stared at her feet when he stated what her pay would be.

He smiled to himself. Bargain basement salaries were always music to his ears, and this strange-looking girl would probably have agreed to work for free if he'd had the balls to ask.

"Now, do you think you could run down to Frederico's and get us a couple of coffees? Freddie's a great friend of mine and his espresso is just the best! Oh, and don't forget to get a receipt, we can make this our first official business meeting and expense them."

"Would you like a double espresso?" asked Elise.

"Oh, God no, a latte for me, but ask Freddie for a double shot, and get whatever you like of course. There's an alleyway straight on to the high street, so don't let my drink get cold."

Elise scuttled off to find Frederico's, feeling relieved that her first task wasn't too onerous.

Gerry sank back in his chair. Elise certainly wouldn't have been his first, second or come to that, third choice, but she looked geeky enough to be able to work a bloody computer, and he was sure that with his public-school confidence and charm, he would soon have her running around doing everything he asked. He smiled to himself. "This would all work out perfectly!" He would enjoy a very cushy ride, whilst he learnt enough about the business to get his own venture up and running. Gerry didn't see, in all fairness, how he could possibly keep the world waiting for him for much longer.

Elise ran down the stairs and down the side alley. The café was just across the road. There were a couple of empty tables and chairs outside. Elise ran in and stood breathlessly at the counter.

A man appeared behind the bar with a huge smile on his face. "Thirsty?" he asked. His smile was very infectious and Elise couldn't help but smile back. "No, just a bit nervous, it's my first day at work. Gerry sent me for coffee." The man didn't appear to recognise the name Gerry, but Elise couldn't remember the rest of his name so she stood there quietly.

"What can I get for, er, Gerry, was it? And what would you like?"

"Two lattes, one with an extra shot and a receipt please." The man nodded.

"What name shall I put on your drink?"

"Elise, please."

The man quickly made the drinks and brought them over to the counter. "There you are, Elise. I'm Freddie, by the way, hope I'll be seeing a lot more of you, now you are working round here."

"Thank you," she answered, picking up the drinks and carefully pocketing the receipt.

"Oh, and good luck," called Freddie as she left.

"Nothing much has changed with her," thought Elise. Trying not to get cramp in her thighs, she gripped the loo seat with both hands, fearing she might do a nose dive on to the tiles if they didn't leave soon.

Then, an alien thought struck her. "Why am I hiding in the loo from that bitch? Come on, Elise, grow a pair." And with that, Elise plonked her feet on the floor, gave the flush an almighty push and flung open the cubicle door.

"Well, hello, girls." Elise smiled at their shocked faces and hanging jaws. "Long time no see. Fermez la bouche, Alice. You wouldn't want to kill a poor fly, now would you?"

Chapter Two

Four weeks earlier.

Elise woke with a start; she lay still, trying to get her bearings. As her eyes adjusted to the dark, she realised with great relief that she was on her sofa in her tiny living room.

Her head was banging and she ached all over. She pulled herself into a sitting position and felt a stinging sensation on the backs of both knees; her left arm was hurting, and just for good measure her back was crying as well. Elise put her hand behind her right knee. Her fingers located a very large hole in her tights; the frayed edges had somehow glued themselves to her skin. Elise slowly stood up and flicked on the light.

She checked her watch; it was one o'clock in the morning.

Half of Elise's brain was desperately trying to recall the events of yesterday evening whilst the other half was doing its best to forget. She decided to go with the 'forget' side for the moment, and headed into her little bathroom. The sleeve on her jumper was covered in dirt and her bare elbow, complete with dried blood, was poking through it. She didn't care much about the cardigan; whilst it may have started life as a 'fashion item', too many dunks in a hot wash by its previous owner had reduced it to a saggy sack with the colour resembling something between mud and grey.

Elise shrugged, she could easily replace it. The charity shop down the road always had a 'sale rail'.

She carefully peeled off the rest of her clothes and squeezed into the shower.

The water hitting her shoulders alerted her to previously undiscovered injuries. She quickly ducked her head under the shower and saw the water turning brown as yet more dirt was released from her tangled mass of hair. Bending her neck was not helping the headache, but unfortunately for Elise, the shower head had not been designed for someone who was five feet eight, and much as she hated being so tall, there was nothing she could do about it. Her only consolation was that at twenty-four years old, she was reasonably convinced that she had at last stopped growing.

Elise wrapped a towel around her head, and pulled on her old towelling robe; it, too, had seen better days, but she had no time for clothes, and could see no point in replacing something that no one else would ever see. She walked into her bedroom and sat on the bed. Memories were starting to flood back, and Elise bawled her eyes out. She checked her watch again, nearly three a.m. She couldn't sleep, her mind was jumping all over the place, and the conclusion that her already pathetic life was going to be even more miserable after her 'evening of hell' made her want to hide under the duvet forever.

Elise lived quite a solitary existence; her Saturday visit to see her grandmother was the only time she went out, unless it was to work, or a quick trip to the shops. She did not seek out friends or acquaintances, and really didn't understand how relationships worked. Her overwhelming shyness crippled her whenever she had to deal with people face to face, so she preferred to steer clear whenever possible of anything that would force her to mix with strangers.

She had always been timid; her mother's open distaste and scathing comments had removed any sense of self-worth at a very early age. The fact that she had been a head taller than all her classmates, and extremely skinny to boot, had made her a target for every would-be bully in the school. It was almost as if they could smell her fear and from day one, they had descended on her like a pack of wolves at every opportunity. The misery went on for thirteen long years, until she was finally able to escape.

The only time Elise had felt confident and capable was when she was behind her desk at work. Alice had managed to take even that away and now she was facing complete humiliation. She knew there was going to be a huge fallout, and as usual felt totally responsible.

Elise gave up trying to sleep, and grabbed whatever came to hand from her wardrobe. She felt happiest when she could walk around unnoticed by everyone, and camouflaged herself with the darkest plainest clothes that the charity shops had on offer. She was suddenly struck by another scary thought. "Where the hell was her car?" Elise had a vague recollection of the two wine reps helping her up the narrow steps to her flat. She knew that she certainly hadn't been capable of driving herself.

She tiptoed from her bedroom across her living room and through the 'cupboard' which served as a kitchen, and peaked out of the window. "Thank God." Her beloved car was sitting calmly in its usual spot. How it got there would be something she could worry about later. At least she would have no excuses to be late for work.

Elise checked her watch, seven a.m. That would give her enough time to get into the office, get herself settled (as she put it) and be extremely busy with her head down and headset in place by the time anyone else arrived. She still wasn't feeling at all well, her head throbbed, and her back ached, but Elise had never taken a day off sick in her life and it had never entered her head to do so now.

As she pulled into the parking lot and, as always, selected the spot furthest away from the office to leave the more sought-after places for her co-workers, Elise's stomach was more knotted than usual, her eyes were stinging and her cheeks burned. The memories of last night's horror were becoming less and less fuzzy and the worst bits kept replaying themselves over and over in her head, like some awful tune that was permanently on repeat.

Elise hardly ever went out; all her spare cash went into her deposit account towards buying a flat. Although the little place above a shop that she currently rented was inexpensive, she considered it a complete waste of money and all she could think about was buying somewhere of her own. She was at a loss to understand why people spent a fortune on drinks in some poncy wine bar, when they could get better quality stuff for a tenth of the price at the local supermarket.

Elise never paid any attention to her clothes; she was "Far too tall and too painfully thin" to do justice to any outfit, according to her mother. Her grandmother had insisted on Elise attending the school prom, and had bought her a beautiful gown to wear. As the taxi pulled up outside their little cottage, her mother happened to be coming out of her study. She gazed critically at her daughter, shook her head sadly and said, "Well, Mother, are you trying to make her into a laughing stock? She looks ridiculous!"

Elise had run up to her room and pulled off the dress. She watched from the window as the taxi drove away and was determined that she would never ever put herself through anything like that again. From then on, Elise had refused to shop anywhere other than charity shops and, even then, headed only for their 'SALE' rails. Occasionally, she felt a pang of embarrassment when she overheard catty comments from the other girls in the office, but generally wore her badge of disinterest with pride; let them others spend hundreds on stupid designer stuff. How could that compare with owning a place of your own?

Elise had decided when she was just a little girl that she was never ever going to be the flirty fun girl that could chat to everyone, and be popular with the boys, so she worked hard to develop the persona of a woman who cared nothing for appearances and everything for being indispensable.

At work, she prided herself on knowing how to do everything and being the person everyone went to if they needed any help; anything from doing the coffee run to tracking down errant delivery drivers fell to her.

Elise loved her job; she felt like part of the furniture, as if she had been there for ever. Everyone appreciated her and she had no qualms about accepting responsibility for even the slightest thing that went wrong, and would happily work around the clock if the necessity arose. She was never required to leave the safety of her office, administrating everything via phone or laptop with quiet confidence, perfect French and great attention to detail.

Everything that could possibly be required by her colleagues was always to hand, and every client knew that one call to Elise would be all that was needed to ensure a successful outcome to even the smallest of niggles.

She had hidden herself quite happily beneath a cloak of 'no nonsense' and had felt so safe and secure inside the 'little bubble' that she had created for herself that she had no thought of ever emerging.

The arrival of Alice changed everything.

Gerry had run in one morning and dumped an envelope in front of her. "Alice will be joining us next week. Can you stick her on the payroll? You'll find everything you need in there."

Elise was intrigued. "I didn't know we had a vacancy," she said.

"Well, obviously, we don't know. Just be nice to her."

Elise was shocked at the new girl's very generous salary, which was several pegs above her own, but she didn't venture any further comments; this woman must be a serious 'highflier'.

Elise had disliked Alice at first sight, and the feeling was definitely mutual, but whereas Elise went out of her way to guiltily compensate for her own feelings, Alice took great pleasure in making Elise's life a misery.

For some strange reason, this nasty, spiteful girl had made Elise's stomach churn from the minute she had first sauntered into the office, caked in make-up, wearing an outfit that would make anyone blush and tottering along on the most ridiculous heels Elise had ever seen. Alice nodded her head at Elise as she wobbled up to her desk.

"Hello, I'm Gerry's new assistant. Who are you then?"

"I'm Elise, I'm the…" Alice cut her off mid-sentence.

"Well, I can't have that. God forbid, someone might mix us up. You'll have to change your name." She paused for a moment, and then with a nasty smile, said, "From now on you can be 'Elsie'. It suits you much better anyway. How old are you?"

"I'm twenty-four," answered Elise, her nerves beginning to show, and her cheeks burn.

"Christ, I thought you were about fifty," said Alice, laughing, "Anyway, run and get me a latte, and hurry up 'cos I'm dying of thirst." Alice then wandered over to Gerry's office and made herself comfortable in his chair.

Elise followed her. "Sorry Alice, I just wanted to let you know that we have a little kitchen, so you can make your own coffee, if you want?"

Alice looked across at Elise. "Make my own coffee? At work? I mean, like, who does that? God, that's like, one of those losers who, like, make their own sandwiches!"

Elise blushed, hoping that Alice wouldn't see her little Tupperware box in the kitchen fridge. Elise was still hesitant; she didn't have any cash on her to pay for Alice's latte. She tried again:

"Do you want a large latte, it's £2.50 or a medium one for £2.00?"

"A large one, of course. Do we have to pay for it?"

"Yes, apart from on Friday when Gerry has a staff meeting, and puts the coffees through as expenses."

Alice sighed and fiddled about in her handbag. She threw a five-pound note across the desk to Elise. "Here," she said. "And keep the change, you can use it when you get me another one tomorrow."

Elise took the money and obediently set off to the coffee shop, still in shock. She had been working there for five years and felt that if, for a reason she could not fathom, a name change was required, it should most certainly be Alice's. However, she could not compete with Alice's sweeping self-confidence and had silently nodded in agreement when Alice had proceeded to inform everyone of the name change, and any raised eyebrows were met with Alice's assurance that it had been 'Elsie's' suggestion. Other colleagues, who appeared to be equally afraid of risking Alice's wrath, quietly still called her by her real name but only when Alice was not within earshot.

Elise's initial dislike had quickly spiralled into fear. She really was terrified of Alice and would go to any lengths to avoid 'annoying' her, which would then mean enduring her vitriol for days to come.

Alice had never made any attempt to hide her utter contempt for Elise, and her forceful nature meant that the other girls followed her lead, perhaps fearing that any hint of dissension would not be tolerated.

Elise had been personally responsible bringing in Armand Duval. Mike had brought a bottle of wine into the office. He, Elise and the reps had all commented on it, and Mike had handed the bottle to Elise. "You couldn't try and track this down for us, could you? It could be a best-seller."

Elise had set about tracing the vineyard, and had soon tracked down Armand, who ran the Wine Makers distribution network. He now supplied them with all of their 'top of the range' wines. He and Elise spoke almost daily on the phone. Armand always sounded full of life; Elise loved hearing his voice and he was always full of compliments about her knowledge of wine, and more importantly, her perfect French.

Elise knew every supplier and customer by name. Her shyness evaporated whenever she picked up a phone. In the office, she treated everyone with great respect, ensuring that their two representatives had everything they needed to go out and win new business.

She tried to impress upon Alice the importance of maintaining excellent customer relations with both their suppliers and their small, but growing list of clients. Elise had never been told exactly what Alice's role was supposed to be.

They already had Kate who did all the cold calling, and Kelly, the office junior, who tried her best; not being the 'sharpest tool in the box'. It had taken the poor girl three months just to master the four-digit code to open the office door.

Arek and Dave were their two 'go-getting' young sales reps. Arek was just as driven as Elise and as knowledgeable about the wine business. The two often worked into the wee hours discussing new customers, working on strategies to increase sales.

Elise had actually gone into Gerry's office and asked him what the role of his 'new assistant' was to be. As far as she knew, she did everything necessary to keep him on track.

Gerry, looking harried as usual, had simply waved her away and said, "Just, you know, show her the bloody ropes, then she can work with Kate, or maybe one of the reps?"

Elise had spent long, pain-filled hours 'going over the ropes' about every aspect of the wine importing business when Alice had first arrived, and had had to hide her dismay at the young woman's complete ignorance of, and lack of interest in the wine business.

Elise had done everything to make Alice welcome, and assumed her apparent indifference was due to extreme shyness. At the end of her first week, Elise had invited her to join her and the two reps at their regular lunch hour wine tasting session, to check out new arrivals from the exporters, and discuss the marketing potential.

Alice was horrified at the thought that she would be expected to 'work' during her precious 'shopping' hour, but thought she may be able to turn a little flirting with the reps to her advantage. She had seated herself opposite Elise and had furtively watched her expertly uncork the wine, and pour a very small amount into Alice's glass. Alice took this as a slight.

"Sorry, are you trying to take the piss?" she said, glaring at Elise. The reps had responded with muffled giggles, and Alice reddened. She watched Elise staring at the wine, sloshing it around in the glass and actually sticking her nose in it. Elise had then invited her to comment.

"So, Alice, would you like to start? What do you think of the bouquet?" Alice was actually thinking about a pair of shoes she had seen beckoning to her from a shop window on her way to work that morning and was fuming that her precious shopping time was being wasted cooped up with this pretentious cow.

She gazed around the room, and wondered what the hell Elise was on about. Elise tried again: "Can you describe the smell? Does it remind you of anything?"

Alice sniffed the glass. "It smells a bit like cherry coke," she offered. She looked up to see the reps nodding and winking at each other; Arek was laughing out loud.

"Coke?" he spluttered. "You are fucking joking me."

Elise bowed her head, realising that her efforts to help had been taken by Alice as an attempt to show off. She could feel her fury from across the room and cowered like a cornered mouse waiting for the cat to pounce.

"Sorry, Elsie, I haven't got time for this shit." With that, Alice threw the contents of her glass at Elise and stormed out, banging the door so hard that the partition walls shook.

Dave burst into laughter. Arek jumped out of his chair, and was about to go after Alice, but Elise, shook her head at him. She knew that she would never be forgiven.

That incident had been the catalyst for Alice's reign of terror.

Alice had a huge repertoire of scathing looks and nasty comments which she unleashed on a daily basis at Elise, who shrank into her chair and tried to hide whenever Alice strode into the office. She bore a striking resemblance to a particularly evil girl at school who had never missed an opportunity to torture her. Elise tried hard to separate the two images, but her brain refused, and instead fused them together creating one huge hideous monster that made Elise's stomach tie itself in knots and her brain to turn to mush if Alice so much as looked in her direction.

Kate had, at the request of Elise, tried to help Alice master the 'cold calling' technique, but Alice's efforts veered more towards 'icy', her calls invariably involving the phrase "You are not listening to me", followed by "Suit yourself" and ending with Alice throwing her headset down on the desk and rolling her eyes.

Alice refused to allow work to interfere with her social life, and had been heard on many occasions telling some poor unfortunate that she would call them back later, as she needed to check her Facebook.

Elise had wanted to cry, and in desperation had quietly spoken to Gerry, but he seemed strangely reluctant to dismiss Alice, or even talk to her about her behaviour, instead she was offered a 'new and exciting role' which basically kept her out of harm's way and prevented her from losing any more potential clients.

Chapter Three

Elise tried to calm herself as she got out of the car; she tugged at her skirt, an offering from yet another charity shop sale rail, and hurried across the car park. She entered the building and waited far too long, as usual, for Sam, the security guard to look up. He gave her a cursory glance before getting back to his crossword and she scuttled across the foyer to the stairs. However hard she tried, she could not get rid of the images of last night, of dealing with the realisation that aside from feeling like a fool, she had, yet again, been the victim of one of Alice's nasty tricks.

Elise's 'nightmare' had started early on the previous morning. By lunch time she had had just about her fill of Alice, who having feigned illness and staggered out early the day before had sashayed in two hours late and then proceeded to bounce around like a school girl, whispering and giggling with her 'side-kick', Kate.

Kate had at least had the decency to look ever so slightly apologetic when Elise had asked them ever so politely to be a bit quieter as she couldn't hear her client; Alice had stuck out her tongue and given Elise the finger.

Elise hadn't been able to resist sneaking a peak at Alice's amazing new hair; it had not only gained glowing highlights, but seemed to have grown a foot overnight. Her eyelashes had taken on the appearance of extremely exotic caterpillars. To cap it all, she had refused point-blank to go near her keyboard for fear of chipping one of her newly painted red pointed talons.

Alice and Kate had spent their lunch break leaning over Alice's laptop, Kate furiously typing whilst Alice with her phone glued to her ear dictated. Elise had no idea what was going on and was by now past caring. She busied herself sifting through her emails. She needed to double-check the restaurant booking she had made for Mike and their main supplier today. Armand was coming in from Paris, to check over the new marketing brochure, and he was bringing a VIP by the name of Jean-Pierre along for the ride.

"Not exactly keen to learn," Armand had said, in his latest email, "but he is just out of boarding school. This trip is part of his eighteenth birthday present, and an introduction to the family business. Apparently, he has been blabbing to your colleagues about it on Facebook! Frankly, I could do without it but he is the son of the vineyard owner, it's his first trip abroad without Mere and Pere, so I am basically the babysitter! He is a spoilt brat, and my boss will have my bollocks if anything goes wrong. I am on my guard, and won't be letting the little shit out of my sight. He certainly seems to have made an impression with one of your colleagues."

Elise was furious; she didn't have to think too hard to figure out which colleague that would be. How bloody unprofessional. Trust Alice to track him down; no wonder she had been banging on about the brochures ever since she had thrown a 'hissy' about having to collect them from the printers. Armand and the vineyard was the main feature, with an article featuring Jean-Pierre as the heir to the 'throne'. Alice seemed to be surgically attached to bloody Facebook, and judging by the office gossip, she certainly had a penchant for younger men.

Thankfully, Armand and Jean-Pierre were booked to return to Paris on the Eurostar at six p.m. so there would be no opportunity for Armand's bollocks to be put at risk. Elise leaned back in her chair, relieved that every 't' had now been crossed. The restaurant had confirmed the booking, and Mike had confirmed receipt of the new brochure, along with last year's figures and next year's predictions, so hopefully all would go well.

Elise checked her watch; it was a nervous habit that she couldn't seem to kick; nearly three o'clock, and no frantic phone calls from Mike. She took a deep breath. "Panic over," she thought.

"Els, could you come in for a minute?" Elise looked up and saw Gerry waving at her. She grabbed her note pad and headed for his office. Gerry was looking more flustered than usual. "Is everything okay?" she asked.

"Sit down, Els. I just need a quick chat."

Gerry, to his credit, had refused to call Elise, "Elsie", but couldn't quite bring himself to say "Elise" when Alice was around, so he settled for "Els", which didn't appear to cause offence to either party.

"I'm just a bit worried, you know, about Armand. I don't think he came all the way here just to see a bloody brochure. Did he say anything to you about any other meeting with our competitors? There's lots of competition out there and they are much bigger than us, there's no way we can compete with the big guys."

Elise suddenly felt really sorry for Gerry, and she knew as well as he did that their company was almost totally dependent on Armand's business.

"It will be fine, Gerry, don't worry. Armand likes the personal touch, you know, he likes small companies and he has told me that he isn't comfortable with big impersonal importers. We speak nearly every day; I'm sure he would have told me if there were any problems. We do treat him like royalty, and he wouldn't get that with anyone else, so I can't see why he would look elsewhere."

Gerry seemed to be reassured by Elise's response.

"No, you are right... don't know why I'm getting stressed. I honestly really appreciate all the work that you do, and I know you put up with shit from that idiot Alice, but she's very young, so you know, I just put it down to immaturity. She's like a good wine, I'm sure she'll be better when she matures."

Gerry laughed appreciatively at his own joke. "Sorry for taking up so much of your time, I know you are busy, but thanks."

Elise smiled to herself; she had only been in there for five minutes.

"No worries, Gerry. It's only ten past three, and there's not much left on my 'to-do list' anyway."

Elise opened Gerry's door, and much to her annoyance saw Alice and her evil twin Kate hovering around her desk.

"Anything wrong?" she asked.

"No," said Alice with her usual grin.

"Everything is absolutely fine, except, we've run out of milk, and you know what Gerry's like about his afternoon tea. Oh, and get some decent bickies as well."

"Who the fuck says 'bickies'?" thought Elise. She was furious with herself as she grabbed her bag and trotted down to the shop. Why the fuck did she act like that nasty bitch's errand boy? Elise had already been the office administrator for two years when she was Alice's age, and she swore she had been more mature at eleven than Alice.

Elise came back with the milk and biscuits, and as always handed the receipt for Gerry to sign so she could sort out the petty cash.

"Thanks for that, Els, perfect timing. I'm feeling the need for a sugar rush."

"I'd better go and put the kettle on then, you hang on to the Hobnobs." Elise headed back to the little kitchenette tucked in behind the staff room.

Alice was in there slathering on lipstick in front of the mirror.

"Sorry, Elsie," she said without turning around.

"The mirror in the bog is too small."

Elise found the smell of Alice's 'Angel' overwhelming, and put her hand over her nose. Alice saw the reflection in the mirror.

"What's up, Elsie, something bothering you?"

Elise ran into the kitchen and closed the door, determined to stay put until Alice and her perfume departed.

A few minutes later, with Alice gone, and the 'Angel' fading, Elise walked back out through the staff room and delivered Gerry's tea.

"Better get back to work," she said, and went back to her desk. As she logged back in to her emails, she heard Kate screaming at her.

"Els, come quick, Alice has fainted. She's in the loo and I can't unlock the door."

Elise jumped up and ran to the toilets. "She's probably been overcome with the fumes from that bloody perfume," she thought, grabbing her trusty screwdriver from her drawer.

"Get out of the way, Kate. How can I open the door with you standing there?" Kate stepped aside, and watched as Elise expertly manoeuvred the emergency release and flung open the door. Alice was on the floor, her arms and head draped elegantly across the toilet seat.

Gerry was banging wildly on the door. "What's going on? Is everything okay?"

"Everything is fine, Gerry, no worries," shouted back Elise. She grabbed Alice's ankles.

"Stop," squeaked Kate. "Watch out for her hair. It cost a bloody fortune."

"Kate, don't be silly, we have to get her out."

Elise looked at Kate who was standing looking on with horror.

"Do you think you can squeeze in and get your arms under her shoulders?"

"You're the skinny one," protested Kate.

"There's no way I can get in there."

Elise let go of Alice's ankles and manoeuvred herself into the cubicle. She managed to get a grip under the girl's armpits and directed Kate to pull her ankles. Between the two of them, they got Alice out and laid her on the floor.

"Watch her skirt; she's going to go mad if it gets dirty," shrieked Kate.

Elise looked at Kate in disbelief. She lifted Alice's legs from the floor, and watched her face. Alice groaned a little and then blinked rapidly.

"Where am I?" she said.

"You are on the bog floor, Alice, get up quick," said Kate. Alice jumped to her feet.

"What the fuck!" She ran to the mirror and started checking her lipstick. Elise was bemused; she had never seen anyone come out of a faint with cheeks as pink as Alice's. Kate nudged Alice sharply in the ribs and she let out another groan.

"I still feel a bit groggy. Do you think you could help me to my chair?" Alice allowed Elise and Kate to support her to the nearest chair, and sat for a moment.

"Could I have a glass of water please, Elsie?" she asked in whispery tones.

Elise ran into the kitchen and returned with the water.

"What time is it, Elsie?" Elise without thinking glanced at her watch and felt the freezing water cascade down the front of her skirt. Gerry suddenly appeared, staring anxiously at Alice.

"Alice, what happened, are you okay?"

Alice batted the caterpillars at him. "Yes, Gerry, I just fainted, we were so busy today, I just didn't have time for lunch."

Elise suppressed a snort, as Gerry shook his head.

"Silly girl, do you need a cab to get you home?" Alice didn't do 'cabs'.

She had a shiny little sports car outside, and wouldn't be seen dead in anything else.

"Oh no, thank you, Gerry, you get off, no worries."

Gerry gratefully headed for the door. As it closed behind him, Alice looked up at Elise.

"Where's my water, Elsie?"

31

Elise turned away, embarrassed and soaking wet. She sat at her desk and shut down her computer. Alice appeared behind her.

"Quick, Els, get your bag, we have to go."

"Go where, what are you talking about?"

"There's been a change of plan; John Pear just texted me, he and Armando are going to meet us at Francesco's."

Elise was stunned. "But that's not possible. They are booked on the train at six."

"No, I just told you," said Alice, tugging at Elise's arm.

"They are getting the train at eleven p.m. and Armando wants to meet you, you know, 'cos you speak the lingo and everything."

As Elise stood up, Alice firmly locked arms with her.

"Come on, Elsie, let your hair down, or at least drag a comb through it. You're always gassing to that bloke, you'll enjoy yourself."

Elise was too shocked to argue. She was beginning to feel faint herself, but allowed herself to be dragged to the lift.

Francesco's was a pretentious-looking wine bar just down the alley.

Elise's stomach was doing somersaults. The thought of meeting Armand face to face was almost too much to bear. She looked down at her soggy skirt, her tights had pulls and her shoes were battered; she could picture the look of disappointment that would be on Armand's face when they met. There would be no more banter, no more jokes and no more compliments; she felt as if her little world was falling in on her.

Alice and Kate propelled her to the counter. Elise leaned on it for support, and heard Alice shriek, "John Pear, over here!"

With much bustle and excitement, they disappeared into the back of the bar and left Elise feeling very alone. She shot a glance at the door, wondering if she could make a run for it, but the eyes of the barmaid were burning holes through her.

"What would you like?" she asked in a bored tone. There was a look of disdain on her face that made Elise shrink back. Elise scanned the list of wines on the blackboard behind the counter. She didn't dare turn her head and focussed all her attention on the list; nothing on it was even mildly drinkable. The waitress was 'tutting' loudly and shrugging her shoulders.

"Shall I come back later, when you've made your mind up?" she said rudely.

Elise's eyes frantically swept the list again; she really couldn't bear the thought of disappointing Armand.

The waitress was now leaning right into her face, so close that they were almost touching noses. She tapped her pen loudly on the wooden surface. Elise was by now paralysed with fear, and jumped with shock when Alice suddenly appeared and stabbed her elbow.

"For God's sake, Elsie, we are dying of thirst." With that she pushed in front of Elise.

"We'll have two bottles of the house white, please," she said and then disappeared, leaving Elise to pay for what she was sure was the equivalent of a sofa, if not a three-piece suite. Elise then had to stagger to the table snagged by Alice. The tray weighed a ton, and the waitress had piled everything on one side of the tray making it even trickier to carry.

No one budged when she eventually reached the table. Elise recognised the back of Arek's and Dave's heads. She could not imagine how they had ended up there. Kelly, the office junior, was also present. Elise realised that there was nowhere for her to sit, so she stood trying to balance the tray, not sure what to do next. "Christ, Elsie, you took your bloody time," said Alice, who had been watching her make her way across the bar with a very nasty expression on her face. Arek turned around and jumped up to take the tray.

"Sorry, Elise, I didn't see you. Here let me give you a hand, sit yourself down."

"Oh, no, Arek, don't worry. I can grab my own chair." Elise had seen an empty chair at the next table and pulled it across to the table. Arek was on his feet again, and Elise wished he would stop making a scene. She shot a desperate look at Arek, and he sat down abruptly.

"Come and sit here, Elsie; here, move your fat bum, Kate," shouted Alice. Kate obligingly moved her 'fat bum' forcing Elise to drag the chair half way round the table. As soon as she got near, Alice moved her chair in closer to Kate and Elise was reduced to sitting a foot away from the table, which meant she had to squeeze her arm between Alice and Kate to reach her drink and felt decidedly out of the loop.

She suddenly caught sight of Armand. She had seen his photograph in the brochure, but decided that it did not do him justice. Realising that he was trying to catch her eye, she quickly dropped her head down.

Jean-Pierre, who looked even younger than his eighteen years, was enjoying being the centre of attention. Alice was on full throttle; she was throwing her head back and laughing uproariously every time Jean-Pierre said a word. His English was excellent, but Alice insisted on speaking her unique version of French.

Elise tasted her wine; it was truly disgusting. She risked a quick glance across the table and felt mortified when Armand, after a quick sniff, set his glass down untouched on its mat. Alice clocked Armand and said, "Elise, what is this crap? I thought you were the wine expert." Elise tried to hide in her chair.

Elise winced at Alice's excruciating massacre of Armand's native tongue, for some reason known only to Alice; she felt that the addition of the letter 'o' on the end of every sentence turned it into French.

Elise swore loudly and luxuriously in her head; thinking of the rudest words she knew and stringing them together, always gave her a great deal of satisfaction. She risked a peek at Armand and he at last caught her eye. He seemed pleased to see her and smiled, rolling his eyes in the direction of Jean-Pierre. He rose from his chair, and approached Alice.

"Perhaps you should sit next to Jean-Pierre, as you seem to be the great friends," he said in heavily accented English.

Alice needed no further encouragement, and much to Kate's dismay, she snatched up her glass and danced around the table to Jean-Pierre.

Armand moved Alice's chair a little way from the table, allowing Elise room to sit a little closer to her glass.

"Mon Dieu!" Armand whispered theatrically into Elise's ear, "Save me from that woman, she should be arrested for murdering my language!" He then took Elise's hand and kissed it. "So delighted to finally meet you."

Alice looked up at Armand, shot Elise a glance and then turned her attention back to Jean-Pierre. Kate shuffled her chair closer to the two reps and Elise found herself chatting in her perfect French to Armand.

"I'm so sorry about the train," she began, feeling personally responsible for upsetting his plans, but Armand waved his hands, in the way that only French people could.

"But it was not your fault, my dear, you are not responsible for the British railway now, are you?"

Elise started to relax, and kept reaching for her glass; it really was awful, but it gave her something to do with her hands. Maybe she should ring the bar in the morning and offer to send over some decent stuff for them to sample.

Armand glared across at Jean-Pierre. He had his head so close to Alice's that her hair extensions appeared to be mating with the designer 'fluff' on his chin.

"That boy is trouble," he whispered. "Too much money and too little brains. I don't trust him at all, I am sure he is cooking something up with your little painted lady."

A little while later, Armand stood up.

"I have to go to the bathroom; I'm leaving you on guard! Please don't let him out of your sight!"

The second he disappeared from view, Jean-Pierre and Alice jumped up.

"We're going for a quick smoke. You boys won't mind keeping the table. Come on Elsie, let's get some fresh air."

Elise felt Kate grabbing her arm with such force that she almost lifted her from the chair. Alice was giggling more than usual, and Elise's nerves suddenly returned. She had never had a cigarette in her life, but found herself nodding in agreement. She generally did whatever Alice demanded, and she certainly had no intention of reneging on her 'promise' to Armand.

Much to the surprise of Arek and Dave, she dutifully followed Jean-Pierre, Alice and Kate out onto the patio. Kelly joined them and following a whispered conversation with Alice, she started handing out cigarettes. Elise took the cigarette from Kelly and Jean-Pierre leapt forward to light it. The cigarette looked strange to Elise; the end looked as if it had been twisted into a knot.

"They're French, Elise; don't forget to inhale, you have to suck really hard on these." Kate and Jean-Pierre had already lit their own cigarettes; they were both smiling broadly at Elise, and nodding with encouragement. Jean-Pierre was sucking so hard that his lips almost disappeared.

Grandmother had often said that "everyone smokes in Paris" so Elise, expecting that Armand would be joining them and wanting to impress, inhaled deeply. She was immediately overcome by the foul taste in her mouth and a desperate urge to cough. She had been trying to copy Bette Davis, in Grandmere's favourite scene from 'Now Voyager' but was beginning to feel more like Dot Cotton.

Elise needed to cough. She tried to take the cigarette out of her mouth but found, to her horror, that it had somehow glued itself to her top lip; she gave the cigarette a desperate yank. It came away with most of her lip still attached. She pursed her lips trying to check on the damage, when suddenly Jean-Pierre leapt in front of her and planted a huge kiss on her lips.

Elise, still feeling dizzy from the cigarette, stumbled backwards; unfortunately, a row of flower pots was directly behind her and she went flying. Elise landed on her backside with her legs across the top of the pot. Alice and Jean-Pierre were 'high-fiving' each other amidst gales of laughter. Elise caught Alice's eye; she was staring at her, with a cruel, triumphant grin on her face.

"Look everyone, Elsie's on the pot," she shouted.

"The prince kissed the Frog! Hand over your fivers, girls."

Elise with tears of embarrassment running down her cheeks, tried to slide her legs off the side of the planter. She saw a sea of blurred faces and her legs refused to move. Lying helplessly, with her shoulders in the gravel, she caught sight of Armand running across the patio. Arek and Dave were in hot pursuit. Armand descended on Jean-Pierre and grabbed him by his shirt collar.

"What have you done, you little shit?" he screamed in his impeccable French. Arek and Dave, standing on either side of Elise, heaved her out of the flower pot and leaned her against the wall. Elise still had the 'cigarette' between her fingers. It looked quite sad and was drooping. Arek grabbed it, dropped it on the floor and hastily stamped on it. An interested crowd of giggling onlookers were gathering.

"Can't you take a joke?" screamed Alice. "We were just having a laugh."

Armand was absolutely furious. "How dare you embarrass my colleague and drag this stupid boy into the middle of it. This is disgraceful behaviour. Where did that 'cigarette' come from?"

"It wasn't mine," stammered Jean-Pierre, who was trying to get his windpipe free of Armand's grasp. "Alice gave it to the little one to give it to Elsie, just for fun; you know, the British sense of humour; they taught us about it at school."

Armand still had one hand around Jean-Pierre's throat, and with the other grabbed Elise's hand. She was shaken, and a trickle of blood from her lip was making its way down her chin. "My God, you are hurt." Armand shook out his handkerchief and started to dab at Elise's chin.

"No, no, I'm fine really." But Elise didn't feel fine at all; she felt sick and woolly-headed and her limbs were shaking uncontrollably.

Jean-Pierre suddenly burst into tears. "It was just fun, a bet, you know, Monsieur Armand."

Armand silenced him with a glare that made Elise wish she were back in the flower pot.

"We have to leave. Right now," he said. "We do not need any further delays."

Arek had thoughtfully brought their cases out onto the patio and Dave ran to hail a cab. Armand, incandescent with rage, turned his fury back on Alice.

"You can tell Monsieur Mike from me that we are finished; as you say, 'All the bets are gone!'."

Dave had managed to flag down a cab, and with Jean-Pierre still dangling from his arm, Armand flung open the door, and having first thrown in the suitcases, shoved Jean-Pierre in head first and disappeared from view.

"Trust you to cause a fucking scene," screamed Alice. "You've probably cost everyone their jobs, everyone hates you," and with that, she gave Elise an almighty shove and sent her flying back into the plant pot.

Elise would have happily remained in the pot for a little while longer. "That wine must have been off" was all she could think of. But Dave had dragged over a chair and bundled her onto it. Arek had taken Elise's car key from her bag and drove her car to the bar, then with Dave following, he drove Elise home, which took a while as she couldn't seem to recall where she actually lived. He helped her up the steps to her flat and made sure she was safely on her sofa before leaving.

Chapter Four

Elise busied herself in the tiny office kitchen, frantically washing up cups and putting on the coffee; she did not want to be trapped in here when the others arrived.

She heard the staff room door bang. Elise froze in her tracks. It was far too early for anyone else to be here. She panicked, realising that there was no escape.

"Get the fuck in here, all of you." Elise heard Gerry shout. This was followed by the sound of feet shuffling and chairs banging. "Where the hell is Alice?" Elise could picture Gerry's purple face; she had seen him lose his rag before. The next stage would be his slicked back hair turning into a bird's nest. She tried to peek through the keyhole. It was very early in the morning for him to be having a meltdown, and, she wondered, why he wasn't asking where she was.

Elise heard the slow click of Alice's heels as she made her way into the room. "For God's sake, what the hell's the matter, waking me up at that hour, and how dare you speak to me as if I'm some bloody office junior?"

"If you were an office junior, you would have been sacked years ago," retorted Gerry.

Elise still at the keyhole was trying hard not to breathe and praying that no one tried to open the door.

"What the hell happened last night? I had a fucking irate phone call from Armand, saying that you had played some stupid practical joke and caused him to miss his train and 'harass' a colleague. At least that's what I think he said. His English is shite and he was fucking steaming! Says he is taking full responsibility for causing injury to Elise and that he no longer wants to do business with us. He's contacting Mike today to sever our contract."

"Uncle Mike won't give a shit if he goes elsewhere and anyway he's gone off to Scotland," drawled Alice.

Elise who was by now standing on tiptoe and trying to hide her head in the biscuit cupboard pricked up her ears; it was the first she had heard of Alice being related to the owner of the company.

"Your fucking uncle may be prepared to pay you for doing sod all here, but he is not going to swallow you pissing off our best client, and as much as you hate to admit it, he thinks the sun shines out of Elise's bum. He's built up this business from scratch and you stupid lot might just have lost the lot."

"Excuse me, who said I did anything? And do you really need to bring Elsie's skinny little arse into the conversation? Don't point your bony little finger at me, why don't you ask Kate, or Kelly what happened?" Alice sounded nettled; she wasn't usually fazed by anything other than a broken finger nail. By now Elise was wondering whether she could escape through the tiny window before anyone realised she was there. She heard Kate's voice, sounding thick as if her tongue had got too big for her mouth.

"Oh, no Alice, please, you can't blame poor Kelly."

"Her fucking name is Elise and the next fucker that calls her Elsie is going to go out of that door with my boot up their backside. Is that fucking clear?"

Elise definitely thought it was clear, but fear of retribution from Alice was making her stomach churn.

"Well, for openers, Duval forwarded me an email he received supposedly sent by Elise yesterday afternoon. So, can we start by someone telling me who was responsible for that?" Silence reigned.

Gerry picked up his phone and started to read aloud. "I've google-translated, so that we can all get in on the act. 'Dear Armand, sorry to let you down but the six p.m. train has been cancelled. I have rebooked you on the eleven p.m., so why don't you join us for a drink at Francesco's? We would love to meet you and Jean-Pierre. Love, Elise'."

Elise doubled over in horror. "Love, Elise?" Never, never ever ever!

"Well, I bloody know that Elise didn't do this, even if it was sent from her laptop, so hands up ladies."

"How do you know she didn't?" piped up little Kelly. This was followed by a muted scream when Kate had the presence of mind to stamp on her foot and hiss "Shut the fuck up!" into her ear.

"Well, firstly the train wasn't cancelled, and secondly when Duval checked it again, he realised straight away that it wasn't from Elise. Thirdly, I checked the time and she was in my office when the email was sent."

"The snotty kid bawled all the way home and spilt his guts out, about dictating the email, switching the tickets and God knows what else. This is a bloody office, not a fucking playground. What the fuck did you lot think you were playing at? You've made us all look like fucking idiots!"

"It really was just supposed to a bit of fun, you know," ventured Kate, her voice sounding even more breathless than usual. "We were trying to help the business, you know. Jean had just finished school, he told Alice that Armand was a real bore and wasn't going to let him have any fun, so we just arranged for them to get the later train so we could meet for a drink. That was all, I didn't know anything else, I swear, all I did was keep Elise away from her laptop in case she saw the deleted messages." Elise shook her head; this was getting worse by the minute.

"So how did Elise end up arse over tit in a flower pot?" Alice burst into peals of laughter.

"Oh, Gerry, it was just the funniest thing ever. Kelly gave Elsie a joint instead of a regular fag, and she'd been guzzling the wine, she just went all dizzy and fell over."

"Jesus, Alice, how the hell did you drag Kelly into this? She's just a fucking schoolgirl and, seriously, you gave Elise a joint in a bloody wine bar... she doesn't even smoke, you are fucking insane."

"I just told you, Kelly gave it to her, not me, and Kate typed the fucking email, not me, so just get your bloody facts right."

"But you made me do it," persisted Kelly bursting into tears.

"I don't give a shit who did what. Have any of you lot checked to see if Elise is okay? She's always here by now. Let's just hope she isn't lying dead somewhere."

This brought on a loud wail and more tears from Kelly, who had by now dissolved into a heap on the carpet.

Gerry stepped over her and screamed at no one in particular.

"We have to figure out a way to put this right asap. If Armand goes to a competitor, we will be history, and I'm telling you now, that I am not taking the blame for any of this. Thank fuck, Mike is out of the picture for a few days. We need to sort this shit out before he comes back to the land of the living. You'd all better hope that his bloody mother-in-law hangs on for a few more days. At least he's got no mobile or internet up there, so it gives us a bit of breathing space."

Suddenly, a very old-fashioned ring tone filled the air. Elise gasped down at her glowing cardigan pocket. Who the fuck was ringing her? Nobody rang her, only her mother and grandmother had her number.

For Elise, death would have been a welcome escape at this point, but she couldn't figure out how even death could get her out of this kitchen without being seen. Suddenly, the door flung open and Alice strode in.

"Oh, so you're hiding in here, you sneaky cow. Trust you to have a fucking phone like that. Letting everyone think you were sick, what is it, trying for the sympathy vote? Can't you take a joke? What did you do, jump straight on the phone to your precious Armando?" Alice barged past her and poured herself a cup of coffee.

"Well, you've probably cost everyone their jobs; I hope you are proud of yourself."

"I didn't talk to anyone, how is it my fault?" Elise had trouble getting her words out, she never ever challenged Alice. To be fair, she never argued with anyone, but the 'Love, Armand' was more than even she could bear.

She leaned against the kitchen unit for support; desperately trying to figure out whether she could squeeze past Alice and make a bid for freedom; even having to face staff room full of people was a better prospect than being alone in the kitchen with Alice. She tried to make a move but it was too late. Alice swung round and emptied her cup of hot coffee all over Elise's skirt.

"This coffee tastes like mud, why don't you make yourself useful and go and fetch me a decent one?"

Elise fought back tears; the coffee was burning her legs and dripping off the end of her skirt onto the floor.

Gerry stuck his head round the door, his face was bright red, his hair was sticking up on end and he hadn't shaved. He didn't notice the huge brown stain eating its way into Elise's skirt, nor the growing puddle in front of her feet.

"Elise, didn't know you were here, really glad to see you. Are you okay? Look, why don't you run out and get yourself some fresh air, and get coffees for everyone?" He thrust a £20 note into her hand and held the door wide open. Elise fled gratefully making a detour to the ladies to try to mop up her skirt. She was in such a rush to get to the towel dispenser that she forgot to close the door. As she was frantically drying off the coffee, she tried to shut out the raised voices that were echoing across the corridor and bouncing into her ears.

"You did that on purpose, Alice! Are you completely nuts, haven't you caused enough trouble already?" Gerry was still fuming. "She already looks like a bloody scarecrow, there's no need to make it worse!"

"I've never even seen a scarecrow dressed as badly as her," retorted Alice.

"And I really don't give a shit what you think."

"Uncle Mike won't have you speaking to me like this; it was just a fucking joke. We just wanted to make sure that John Pear had a good time. Don't forget that he's the one that owns all the fucking grape trees. Armando is just his lackey, and as far as I remember John Pear had the time of his bloody life last night, so lay off, okay."

"Bollocks." Elise heard Gerry retort. "If Armand goes, we are in deep 'doodoo', and who the hell is going to do all the shit around here if Els walks out? He's already back in Paris and in a couple of hours he will have found another UK distributor and we will be finished."

Elise scurried out of the ladies and, breaking the rules, a first for her, she switched off the alarm panel, opened the fire exit and escaped down the steps to the back alley.

Chapter Five

Elise breathed deeply, relieved to be out in the fresh air. She suddenly remembered her phone had rung. She grabbed it out of her pocket. It wasn't like Grandmere to ring during the day; something must be wrong. Elise looked at the number, and was surprised to see that it didn't belong to her grandmother. Elise quickly hit the 'return call' key and was truly shocked when she heard her mother's voice on the end of the line.

"Well, at last! You took your time."

"Sorry, Mum, are you okay?"

"Not really, your grandmother passed away during the night, just thought I should let you know."

Elise felt herself folding in half. Grandmere had been feeling poorly for a few weeks now. Elise had been concerned at how much she had deteriorated when she last saw her, but Grandmere had adamantly refused to even allow Elise to call the doctor.

"I'm nearly ninety, my dear, you have to expect this when you get to my age, please stop making a fuss."

"Oh, Mum, I'm so sorry. Do you want me to come home now?"

"There's no point; it's all finished. You could come over tomorrow, there are a few things that I need you to do."

"Of course, Mum, I really am so sorry, I'll be there first thing." Elise felt her voice starting to break mid-sentence.

"Oh, Elise, for goodness sake, pull yourself together, she was eighty-eight after all. Get over it." Elise shrank from her mother's odd matter of fact tone; she sounded as if she was reading for a self-help guru rather than talking about her beloved mother.

"Maybe she's in shock," thought Elise. Trying her best to adopt a more cheerful tone, she answered with a breezy, "Okay, Mother, see you tomorrow."

It took all Elise's strength not to burst into howls of tears in the middle of the high street. She took a deep breath and headed for the coffee shop.

"Are you all right, Elise?" asked Freddie. He was a sweet man and both he and Elise always looked forward to their morning chats, when she did the coffee run.

"The usual?" he asked. Elise nodded, still not trusting herself to speak.

"You don't look so good, are you sure you are okay?" Elise felt the floodgates open.

"Sorry, Freddie, I've just found out that my grandma died last night, it's a bit of a shock."

"How old was she?" asked Freddie, as he stacked up the cups on the counter.

"She was eighty-eight," whispered Elise.

"Wow," retorted Freddie. "You should be celebrating her life, not mourning her death. Come on, I don't like to see my favourite customer looking so sad. Is there anything I can do to help? I've got my car out back if you need a lift anywhere."

"Oh, Freddie, that's so sweet of you, I'm going to go home in the morning. I just need to sort a few things out at work."

"I know you run that place, but surely they could manage without you today. You shouldn't really be at work, it's not fair."

Elise was trying not to look up; red eyes, snotty nose and a pale blue skirt with a great big brown stain down the middle was not a pleasant sight, even for Freddie.

He carefully placed the cups in two carriers. "That one's yours," he added. Elise nodded. For some reason, Freddie always wrote her name on her cup. Elise gave him the note, and as he handed her the receipt, he slipped a cookie into her hand. "Just to cheer you up," he said, and smiled as Elise nodded her thanks and ran for the door.

Elise, staggering under the weight of the coffee, made for the alleyway at the rear of the office. She leant against the wall, and suddenly felt desperately alone for the first time in her life.

She closed her eyes and a memory flooded back. Elise had been chosen for a role in the chorus at the little ballet school that Grandmere had insisted on her attending.

"It will teach you how to walk and hold yourself, my dear," she had said, and Elise had dutifully trotted along behind her every Saturday morning. Mother hadn't objected too much. If Grandmere wanted to waste her money, who was she to complain? It would certainly afford her some much-needed rest after another exhausting week at work.

Elise had returned triumphantly one morning, clutching a large bag close to her chest. Grandmere had been so proud. The minute they got in the house, Elise's beautiful tutu came out of the bag and Grandmere had carefully dressed her in it, putting her hair up into a beautiful chignon and adding a red-rose brooch to finish off the outfit.

"Let me go and show Mother. Do you think she will like it?" Elise still shuddered at the memory of herself as she pirouetted towards her mother's study and knocked.

"It's me, Mother, please may I come in?" Elise had opened the door, stood in front of her mother's desk and performed a deep curtsey, looking up proudly at her mother with a huge smile on her face.

Her mother looked up from her newspaper and glanced over at her little girl.

"Why are you disturbing me when I am so busy? I have so many important documents to read and sign today and I mustn't fall behind."

Elise's smile had started to falter and her legs were beginning to ache from the curtsey. She felt her mother's eyes staring at her and her knees started to wobble. She had reached behind her and grabbed on to Grandmere's skirt for reassurance.

Grandmere had placed her hand on Elise's shoulder as they both waited in silence.

"It's so strange," began her mother, "Mother and I carry red so well, and yet, on you, well, it just drowns you, my dear. I think your teacher has been very cruel, making you wear that." Her mother paused and looked back down her newspaper.

"Why would you want to stand on a stage, and risk making yourself a laughing stock? You are not Darcy Bussell, and you are far too tall to ever be a dancer, so why are you wasting your time and spending all your poor grandmother's money?"

Elise's mother, looking thoroughly irritated, turned her attention to Grandmere.

"Why are you wasting your time with her? You are being just as cruel, putting these silly notions in her head, and setting her up for failure. I haven't got time for this nonsense, I have a deadline to meet; and Elise please straighten your legs, before one of them snaps off!"

Elise had backed out of the room, falling over Grandmere's feet in her haste to escape. Louise Jacobs caught her mother's disapproving glare, shrugged her shoulders, and turned back to her paper.

"Goodness me, Mother, stop looking at me like that. I'm only telling her the truth. Why do you persist in all this nonsense? You are just filling her head with ridiculous dreams, and when it all ends in misery, what will you do then? Just stop with the fairy stories, it's time she realised that ugly ducklings never ever turn into swans."

Grandmere had almost slammed the study door, but not before Elise had heard her mother's remarks. Grandmere never slammed doors, and she never muttered either, both were completely unacceptable in her world, but Elise had definitely heard "Garce" escape from Grandmere's lips. Something told her not to ask for a translation. That had to wait until she was safely under the duvet with her French dictionary and torch. Later that night, Elise thought she must have misheard, since the only translation she could find said 'female dog'.

Elise had always had a very strange relationship with her mother, who resented everything about her. Her 'gangly limbs and stringy yellow hair' proved to be a constant source of irritation. Elise grew to hate her hair, she simply bundled it into a pony tail and when the need arose, hacked at her fringe with a pair of kitchen scissors.

She kept her arms and legs covered, even on the warmest of days with oversized bulky clothes that she purchased from the local charity shops and did her best to stay out of her mother's way. Louise Jacobs tried and, for the most part, succeeded in pretending that the quiet skinny little girl did not exist.

Elise had found school almost as intolerable. She suffered at the hands of the school bullies, and chose to hide herself in her studies; the teachers sympathised with the sad little girl, and allowed her to spend her breaks and lunch times in the school library. Feeling safe under the watchful eye of the school librarian, Elise devoted herself to her studies, dreaming that one day her mother would hug her and tell her how proud she was to have such a clever daughter.

At home Elise spent every possible minute with her beloved Grandmere. They were the best of friends, and did everything together. Grandmere had spoken only in French to Elise from the day she was born, and over the years she took great pains to teach Elise about all things French. Elise grew up completely bilingual, with a passion for and depth of knowledge of all things French.

The loud revving of a car engine jolted Elise back to the present, and she ran for the stairs, hoping firstly, that no one had locked the fire door and secondly, that the coffee hadn't gone cold.

Everything appeared to be calm in the office, everyone's head was down and the telephone chatter was subdued. Elise quickly deposited the appropriate coffees on each desk, and received a muttered "thank you" from everyone except Alice, who had simply glared.

The door to Gerry's office was closed. Elise stood outside. Should she knock, or creep away and come back later? Reasoning that his coffee was already getting cold and that he would be getting antsy about the receipt if she didn't take it into him now, she threw caution to the wind and knocked as quietly as she could manage.

"Is that you, Elise? Come in, come in and close the door." Elise walked in and placed the coffee and the receipt on Gerry's desk. His hair looked even wilder than before; he was beginning to take on a Davy Crocket appearance that did him no favours and the stubble on his chin was anything but 'Designer'.

Gerry looked up at her, his eyes as wild as his hair. "Sit down, Elise, please." Elise plonked herself in the chair in front of his desk; Gerry took the lid of his coffee.

"Oh, I'm sorry, Gerry; your smiley face has melted."

"My smiley face?" Gerry looked puzzled.

"In your coffee, I meant. I took longer than usual."

"Els, my coffee looks the same as it does every morning. What are you on about?"

"Oh, er, nothing." Elise was equally puzzled, her froth always had a perfect smiley face in it. She suddenly blushed and stared down at her feet.

"I'm so, so sorry about all this; some stupid prank of Alice's that got out of hand, and now Armand thinks he's going to get sued or something and well, to put it mildly Elise, we are in the shit."

Elise fought the urge to apologise profusely, not because she didn't want to but because she was desperately trying not to burst into tears again and she had just agreed to go and visit her mum on a work day, which meant she would have to ask for a day off, which she had never dared to before.

Gerry appeared to be waiting for her to speak, his eyebrows had disappeared under his hair line and he had taken on the appearance of a condemned man.

"I'm really sorry, Gerry, I will do anything within my power to help you. Alice was stupid, but that's nothing new, is it? I'm really sorry but I've just received news that my grandmother has died and I need to take some time off."

Gerry's eyebrows rose even higher, this was all he needed, and then a thought struck him. "Is that the French one? Does that mean you'll need to go to France for the funeral?" Elise was about to explain that her grandmother lived in Surbiton, but was reluctant to contradict him.

"Please accept my condolences, of course you can have some time off, you never take any and we owe you at least four weeks." Elise was relieved that he wasn't having another 'meltdown' but he was right; she had never taken any in all the years she had worked there, preferring instead to buy her leave back and get an extra month's pay.

Gerry had never complained. It was much cheaper for him not to have to pay for a bilingual temp, and he couldn't bear the thought trying to manage the office without her, so everyone was happy. "Whatever you need," Gerry announced.

"In fact, you could do me an enormous favour. While you are in Paris, do you think you could schedule a meeting with Armand and sort out all this mess? As soon as you explain that it was all just a bit of fun, you can tell him that you weren't injured and that we British play these 'pranks' on each other all the time. He'll be fine and we won't lose the contract. In fact, I mean obviously… we will pay for your ticket and of course your hotel for two or three nights, and any, erm, expenses that you incur. Just use your credit card, and I'll reimburse you when you get back."

"I don't have a credit card," said Elise, feeling her cheeks redden again.

Gerry was thunderstruck. "Who the hell doesn't have a credit card?" He quickly regained his composure.

"No worries, we can just nip down to the bank and arrange for you to be issued with a company credit card. They should be able to get it to you in a couple of days if I ask them to put a rush on it. You could take out the new brochure that Armand was checking out yesterday for our new campaign."

Gerry paused for breath, his face had gone back to beetroot and his forehead was perspiring, Elise was staring at his hands which appeared to be shaking.

"Oh, and by the way, Mike had to shoot off to the wilds of Scotland with his wife last night. His mother-in-law is on her way out, so hopefully, we can sort all this out before he gets wind of it. I don't need to tell you, Elise, how important that account is to us. Please, just do what you can to put things right."

She needed a minute both to get her head around Gerry's offer and to wonder whether he really thought it was possible to convince Armand, that lying, committing fraud, along with drugging and punching someone, was what the Brits did every day for fun!

Elise had never been out of England, though she had a passport; a birthday gift three years ago that had been obtained at Grandmere's insistence. Maybe it was time to get it out of the envelope.

Gerry was becoming agitated by Elise's silence. The office door opened and Alice sashayed in. "What are you two planning?" she said accusingly. Elise didn't dare look up; she could feel Alice's eyes boring holes in her neck.

"Just trying to repair the damage, Alice, and why don't you try knocking?" Alice didn't deign to reply and slammed out of the office.

"What about it, Elise? Four weeks' leave and we'll meet all your expenses. I know Armand would really appreciate your visit and you would help us by getting some feedback on the brochures."

Elise was confused, everything had been triple-checked and approved weeks before, but she could see that Gerry was struggling so she let it go. A trip to Paris, all expenses paid, was beyond her wildest dreams.

"I… I would have to spend some time with Mum first," said Elise, "but if you think it would help, I mean I'm really sorry about what's happened, I don't want any of us to lose our jobs."

Gerry heaved out a sigh of relief and jumped up from behind his desk.

"Jesus, Elise, please would you stop apologising? Look, I know I let that bloody Alice treat you like shit. But her mother owns half the company and I don't want to make any enemies. Honestly, Elise, if you can pull this off, things will be different, I swear. That Armand bloke really likes you; do you think we have a chance?"

Gerry paused to take a breath.

"Brilliant, well, that's all settled then. I'll get Arek to cover for you here whilst you're away. I'm going to leave everything in your capable hands; you know we are all depending on you, and I'll see you back here on the first."

Elise was still having the greatest difficulty trying to process Gerry's offer. It had been Grandmere's dream for them to one day visit Paris together and it seemed so bizarre that the opportunity had suddenly come up on the day after her death. But Grandmere had always urged Elise to 'grab life and live it'. So perhaps this was meant to be.

Gerry ran to open the office door for Elise.

"Come on, we'd better hotfoot it down to the bank and get the ball rolling."

He paused for a moment.

"Why don't you send Armand a quick email, you know, just to let him know that everything is fine and settling a day for you two to meet up?"

Elise dutifully walked over to her desk, and in her finest French informed Armand that she was absolutely fine, and would be coming over to Paris to personally hand over the brochures, and that she would let him know the date and time of her arrival, once she had made her travel arrangements.

Gerry was hovering behind her as she wrote the email, she could hear his heavy breathing; he was actually mouthing the words as she typed them.

Gerry's French was non-existent, but she heard him exhale loudly when she hit the send key.

Gerry disappeared into his office and slumped in his chair. He felt for a minute that he had been rather rash offering to pay for her trip to Paris, but he reasoned, Armand Duval's account earned the company in excess of four hundred thousand pounds last year. Without him, they would almost certainly go under.

"Besides," he thought, "she such a bloody cheapskate, she will probably stay in some youth hostel and eat bread and cheese for the duration of the trip." He quickly calculated that even if the trip cost them a thousand pounds, it was a hell of a lot better than losing Duval's business, and in any case, they could class it as a business trip if she took the bloody brochures, so it would be tax deductible.

Gerry relaxed for the first time since he had received the irate and slightly bizarre call from Duval. It was 'sortable' and if she got over there quick enough, it could all be over and done with before Mike got back. Arek could sort out the office and Mike would be none the wiser.

"Job done!" Gerry said to himself. He couldn't help but feel impressed with his skilful handling of the situation. Even if 'Weird' Elsie's grandma dying was a bit inconvenient, he had still managed to come up with a solution, although it would be a bit of a bugger not having her in the office to deal with all the shite. Hopefully, Arek would cope!

He emerged a few moments later to find Elise waiting for him by the door. He really didn't relish the thought of being seen in public with her, but desperate situations called for desperate measures, so he had no option, but to hope that no one recognised him.

The bank clerk had obligingly organised a company credit card for Elise. Whilst they were there, Gerry withdrew some euros. He was determined to leave nothing to chance, and immediately handed the money over to Elise.

"Gerry was certainly suffering from an attack of something awful today," thought Elise; though she did feel slightly more reassured when he hung on to the envelope for just a fraction too long.

"For your taxis and incidentals, try and keep the receipts, only if you can, though." Elise was shocked. Gerry insisted on receipts for everything, the sales reps fumed at his meanness, but had had to accept that no receipt meant that they would personally be footing the bill.

Having returned from the bank, Gerry dived into his office and returned with another large envelope containing several copies of the slick new company brochure. Then making a great show of escorting her to the lift, he waited until the doors were about to close before saying:

"Sorry again about your grandma, please do your best for us in Paris."

Chapter Six

Elise drove the short distance back to her bedsit. The commute to Surbiton was eminently doable and would have saved her the rent money, but her mother had insisted on her getting a 'place of her own' the day her first pay cheque had arrived.

The bedsit was gloomy and cheap but as it was above the shop on the high street and miraculously had a car parking spot, Elise persuaded herself that it was perfect. She slotted her car expertly into the gap. Looking at her watch, she noted that it was just the right time to go shopping. Elise had this activity honed to perfection. She knew exactly what time the supermarket started to reduce the 'best before' and 'Use by' products. She usually hovered in the doorway, pretending to take a call on her obsolete mobile so that she didn't look too eager, and always made a point of buying one item that was not reduced, so she didn't look too much like a bargain grabber.

Elise tried to spend as little as possible on food. As long as she had enough to make a sandwich for work and food to eat when she got home, she was content.

Grandmere had always made a point of preparing beautiful meals out of cheap ingredients, and presenting them with great passion on the plate on a beautifully laid table. Even breakfast was served with napkins! Elise had grasped the idea of the cheap, but had never bothered to get to grips with Grandmere's concept of 'first eating with your eyes'.

"After all," she reasoned, "there's only me looking at it and I couldn't care less."

As she walked towards the store, Elise couldn't help but picture her beautifully dressed, manicured and coiffured grandmother. Even as a very old lady, Grandmere took great pride in her appearance, she was always beautifully dressed, carefully altering all her clothes so that they fitted to perfection.

"Poor Grandmere, how excited you would have been to hear that I am going to Paris." Elise was trying to decide on an appropriate poem to read at the funeral and what hymns Grandmere would like. Hopefully, her mother would be 'too busy' and would let her arrange everything just the way Grandmere would have liked.

Elise drove slowly up the drive to Grandmere's 'chocolate box' cottage. Elise had been born there and loved every inch of it, especially the little garden at the back where she and Grandmere had spent many happy hours growing vegetables and herbs. It was overgrown now and lots of weeds had sneaked their way in since Grandmere had become too ill to remove them. Her mother had no interest in their 'little patch of heaven' and on Elise's fleeting visits home over the last few years, she had always spent the precious time they had, chatting in the kitchen, and in the last few weeks sitting at her bedside.

Chapter Seven

Elise carefully parked at the side of the garage. God forbid she should block the drive or allow her shabby little car to be seen by the neighbours! She felt a slight jolt as one of the overhanging branches snagged itself on her rusty roof rack and prayed that it hadn't loosened any of the bolts. Elise was fighting back tears as she walked up to the front door. At least Mother had let her keep the door key.

"You can let yourself in when you come to see Mother and you won't need to disturb me," she had said when Elise had held out the key the day she moved out.

"Message received," Elise had thought.

"Good heavens, don't be ridiculous, Elise, why on earth would we have a funeral? There are only the two of us. Anyway, Mr Forbes was here and he's sorted everything out for me. They actually have a slot at the crematorium tomorrow afternoon, would you believe? He said if you wanted to take an outfit or something to put on her, you could go over today. She could just keep her nightie on, but if you want to go, you can and you can drop the rest of her stuff off at one of your charity shops whilst you are there. I need the space, I might even sell the place, I don't want to live here now I'm all alone."

"But you're not alone, Mum, you've got me," said Elise.

"Well, I don't want you," her mother answered.

Elise sank into the nearest chair. She had known for a very long time that her mother was a self-centred and cruel woman, but this was going too far even for her. No service, and dumping her Grandmere's beloved clothes were horrific.

"I'd like to keep her things if that's okay," Elise managed to stammer. Her mother stared at her, not even trying to keep the look of disdain from her face.

"Do what you want, I don't think they are worth much, but even Mother's fifties specials have got to be an improvement on the usual rags you walk around in. Although I'm sure she would turn in her grave at the thought of you shambling around in her couture." Her mother paused for a moment.

"I'll go and sort out an outfit," Elise said, getting up from her chair.

"Just get everything out of this house today, make sure there is nothing left hanging around when I get back from work."

"Surely, they can't expect you to go in today, Mother?" Elise tried to disguise the shock in her voice, but it still shook as she spoke.

"Why on earth would I want to stay here? Just do as you are told, you don't need to stay. Soames will sort everything out. They should have the death certificate from Mr Forbes by now and anyway, I've got so much to do, documents to read, and deadlines to meet."

"Mother, why was Mr Forbes here so early?" Elise was puzzled by her mother's mention of their solicitor's visit; it wasn't even nine o' clock.

"Don't be silly, Elise. He didn't come this morning, he came yesterday to see Mother. She asked me to call him and he came straight over. Stupid man couldn't do anything; I told him not to let her die, but he just shook his head and sat there, holding her hand, as if that was going to do anything. Then he phoned the doctor and the doctor came and he couldn't stop her either. I told her that she couldn't die and leave me on my own, but she did it anyway. I've always hated that nasty Mr Forbes, always sticking his nose in other people's business; God knows why Mother thought she needed him. The house is mine, obviously and there's nothing else to speak of. I think she just liked nattering to him; he was always coming round, and sending her those expensive bloody flowers every week. He really got on my nerves."

Louise paused for breath and glanced out of her study window.

"My car is here, I have to leave now, I told you, I have an extremely important meeting."

"They've sent a car for you?" Elise had never known that to happen before.

"Oh, I don't drive anymore. I have my own driver, you can have the car if you want, and it's only cluttering up the drive. I'm extremely busy, and you are going to make me late."

With that Louise pushed her daughter out of the way and with a last withering glance in her direction, she pulled on her jacket, grabbed her bag and strode out of the room.

"Bye, Mother," Elise called after her. Her mother's breakfast tray was sitting in the middle of the desk, Elise picked it up to take to the kitchen, the toast looked very old and the half-drunk coffee had mould growing on the top. Elise, suddenly feeling very sorry for her mum, walked into the kitchen. She went over to the bin and lifted the lid. As she leaned over, something caught her eye. Elise quickly put down the tray and reached inside.

"Oh, no," she cried, as she pulled out the gold damask cloth which was wrapped around her grandmother's treasured hairbrush, comb and mirror. They were beautifully crafted; the comb was made of ivory, decorated with exquisitely painted sprigs of lavender, with an ornate gold surround. The matching brush and mirror were decorated on the back with matching lavender tapestry, protected by a glass cover with the same gold edging and handles. Elise started to cry. How could her mother have thrown these away? Elise visited her grandmother every week and had noticed that her grandmother's hands were getting much worse. Her fingers had been swollen and bent for as long as Elise could remember but now she seemed to have great difficulty holding and manoeuvring the heavy brush.

"It's getting too much for you, Grandmere. Why don't you let me buy you a lighter brush, or maybe next time I take you to the salon, you could ask Madeleine to cut it a bit shorter for you?" Elise wasn't sure whether it was the mention of a plastic brush or the suggestion that she had a new haircut that caused Grandmere's face to glow.

"Your grandfather bought this vanity set for me on our tenth wedding anniversary. He loved my hair; I would never dishonour his memory by not using them. Your grandfather would turn in his grave if I ever let anyone cut off my hair."

Elise then took on the task of washing, brushing and plaiting her grandmother's waist-length hair during her weekly visits, there were no more conversations about replacing the vanity set and Madeleine would have cut her own throat before contemplating trimming away anything more than a centimetre from Madame Jacobs' crowning glory!

Elise carefully laid out the damask cloth and anxiously checked to see if any of the set was damaged. The cloth had a couple of damp patches, but the set itself was intact. She quickly folded the cloth back around them, and placed them in her handbag. Elise then grabbed the bin liner, pulled it out of the bin and emptied it onto the kitchen floor. She gasped in horror as she saw Grandmere's 'secret box' lying on a mass of old damp teabags. This was her Grandmere's most treasured possession. Elise had always been fascinated by this strange wooden box; it was made from lacquered wood inlaid with intricately carved ivory.

"How is it a secret?" she used to ask. Grandmere often gave her the box, and Elise spent many hours trying to open it without success. Then one day, when her mother was away on one of her frequent business trips abroad, Grandmere had sat her down and showed her how to press one of the ivory squares; it sank in slightly, allowing Elise to slide a tiny panel out over the edge of the box which in turn revealed a metal catch. Elise pressed the catch and squealed in delight when the end of the box sprang open like a drawer. Inside the drawer was a folded piece of paper and a shiny key. Elise went to take out the key, but Grandma shook her head. "No, Elise, this is very important. I know this won't happen for a very long time, so please don't worry, but one day when you are grown up, and I am very old, I shall die and go and be with your grandfather."

"I don't want you to be sad, because by then, I will have taught you everything you need to know and you will be fine without me. Now listen very carefully, this box is our special secret. No one else knows how to open it and when I die I want you to have it, and then you may take out the piece of paper and the key because they are for you."

Elise had been very scared at the thought of Grandmere leaving her, but Grandmere had laughed and said, "Now don't you worry, I am not going anywhere for a very long time." With that, she had closed the box, placed it back on her dressing table and they had both gone downstairs to bake an extravagant chocolate cake for tea.

Elise had never forgotten their conversation and had often looked at the box, but had refused to even stand too close to it after that day.

Now with her hands trembling, she picked it up and ran out of the kitchen. Elise went straight to the front door and drew the bolt across, she ran down the hallway, took the stairs two at a time and pushed open the door to Grandmere's room, carefully locking it behind her.

Chapter Eight

The room was a mess. The bed was already stripped. Grandmere's beautiful bed linen and exquisitely embroidered cushions had been thrown on the floor in a heap. Elise bent down and lovingly picked up the cushions, one by one and placed them back on the mattress. She could still smell Grandmere's 'Lilly of the Valley' perfume on them. Tears filled her eyes again, as she folded up the sheets and counterpane and put them back on the bed. Elise then turned her attention back to her box, it took her less than a minute to open it and inside lay the envelope neatly folded in half. The key was still sitting on top. Elise opened the envelope and pulled out a letter. She placed the key on the cushion beside her and looked at her Grandmere's shaky but still beautiful handwriting. The letter was short, and as always written in French.

"My dearest Elise, as you are reading this, I know that the end has come. Please don't feel sad, I've had a long and happy life and you have been a source of great joy to me.

This isn't the same letter that I showed you when you were little, by the way. I write new ones every few months, but I am fairly certain that this will be the last, and as you are obviously reading this, I was right as usual.

Now, you know your mother has a real fear of anyone opening the little door to the attic; you must only do this if you are sure that your mother is well out of the way. Don't leave any trace that you've even been in there, or she will have a panic attack about the spider again."

'The Spider' was legendary. Grandmere had told Elise that Louise forbade anyone to even mention the attic. Following a traumatic episode with a huge hairy spider, she had demanded that her father get rid of the attic. Tom being Tom, put a piece of wood across the door, and wrote 'No Entry', which appeased her, and as far as Louise was concerned, it had ceased to exist.

"There is a big cabin trunk in the corner, it's under a pile of curtains and well-hidden from view. Make sure you get it out of the house when your mother is away and take it somewhere safe, and please don't leave my mirror behind; I brought that with me all the way from Paris and I want you to have it."

Elise looked across the room at Grandma's huge cheval mirror, and shuddered. She hated mirrors, the only one in her flat was on the bathroom cabinet, and Elise tried to avoid looking at that, other than to make sure she didn't have toothpaste all over her chin.

"You were always asking me about what had happened 'in the olden days' as you so quaintly put it, about your grandfather coming to Paris and how I ended up in England. I could never really talk about it because I knew you would be full of questions, which would have caused great pain for your mother. She could not bear the thought of you and I talking about your grandfather and made me promise never to discuss his death. But, well, I am dead now, and you have your own place so I'm trying to put everything right and try to help you understand things a little better.

Anyway, hurry up, grab anything of mine that you can, your mother will destroy everything otherwise, and I couldn't bear that. I know that you will do everything within your power to be with me at the end, but please don't be upset if you didn't make it. You are here now and that is all that matters, so don't spend any more time with this letter; please get everything that you can out of the house and put them to good use. Now off you go, I'll speak to you again later."

"Whatever does she mean?" Elise was mystified, but knowing that she had lots to do, she pulled Grandmere's ancient suitcase out from under the bed and began to pack.

Only once every surface was clear and every drawer emptied, and carefully loaded into the boot of the car, did Elise open the big oak doors of Grandmere's wardrobe. 'Lilly of the Valley' filled the room as she carefully laid the clothes out on the bed. All the beautiful skirts were on the left, blouses, cardigans and jumpers in the middle and jackets and coats on the right.

A beautiful red cashmere skirt, with a cream silk blouse and matching jacket caught her eye. "Trust Grandmere to have the whole outfit ready and waiting on a single hanger." Elise had to smile. Grandmere certainly left nothing to chance, and would definitely not risk Elise's 'eclectic taste', no hunting around for matching bits required. Elise pulled out the box that contained Grandmere's matching shoes. She had no trouble finding it as each box had a square label attached to the side, with a description of the contents. She picked out the one which read 'court shoe: red' and placed it alongside the ensemble.

Grandmere always kept her shoes in their original box; inside the box each shoe would be carefully packed into a separate bag, and were always scrupulously cleaned and polished before being put away. The matching handbags each in their own labelled dust jackets were kept on the top shelf, but, although Grandmere would never leave the house without one, Elise reasoned that on this occasion, it was definitely not required. Elise took the shoes out of the box. The writing on the lid was French and the shoes were certainly more than fifty years old.

They were exquisitely stitched, and the leather was still soft and barely marked. Elise placed the shoes on top of the outfit. She carried the clothes encased in one of Grandmere's garment bags down to the car. The boot was almost full, but she managed to fit everything in. She hung Grandmere's ensemble on the tiny hook just inside the rear door. Then with a heavy sigh went back for the dreaded mirror.

She positioned herself behind it and, lifting it slightly, she managed to rest the mirror on the stand. With great difficulty, she turned the mirror on its side and very slowly and carefully edged her way down the stairs. She laid the passenger seat as far back as it would go, but still could not manoeuvre the mirror into the car. In desperation, she ran back into the house and returned with the step ladder. She grabbed the spare duvet from the airing cupboard, knowing her mother would be furious to find it missing. She mouthed an apology.

Elise climbed onto the step ladder, threw the duvet over the roof rack and then heaved the mirror up. She leaned over the roof and wrapped the remaining duvet over the mirror, tucking the edges carefully between the two halves. She then took the roof rack ties out of the boot and secured the mirror with them. Feeling hot and sweaty, she brushed her fringe back from her forehead. She suddenly remembered the brush and comb set, and hastily went back into the kitchen to retrieve them. Elise was exhausted, but she had no intention of stopping until she had carried out her grandmother's wishes.

Elise looked around Grandmere's bedroom; she wanted to be sure that nothing had been left behind. Satisfied that the room was empty, she wandered over to the window for a last look at the garden, and spotted a silk pin cushion tucked behind the curtain.

Years ago, Elise had picked up a strange object in the garden and run over to her grandmother to show off her treasure.

"Is it a stone?" she had asked.

"No, my darling, you have found something very special! This is a chrysalis. Inside is a beautiful butterfly, just waiting to spread its wings and fly."

"Can't we let it out?" Elise was jumping up and down with excitement.

"Oh, no, you will injure it if you do that. The butterfly will only come out when it is ready."

She and Grandmere had gone into the house, and Elise had watched, fascinated as Grandmere had carefully removed all the pins from her little velvet cushion. She then gently laid the chrysalis on the velvet, and turning to Elise had said, "Now we must be patient."

Elise could not remember how many times she had run up the stairs and gazed at that cushion, but nothing ever happened and after a few days she forgot all about it.

One afternoon, she and Grandmere had been out in the garden, when Grandmere said, "Look up at my window, Elise." She looked up and saw a beautiful butterfly flapping its wings at the window. Elise remembered how she had run up the stairs, opened the window, and watched with her grandmother as the butterfly flew away.

She grabbed the pin cushion and put it in her pocket.

Elise left the room and locked the door behind her. She then made her way up to the attic. She and Grandmere only entered this room on the rarest of occasions. Elise always had to wait at the door. Grandmere would tiptoe in and out as quickly as possible. It was always dark in there even in the middle of the day. Elise had never been allowed to go inside, as the floorboards creaked loudly and Grandmere was afraid that Elise's mother would hear, or even worse that Elise might end up crashing through the ceiling beneath.

Chapter Nine

Elise didn't have a torch and wasn't even sure whether the light switch still worked. There was just enough daylight coming in behind her when she stepped out of the doorway to spot the old-fashioned pull-down cord; she tried a gentle pull, but nothing happened, she then tried a quick tug. Joy of joys, the light came on.

The attic didn't look as if anyone had been in there in years. It was very hot and cobwebs hung from every beam. An assortment of rusty tools, also coated in cobwebs was attached on equally rusty nails to the joists. Elise saw an old high chair and an antiquated pushchair that must have been her mother's, gathering dust in the far corner.

"Mother would definitely have chucked those out, so it must have been Grandmere who brought them up here." Elise decided that the far corner was as good a place to start as any. She picked her way through the cobwebs testing each floor board before stepping on it, and made it in one piece to the corner.

She pushed aside the high chair and moved the pushchair and an equally ancient-looking rocking horse to one side to reveal a pile of old blankets. They were full of dust, so she tried to slide them to the floor without releasing a massive cloud. It took her a few minutes to remove all the coverings, but underneath she found a huge trunk. It looked like one of the things she had seen in the old Hollywood movies that she and Grandmere had loved to watch.

Elise, throwing caution to the winds, tugged it into the middle of the floor; she let out a loud scream as something yanked her head back. Elise stood stock still, there was no sound other than her own very heaving breathing, so she slowly put her hand up to her head. She realised that her pony tail had tangled itself around the teeth of an ancient electric hedge trimmer. It took several minutes and lots of swearing to free herself from the blade, but she eventually dragged her hair through the teeth to free it and then concentrated on piling everything back in its place, bulking up the blankets and inhaling mountains of dust as she did so to hide the fact that the trunk was no longer in its place.

Elise then dragged the heavy trunk to the doorway and carefully manoeuvred it down the short staircase onto the main landing. She then retraced her steps and used her jumper to eradicate any evidence of her footprints. She flicked off the light, closed the door and started one stair at a time to get the trunk out of the house. Elise didn't feel safe till the trunk was stashed on the back seat of her car.

It had been a squeeze; Elise's knuckles were bleeding where she had scraped them on the door frame. She felt as if it had taken forever, and was getting worried about getting to the undertakers in time. Placing the trunk key in her bag, she ran back into the house, and taking a dustpan and brush from the kitchen quickly swept the landing and stairs. Once she was satisfied that no evidence of her clandestine activity remained, she wiped the dustpan, shook the brush, returned the bin liner to its rightful place and locked the door behind her.

Elise desperately wanted to open the trunk but for now it would have to stay locked. Instead, she started the car and headed for the High Street.

Not sure of the etiquette involving funeral directors, Elise hesitated before knocking on the door of Soames and Soames's. A lady sitting behind a desk noticed her peeking through the glass and hurried to open the door.

"Come in, please, how can I help you?" The lady had a friendly smile, but it seemed to turn a bit manic when Elise tiptoed in, clutching a large polythene bag.

The lady took a step back, glancing over her shoulder towards a little door at the back of the office. Still not sure what she was supposed to do, Elise whispered to the lady, "My name is Elise, I've come to bring these clothes for my grandmother." The lady still looked puzzled and slightly alarmed.

In desperation, Elise raised her voice. "Giselle Jacobs, my mother told me that she was here."

Elise panicked. What if her mother had given her the wrong name, what if Grandmere was somewhere completely different.

The lady heaved a sigh of relief, but still stared quizzically at Elise.

"You are Louise Jacobs' daughter?" she asked.

Elise was beginning to feel very nervous; maybe she was supposed to show some ID, before they would let her see her grandmother. The lady's worried expression had gone and wearing a sympathetic smile, she reached out for Elise's hand.

"Hello, Elise, I'm so pleased that you were able to come. Alex Forbes said you would probably be popping in this morning. Come in and sit yourself down, can I get you a cup of tea? You look worn-out."

"I'm not really sure what I'm supposed to do; I've brought some clothes for my grandmother."

"Oh, yes, I understand that your mother has spoken with my husband, and that she has insisted that there is to be no service at the crematorium. Is that what you both wanted?"

"Mother had spoken to him before I arrived, but she told me this morning that that's what she wants."

"Well, you could go and spend some time with your grandmother before she leaves us if you would like."

"Is that all right? I mean, I would like to if that would be possible."

"You do whatever you feel happy with."

Mrs Soames took the garment bag from Elise, and unzipped it.

"These are perfectly lovely; you have excellent taste, Elise."

"It's one of her favourite outfits, and yes, I would like to sit with her for a while."

"That's absolutely fine. Why don't you go and get yourself a coffee? Give us a couple of hours and we'll have everything ready for you."

Elise was trying hard not to let her chin wobble. She looked at her watch. It was only twelve o'clock, but she already felt exhausted. She wasn't sure that she could keep going for another two hours, but she quietly nodded, and decided to go back to her car.

Chapter Ten

Elise climbed into the driver's seat, and stared at the trunk through the rear-view mirror. She really wanted to see what was inside. As far as she knew, Grandma kept everything that mattered to her in her bedroom. Elise could not bear the agony of not knowing for a moment longer, and wondered if it would be possible to open the trunk whilst it was still on the car seat.

She soon realised that that was not an option and reluctantly set about dragging it out of the car. Elise eventually managed to manoeuvre the trunk onto the tarmac. Sweat was dripping unceremoniously off the end of her nose, and her back was starting to ache.

She didn't know whether the mirror, the trunk or the plant pot was responsible, and decided to focus all her attention on the task in hand. She could see now that the trunk was supposed to be standing on its end before being opened. The gold padlock was on the top left, and the 'lid' acted as a small door which opened horizontally. Elise debated about opening it. "What if everything falls out?"

"No," she reasoned, "Grandmere was far too organised to ever let that happen." Elise took the key from her bag, the envelope containing her euros was clearly visible. Elise had forgotten all about them, and was annoyed with herself for not leaving them in her flat for safe-keeping.

The sight of them gave her a sudden burst of confidence and she slid the key into the lock. The padlock opened and Elise was able to swing the door back. Inside, on the left, was an array of little wooden drawers. The right-hand side of the trunk had a fabric curtain stretched across it, covering the contents, held in place by a zip. Grandmere had attached a card to the curtain. It simply said, "Do not open." Elise carefully pulled open the top drawer, and saw a large thick envelope addressed to her. She placed the envelope in her bag, and relocked the trunk; the thought of having to get it back into the car was agonising, and she scolded herself for being so impatient.

She suddenly saw an easier way to get the thing back, and pulled her dust-covered jumper out of her bag. First, she leaned the trunk at a forty-five-degree angle so that the top of it leaned against the car seat. She then walked around the car and pulled open the other rear door. She threaded the sleeves of her jumper through the sturdy metal loop on the top of the trunk and slowly began to ease it across the seat. As soon as a third of it was in the car, she ran back around and pushed the rest of it safely inside. Elise closed the door and retrieved her jumper before locking the car. The heavy trunk and warm sunshine had caused another bout of sweating and Elise quickly mopped her forehead with the sleeve before dumping it into her bag. It wasn't even one o'clock, she still had an hour to go before going back to see Grandmere.

Elise never treated herself to 'posh coffee' outside of work. Gerry was addicted to the stuff and sent Elise out to grab coffees for everyone at least every other day.

'Grabbing the coffees' was a task that Elise always enjoyed. She looked forward to chatting with Freddie and to his 'perfect smiley face' that greeted her when she took the lid off her cup of latte. She was still a bit puzzled by that. She had always assumed that Freddie put them in everyone's froth, but apparently not.

Buying it for herself outside office hours, however, was far too extravagant, but she reasoned, today was a special day and she did need somewhere quiet and preferably out of the sun to sit and open Grandmere's envelope. She was also feeling extremely thirsty and light headed. So, she set off once again for the High Street in search of a coffee shop.

Elise spotted a small but inviting-looking café. She walked up to the counter admiring the family photographs adorning the walls, and the little lamps with pale cream shades in the centre of the small tables set against the wall.

"Perfect," she thought to herself. "Grandmere would be proud." Memories of the nasty waitress in the wine bar started flashing before her eyes, and Elise nervously checked that she had enough cash on her to pay for the coffee. The man behind the counter was busy replenishing the chilled display cabinets.

"Please take a seat; I will bring you a menu."

Elise panicked; did this mean she had to order food? She wasn't quite prepared for that expense.

"Oh, I only want coffee. Is that all right?"

The man straightened up and said,

"Yes, of course, what would you like?"

Elise looked around for a drinks list, gave up and said, "Cappuccino?"

The man nodded. "I will bring it over, large or small?"

"Better make it a large," she replied. The man was still staring at her and Elise wondered if he was waiting to be paid. Red-faced she dived into her bag and pulled out her battered old purse. The catch was fiddly and was becoming more temperamental by the day. Elise, after much fumbling, managed to pull out a five-pound note. He seemed to change his mind and waved her away.

"I will bring the bill, don't worry."

Elise thought the man was getting annoyed with her dithering and quickly headed for a seat in the far corner of the café.

She sat as far away from the counter as she could and with shaking fingers, pulled the envelope out of her bag, checking that nothing else had fallen out with it. The envelope, full of euros, was making her very nervous.

She carefully placed her jumper over the euros before zipping up the bag. It was falling apart and the zip didn't close properly; no doubt that was the reason the previous owner had dumped it in the charity shop, but it would have to do for now.

She held on tightly to the envelope as the waiter approached. He eyed her up and down as he placed the cup on the table in front of her, and lingered a moment too long.

"He probably thinks I don't have enough money to pay for it," thought Elise, but to be fair to him, she probably did resemble someone who normally got their coffee from dumpsters, and proceeded to ferret around again in her handbag for her purse.

Elise triumphantly threw the retrieved five-pound note onto the table.

"Keep the change," she heard herself say. The waiter smiled and scurried away.

"That will show him," thought Elise, before berating herself for being so reckless. "Well, I'm going to be here for a while, so hopefully he won't mind!" Elise turned back to the envelope, took out the long letter and settled herself in the chair.

"My dearest Elise,

Please don't be sad, I am not. I've had a wonderful life, but have been waiting for a while now to join my beloved Tom, so please be happy for us, together again after all these years.

I know now that we will never take our trip to Paris together. Your mother would never even discuss it. I had hoped that one day she would change her mind, but I very much doubt that this will ever happen. I'm getting older now and would not be able to do the things that I have dreamt about any longer. Paris is about walking and discovering the beauty of its tiny back streets and the atmosphere and charm of all the wonderful little shops and cafés just as much as it is about visiting the Sacré Coeur, Notre Dame and of course the Tour Eiffel. I cannot walk very well now, and would be so very cross with myself if I could not manage. I am writing this letter as it is your twenty-first birthday soon. Please don't be too upset about the passport. You are such a wonderful girl, well, I should say 'woman' now, and it's time to see the world.

Please believe me when I say that I did everything possible to help you and your mother stay together. I know that she has not been a good mother, but I hope that you can find it in your heart to forgive her one day. I also hope that I managed to make your life more bearable. You have given me so much, now it is my chance to try and repay just a tiny bit.

I desperately wanted to tell you everything about my life, in Paris, when I met your grandfather, and then my life in England, when we bought our dream cottage and expected to live happily ever after.

Sadly, as you know our fairy tale ended far too soon. I have suffered so much because your mother would not allow me to talk about her father. Louise would have been furious with both of us. She did not cope with his death at all, and strove to remove everything from her life that reminded her of him. So, please don't be shocked if she does the same to me. I am so sure she will that I have given a copy of this letter to my solicitor, Mr Forbes. I doubt if you will remember him but he has been a true friend and counsellor to me ever since Tom died, and I know that I would not have been able to give you what little I did without his guidance and support.

You must thank dear Alex who went to such lengths to carry out my wishes. Bless him; he did get quite dirty crawling around in the loft to hide this letter in my beautiful cabin trunk. It's been quite an adventure for the two of us. I can't stress strongly enough all that he has done for us and will no doubt continue to do now that I am no longer here. So, please tell him when you see him, how much he was appreciated. Now I can talk freely and you can listen without any fear of retribution.

I met your grandfather in Paris just after the war. We had all suffered a great deal, food had been very scarce, and my parents had struggled to keep going. My father was a tailor, and my mother a seamstress and lace-maker. We had a shop on the Rue Legendre, in Montmartre, and my father had managed to keep us going by making clothes out of old curtains and blankets, anything he could get his hands on, really; my mother was skilled at repairing dresses and coats, and reusing any bits of salvable fabric to make up new things. So, we managed to survive through those dreadful years.

Your grandfather was a soldier and was having a last look around before returning to England, and well, he met me and we fell in love and he stayed! He told me that he had no family. His parents had died of Tuberculosis, when he was only a child, and he had ended up living with his grandmother.

At the age of fifteen, he had been apprenticed to a tailor in the centre of Manchester, but when his grandmother passed away, he found himself with nowhere to live and joined up. He had nothing to go back for, and my father was happy to take him in the shop, so everything turned out wonderfully for both of us.

We were a source of great amusement amongst our customers and neighbours. I hardly spoke any English and he only knew about three words of French, but we had both studied Latin at school, and used that to communicate. Tom worked at his French every day and I tried hard with English; he would often chat in English and I would answer in French; it became so natural that we didn't realise we were speaking to each other in completely different languages, but it was frustrating for anyone who was trying to eavesdrop.

Sorry, my dear, I am digressing. Tom loved working with my father in the shop. He had always been interested in clothes, and was a very quick learner. My father taught him everything he knew and Tom became an extremely skilled craftsman, cutting patterns and making wonderful shirts and suits. Men would come to our little shop from every corner of France and some, even from abroad to have Tom make the most wonderful clothes for them. He used only the finest fabrics, and fussed over the smallest detail to ensure perfection.

Mother and I loved creating wonderful ensembles; she was famed for her lace-making and was an amazing seamstress. We used to make costumes for the show girls at the 'Folies Bergeres'. It was a wonderful place, and was world famous! Even Charlie Chaplin played there once. Sadly, it closed for a while during the war. The Germans didn't like the fact that our friend Michel worked there, but Mr Derval refused to let him go and just made sure he stayed out of sight. So, everything re-opened and Mother had plenty of work then. Of course, she also had a very discreet clientele of beautiful courtesans who wore the most beautiful clothes and the 'Mesdames a cinq heures', as they were known, who always insisted on having the very latest fashions. I do believe that the famous Princess Fahmy Bey was a client, she was just plain 'Maggie' then, but my mother treated every customer with great respect, and was known for her discretion.

Your grandfather and I were often given tickets in exchange for my work. The costumes were always getting torn, and the girls didn't earn much money. We would love to walk up together in the evenings and see the shows. One of our favourite places to visit was the Cimetiere de Montmartre, I know that might sound a bit macabre, but it's a beautiful and peaceful place.

Your grandfather loved the ballet and there was great excitement when Nijinsky was finally laid to rest there in 1950. His tomb is a work of art with a beautiful sculpture of him seated on the lid. I hope, my darling, that now that I am no longer here, you will at last seize the opportunity and travel to my wonderful city and see the sights that we have talked about all these years.

I would have loved to have taken you, to have walked down all those familiar streets and seen all the sights together, but it would have destroyed your mother. You can go now and think of me whilst you are there. I will try to help you understand why your mother is the way she is, and why she hates all things French.

I have no wish to excuse her, but hopefully you will find your own peace and learn to love yourself a little more if you manage to find the strength in your heart to forgive her even just a little.

Your grandfather and I always wanted children, but it seemed that a child did not want us! Over the years, we got used to there just being the two of us and we were so happy and felt very blessed to have each other. Then, in 1970, I realised that I was pregnant, and we were beside ourselves with delight, but full of fear. I was far too old to be having a baby, and the doctors warned us not to get our hopes up.

Your grandfather was determined that all would be well, and insisted on us moving back to England. He had always talked about little country cottages with their own private little gardens at the back where you could have a swing and run around and wanted his child to have that. Of course, I was terrified. I had never lived anywhere but Paris, and never wanted to live anywhere else. But your grandfather had stayed in France for me and I loved him very much, and thought it was only fair that I move to England for him.

My father had died years earlier, and my mother wanted to retire; without us, she could not continue with the shop, but she refused to move to England. I think Tom was surprised; it had never crossed his mind that she would prefer to stay on alone in Paris rather than coming to England to help raise her grandchild. But my mother was adamant that she was going to stay put. I knew that she was not well, and could not face the upheaval of the move, but she forbade me to tell Tom, as she knew that he had set his heart on going home.

She sold all the sewing machines and equipment and rented a tiny apartment nearby on the rue L'Epic. She gave your father and me some money to bring to England to help us get started.

Tom was not happy with having to bring my mirror, but it was the one thing that I insisted upon, so he had it shipped here by a very special company who took great care of it. I hope that you managed to save it and that you will treasure it as I have."

Elise couldn't help shaking her head when she read this. "Please Grandmere," she thought, "you know I cannot bear to look at that thing." Feeling slightly silly then, she looked around to see if anyone had noticed and had a quick gulp of the lukewarm coffee, before turning back to the letter.

"England: We arrived, and found our perfect cottage in Surbiton. Your grandfather found a position with a very fine tailor's shop in Savile Row, as we knew he would, and I started making layettes and christening robes to help pass the time.

My hands were getting worse every day, and your grandfather spared no expense in trying to find a cure. The consultants diagnosed me with rheumatoid arthritis and explained to Tom that although they could slow down the progression, there was no cure. Poor Tom was heartbroken and kept insisting that we seek a second opinion. I told him that God Willing I should soon have a baby to look after and that was far more important to me than sewing.

The doctors insisted on me having complete bed rest for the last four weeks of my pregnancy, I could still sew a little and enjoyed doing a little embroidery. It helped me to pass the time, and I ended up with a thriving little empire!

Well, obviously, your mother arrived, and your grandfather was completely besotted with her from the moment he held her in his arms. We named her Louise, because it was a name we both loved, and it worked in French and English. Of course, I insisted on speaking to her only in French and her father spoke only in English, that way she spoke both perfectly and was very proud of herself."

Elise re-read that line, as far as she knew her mother could not speak a single word of French and always turned on her heel and stormed out of the room if she and Grandmere were chatting to each other. Elise turned back to her letter.

"My mother came to stay for a while when Louise was born, but she was not well and stayed only a short while. She passed away when Louise was two, and I went back alone for her funeral. It was hard for me to leave Paris after losing her. The trunk was her pride and joy. She had had it for as long as I could remember, and used it to store her most treasured possessions. She told me that an impoverished lady had given it to her as payment for some dresses that she had made for her just before the war. I packed what few bits were left in my mother's little apartment and brought the trunk back to our cottage. It had pride of place in your grandfather's workroom.

When Louise was ten years old, your grandfather and I decided to take her to Paris for a special birthday treat. I was becoming more than a little concerned about her. She was to be fair, completely spoilt by her father. She was an extremely pretty little girl, and she knew that her father would give her whatever she wanted; one summer it was ballet, after her first lesson Tom was telling her that she was going to be as famous as Margot Fonteyn, and so on. Her ballet teacher was less than impressed with her complete lack of self-discipline and when she tried to correct her, she flounced out of the class. Of course her father blamed the teacher, and then it was music, then singing and so on. Louise expected all the glory but could not grasp that success depended on hard work and endless hours of practice.

Tom refused to accept that at ten years old she was still behaving like a two-year-old. He laughed at her very public tantrums and appalling rudeness. I tried to tell him that spoilt children do not always end up being happy adults, but he refused to hear a word against her, and Louise used it to her advantage. If I ever said 'no', she would simply stamp her feet and scream and say, 'tell her Daddy, tell her to say yes', and then she would laugh triumphantly, knowing that she had won and that he would give her whatever she wanted.

He never tired of telling her that she was the best, that whatever she wanted she would have, and that she would grow up to be the most beautiful princess in the world and that her every wish would be granted.

(Oh, dear Elise, I think I just got a little carried away, but I have just realised that this is the first time that I have been able to get all this off my chest. Sorry, back to Paris, 1980) Well, off we went to Paris. First, we took her to see all the sights, but Louise was more interested in ensuring that she remained the centre of attention. She loved impressing everyone by switching constantly between perfect French and perfect English, skipping around in her beautiful dresses.

Tom and I still managed to have a wonderful time, meeting up with old friends and catching up on everything. I hadn't been home for eight years, and there just didn't seem to be enough hours in the day and soon it was time to return home.

On our last evening in Paris, we decided to take Louise to the Cimetiere to show her Nijinsky's grave. We wanted to share with our daughter a place that had always been so special for us. Louise, for once, was fascinated and insisted that her father took a whole roll of film of her dancing next to the sculpture so that she could show her friends at school. It was getting late and we had an early flight in the morning so we started to walk back to our hotel.

Then it happened: A motorbike came out of nowhere, it crashed into one of the tables outside a little café, and both the bike and its rider were sliding across the road, heading straight towards us. Your grandfather pushed Louise and me out of the way, but the front wheel caught him and dragged him down the road. Louise was screaming, there was pandemonium, the gendarmes arrived, ambulances, everything, but it was too late, the motorcycle rider and your grandfather were dead.

The next few days were a nightmare, but luckily, I had good friends who took care of everything. The embassy was wonderful and your grandfather's body was flown back to England. Louise and I returned to our little cottage. She blamed me of course, and refused to accept that her father was gone. She hated Paris and swore she would never speak another word of French.

Worse still, she refused to go to the funeral. Her school teacher even came to see her and tried to convince her to go, saying that it was her chance to say 'Good bye'.

'How can I say *goodbye* to him? He can't hear me. I will not go.'

So, Louise stayed with her teacher and I went alone. Louise never ever forgave me. She made me throw everything out of the house that reminded her of her daddy. She emptied his sewing room and even threw his beloved sewing machine into the bin.

She insisted that I threw away my mother's trunk. I could not bear the thought of it, so Mr Forbes came to the house when she was at school, and we hid it in the attic. I knew that it was very unlikely that Louise would ever go in there as she pretended that it no longer existed. But we hid it in the farthest corner under piles of clothes.

Mr Forbes, and later his son, used to dread having to hide things in there, but they were wonderful friends, and would have done anything for me, even if it meant crawling through all that dust!

Louise did not get any better, she would not even allow me to mention Tom's name. Her teacher told me that it was her only way of coping with the stress, and not to try to intervene; of course, I loved her very much and did whatever I thought would help her to deal with losing him.

After a few short weeks, Louise started to behave as if her father had never existed. It was as if she had shut every memory of him away. She went back to her old ways, still expecting to have everything that she wanted, and she was furious with me when I refused to give in to her. She still inhabited this strange make-believe world, filled with magical stories of princes and fairy princesses. Even at the age of sixteen she was still convinced that she was going to marry a prince, and complained endlessly that she couldn't be expected to meet one if she didn't have the money to go to all the right places. She left school without even finishing her A levels.

'It's all a waste of time: I just need to move in the right circles,' was all she would say. Louise was a very pretty girl, heads turned whenever she entered the room, so I thought that maybe she would find her Prince Charming after all. She spent every minute in London, often not coming home for days on end. Of course, I was worried, but I knew that if I said too much, she might never come home at all.

One day she came running into the house, she couldn't stop smiling and told me with great excitement that she would be moving into a flat in London at the end of the month. I was very surprised, as flats don't come cheap, but when I asked her about the rent, she said she had got a wonderful job working for a Danish company and that she would be sharing with lots of friends, so the rent was not a problem.

She seemed to be so happy and full of life; she told me that she couldn't move into the flat until after Christmas, and so we had a couple of weeks together. I couldn't believe the change in her. She was up every morning at the crack of dawn, spending ages with her makeup and agonising over outfits. She gave me a beautiful 'Mont Blanc' fountain pen for Christmas; it had the name 'Jesper Andersen' inscribed on the side and I asked her about it. 'That's the name of the company, Mum. It's a company pen; I thought you might like it.' I was very shocked, the pen must have cost a fortune, but Louise insisted that the company was very prestigious and that they never had anything but the best.

I was devastated the day that she left, but I had to let her go, her dreams seemed to be coming true and I was delighted for her.

Then, everything fell apart. I hadn't seen Louise since she moved out, but she phoned occasionally and was full of stories of restaurants she had been to and nights out in the best clubs in London. The phone rang; it was quite early in the morning, so I was surprised to hear her voice. She sounded strange, very quiet, and very odd. She just said, 'Mother, I have decided to resign. Can you come and get me?' That was it; she just put the phone down. I rang back, but just got an engaged signal. I felt myself starting to panic, she had never given me her address, but had often mentioned the location of the company headquarters, and of course, I remembered the pen. I grabbed a cab all the way into London, and the driver dropped me off outside the grandest building on the street.

The name on the sign didn't match the pen, but it was definitely Danish, so I went straight up to the reception desk. I asked the lady if she could direct me to Louise Jacobs, she looked at her computer screen and told me that they had no one of that name working there. I just stood there, I had no idea what to do next, so in desperation, I took out the pen and showed it to her. 'My daughter works for this company. Do you know where their office is?' I asked. She immediately picked up the phone and told me to take a seat.

A few moments later, a very smartly dressed lady hurried over to me. 'I'm Anne Walter, the head of H.R. Please may I see the pen?' Well, I showed her the thing! I was getting more and more upset, and told her about the strange phone call. The woman asked me to wait. I was in agony, but I didn't really have much choice. She reappeared after a few minutes holding a glossy magazine. She flicked through it and then showed me one of those society photographs, and there was Louise, holding the arm of a very tall blond man. I nodded and said, 'Yes, that's Louise.'

She pulled out her phone and made a call. 'Just wait here for a minute, and please stop worrying, I think I know where your daughter is,' she said.

A huge car pulled up outside the door and we jumped in. The woman said something to the driver and off we went. We came to a stop, maybe half a mile from the office, outside some sort of hotel. It was a very grand-looking building. There was a doorman, who nodded at us and opened the door. Ms Walter told me to go inside and wait for her. I could see her talking to the doorman, but didn't want to eavesdrop. She followed me into the lobby and pressed the button for the lift. She was just standing there in silence, and I couldn't wait any longer, everything was so confusing, and I didn't have a clue where we were going. 'Ms Walter?' I asked. 'If Louise is not employed by your company, how'd you know where she is?' The lift arrived and we jumped in. As it started to move, she took my arm again. 'I do not know your daughter, but I do know Jesper Andersen.' I should have felt relieved, but I just didn't.

The lift seemed to go on for ever, Ms Walter had taken a card out of her bag, and as soon as it stopped she marched out and walked straight across the hall. There was a big oak door directly in front of us. She pushed the card into some gadget on the wall and then knocked and shouted Louise's name. There was no answer; she just opened the door and in we went. It was a huge and very lavishly decorated apartment, certainly not an office of any sort. She led me through a beautiful room, one of the walls was completely windows, I had never seen anything like it before, and then she knocked again on another door. 'Louise, your mother is here, may we come in?' I'm afraid to say that I forgot my manners for a moment and almost pushed her, but I was so scared. I ran into the room and saw my Louise; she was sitting in a huge armchair with a large suitcase on her lap. I could see that she was very pale, and had tears running down her face.

'Where have you been?' was all she said. Mrs Walter was so calm, she walked over to the chair and tried to lift the suitcase off Louise, but Louise would not let go. I tried to hug her, but the case prevented me from getting near her. 'Let me take that,' I said, 'you look very pale, whatever has happened?'

'I told you, on the phone, Mother, I've resigned,' was all she would say.

Mrs Walter smiled at Louise, and said, 'I think you could do with some breakfast, let me go and see what's in the kitchen.' She left the room and I took hold of the case.

I sat down on the arm of the chair and stroked her hair. I tried to be as bright and cheerful as I could manage, and said, 'Come on now, let me go and put this in the hall and call a cab to take us home.'

Louise brightened up a little. 'Yes, please, can we go right now, straight away?'

Mrs Walter was so calm, she nodded her head, and said, 'You look as if you haven't eaten, why don't we have a drink at least and then I promise you we will go straight home.'

'You can sort everything out then, Mum, can't you? I don't want this anymore, and I've changed my mind.'

Louise was staring at the suitcase as she spoke. I still didn't really have a clue what was going on, but I could see that she was not herself and I just wanted to get her home. I pulled the suitcase onto the floor, and helped Louise out of the chair. I realised then that she was not talking about the case.

Mrs Walter bustled back in with some tea and toast, she paused at the door, when she saw Louise standing up, but carried on as if nothing had happened. 'Come on, dear. You'll feel better when you have had some food.' Louise picked up the toast and started to eat. Mrs Walter pulled the handle up on the case and wheeled it into the hall. I followed her. I was too shocked to speak, but she put her arms around me and gave me a hug.

'I'm so very, very sorry,' she said, 'I saw the pen and just put two and two together. Mr Andersen is in charge of all our Northern Europe Territories; he came over in November and decided to stay for a while. This is the company apartment, we keep it for all the bigwigs to stay in when they come from abroad. He called me yesterday and said something had cropped up and that he had to return to Denmark immediately. He asked me to arrange for his stuff to be shipped home. When the receptionist told me about the pen, I knew straight away. He had us turning the office upside down looking for it. Apparently, it was a gift from his wife, and he didn't want to go home without it. Andersen may be a highflier in this company, but believe me he is a real lowlife in everything else.'

Louise appeared in the hall. 'Is the cab here?' she asked. Mrs Walter nodded, and then smiled at Louise, 'Yes, my dear, come on, let's go.'

We all walked back to the lift; Louise looked so dejected and miserable.

I felt so helpless and so sorry to see her like that, it broke my heart. I just told her, 'It's time to come home, my darling.' She just followed me; I couldn't believe it was happening, but it was like her spirit was just broken.

The car was waiting outside for us. The driver put Louise's case in the boot and we all got in. 'Steve will take you home,' she said. 'I don't want to hold you, I can see you need some space, but please give him your phone number. I will be in touch. I promise, I have a daughter myself.'

Mrs Walter was true to her word, she actually came to see me two days later. She really tried her best to help. The doorman had recognised the photo of Louise and said that she had been living there with Jesper Andersen, and there were a few photos of the two of them together. She said that Jesper had slipped the doorman a very large tip and told him to get rid of Louise. Fortunately, John is a decent man, with children of his own. He had taken a shine to Louise, so he had gone straight up to see her, told and made up some story about him having to rush off to attend some important meeting back in Denmark. He told her to resign herself to the fact that Jesper wouldn't be back and that she needed to go home.

He had helped her to pack up her belongings, and told her to contact you. He was praying that you would come; otherwise, he would have been left with little choice other than to get the security team in to evict her from the flat.

Mrs Walter gave me Andersen's home and work address and told me to hand everything over to my solicitor. According to her, and strictly off the record, she told me that your father was irreplaceable as far as his company was concerned, and that they would fall over backwards to protect him, if necessary.

You were well on your way, and there was no way to hide anything. Gradually over the next few weeks, your mother told me bits and pieces. Of course, she had gone straight to the top, seeking out the 'Highest Flier' and, knowing your mother, getting what she wanted. Well, she got the posh apartment and the fancy clothes and lifestyle, but she was greedy for more. Andersen was much older than her and had a family back in Denmark. It appears that Louise took a liking to the pen and simply took it from his briefcase one day. I have no idea why she ended up giving it to me. I never dared mention it again.

He had made it clear that it was just a fling and that he had no intentions of leaving his wife. Mrs Walter had told me that he was known for being a player, but Louise, was so arrogant, and so sure of herself that she actually believed that he would not be able to live without her. Being the silly naïve girl that she was, she decided to present him with a baby, assuming that he would be a doting father just like her own and would refuse the mother of his baby nothing.

She was a selfish, naive girl, who thought nothing of the child she was bringing into this world; it was just a means to an end. Once she realised that she was not going to get what she wanted, she somehow expected me to be able to wave a magic wand, say 'Hey Presto' and make the baby disappear.

Louise was so angry, she screamed and shouted and threw terrible tantrums, and the doctor was really worried about both her and the baby. 'You need to calm yourself,' he said to her. 'All this is not good for you or your baby.'

'I don't want the bloody baby!' she screamed at him. 'Just get rid of it.' Louise was about seven months pregnant by now and the doctor was shocked and, I dare say, quite disgusted at the way she was behaving. I really lost my temper with her.

'This baby is not to blame for what has happened, he or she will be in the world soon, and there is nothing we can do about that'

'Oh, yes, we can! Jesper has to pay for what he's done to me. What am I supposed to do with a baby? I don't want it and I'm not having it. If my daddy were here, he would sort everything out for me, he would make him marry me and buy me a big house and pay for nannies and everything.' She was twenty and still thinking and behaving like the spoilt little girl from ten years ago.

I managed to track down your father with the help of Mrs Walter (again, strictly off the record) and dear Mr Forbes. It wasn't that hard, everything went through the solicitors. Mr Andersen was a very wealthy man and agreed to support you financially as long as your mother agreed never to try to contact him or any member of his family. When your mother finally realised that her plans had failed, she did her usual foot stamping and said she wanted nothing, but we didn't have much money, and Louise finally agreed to allow my solicitor to do the negotiating. Mr Forbes took control of everything. It was agreed that he would support you until your eighteenth birthday.

I am truly, truly sorry and terribly ashamed for the way Louise treated you. I can only hope that I made up for her lack of love as you know that I loved you more than I could ever say. Please just begin to love yourself a little more. You are intelligent and beautiful, but you always blamed yourself for your mother's lack of interest. She has lived in a make-believe world of her own all her life, everything has to revolve around her, and you felt as if you had to apologise for your very existence. She made you think that you are to blame for whatever goes wrong, even when you have done nothing wrong. You allow people to bully and criticise you without ever even trying to defend yourself, because that is how your mother treated you, and you think that because she did it, it's acceptable for everyone else to do it too.

I have been in despair over the years, watching you wear those awful, ill-fitting clothes, chopping at your hair with blunt scissors, and refusing to allow yourself even the tiniest of pleasures. Your mother made you feel worthless and despite all your achievements and your exceptional intelligence, you seem to be unable to accept that you are entirely blameless.

Your mother is so self-centred; she is unable to put anyone or anything before her own needs. I know it has been so hard for you, growing up without loving parents to support and nurture you, but you are an adult now. Let your mother do as she pleases, she is not your responsibility. You must put all of it behind you and find the strength within you to start afresh.

Now put this letter away and go and see the solicitor. I did not trust your mother to carry out any of my wishes, so I handed over everything to dear Mr Forbes. He knows exactly what is required and has promised me that he will ensure that my ashes are placed next to my beloved Tom, which is all I want. I know your mother will refuse to have a funeral; she has never been to one in her life. So please say your goodbyes to me now and run along to see Mr Forbes as he has a letter for you. I also gave him a copy of this and a spare key to the trunk in case your mother did not give you the box.

So please, my dearest Elise; you have your passport, your trunk is packed, and Mr Forbes has everything else that you need. Leave as soon as you can for Paris. xxxxxxxxxxxxxx"

Chapter Eleven

Elise looked up from the letter. Her coffee was cold, and she felt nauseous; she shivered and dived into her bag to retrieve her jumper. As she pushed her hands through the crumpled sleeves, she looked at her watch. It was time to say 'Goodbye'.

Elise walked slowly back up the high street and entered Soames and Soames.

She was filled with dread at the idea of seeing her grandmother, but equally could not bear the thought of not having just a little more time with her.

Mrs Soames quickly came up and took her arm.

"Are you sure that you would like to do this? A lot of people prefer to remember their loved ones as they were when they were alive. Nobody would think the worse of you if you prefer not to see her now."

Elise shook her head, "Thank you, Mrs Soames, but I really think I would like a little time, just to say goodbye to her properly."

Mrs Soames led Elise through a door at the back of the office into a small corridor. There was a door on the right.

"Madame Jacobs is in here," she said and opened the door slightly. Elise tried to visualise what was behind the door, but really had no idea what to expect.

"Would you like me to come in with you, Elise?" asked Mrs Soames.

"No, thank you, I won't stay long, just a few minutes." Mrs Soames turned around and headed back up the corridor. Elise took a deep breath and pushed open the door.

She was horrified to be greeted by a coffin on a trestle, with a large bouquet of lilies in front of it. A red velvet chair was placed at the side of the coffin.

Elise focussed her eyes on the chair, and made a grab for the seat. Once she had a hand on it, she closed her eyes and didn't open them again until she was securely seated on the cushion. She glanced quickly into the coffin, hoping that her grandmother would look as if she were sleeping.

Madame Jacobs was lying in the coffin, dressed in the outfit that Elise had brought in. Her hair and makeup looked almost the same, but there was nothing else there that Elise recognised. She desperately wanted to feel as if her grandmother was still with her, but the realisation that she was completely alone, suddenly hit her.

Elise sat for a moment, trying to gather her thoughts and started to have a silent conversation, filling her grandmother in on all that had happened during the last few days, although she did leave out the bit about the 'joint'. That would definitely be too much information for Madame Jacobs's delicate ears!

She sat with Grandmere for more than an hour, telling her all about her trip to Paris, and promising that she would visit the Cimetiere in Montmartre and see Nijinsky's tomb, just as they had talked about over the years.

Elise leaned over into the coffin and after kissing her Grandmother on both cheeks, she slowly walked back to Mrs Soames's desk and after quietly thanking her for her kindness, she asked for directions to Mr Forbes's office.

Elise's mind was in knots, the father she had never known had turned out not to be the secret prince, after all. Well, maybe 'Hamlet', but then he wasn't much cop, as she recalled. At least she actually had one, though sadly he seemed to dislike her almost as much as her mother did. She smiled to herself in spite of everything, at least it kind of explained why she didn't have the raven black hair of her mother and Grandmere.

Grandmere had shushed her whenever she tried to ask questions about him. She had only seen her birth certificate once, when Grandmere had insisted on paying for a passport for her 21st birthday. She had wondered at the strange name in the 'Father' space, but assumed her mother had just made one up. It was never mentioned at school. She knew lots of other children who only had one parent at home, but most of them talked about their fathers and going to visit and special days out. Elise never got involved in such conversations. She had no close friends; nobody asked her too many questions, nobody was particularly interested in her, to be fair, and that was the way that Elise liked to live. So, now she had a father who was alive, but seemed to care for her even less than her own mother did, if that were possible. She had managed without him up until now and felt no burning desire to seek him out.

Elise stopped outside the solicitor's office, it looked very swish; 'Forbes and Forbes' in gold rimmed letters. This time Elise didn't knock. She walked up to the lady, who was seated behind a very ornate desk, and waited. The lady glanced up at her and frowned. "Can I help you?" she said in a tone that implied that she would rather not.

"I'd like to see Mr Forbes, if he's here."

The woman looked on her computer screen. "I'm sorry but Mr Forbes has cancelled all his appointments today, he is expecting a visit from one of our V.I.P. clients this afternoon, so perhaps you could telephone next week, and I'll see if we can fit you in." The woman had already got up from behind the desk and was heading for the door, beckoning at Elise to follow her. There was a distinct expression of distaste on her face that was causing Elise's knees to knock.

"I don't have an appointment," Elise said in desperation. "My grandmother died and she told me, well she didn't actually tell me, I mean..." Elise could barely speak, her nerves and shyness had taken hold and she felt that she was about to burst into tears again. The woman let go of the door and it closed with a loud bang. The expression of the woman's face had changed from distaste to utter disbelief.

"Surely not Madame Jacobs?"

A flood of relief overcame Elise and fresh tears started to run down her cheeks. "Yes, I'm Elise, Grandmere told me to come and see Mr Forbes, but if he is expecting someone, I don't know what to do."

"I'm so sorry, my dear, no please take a seat, let me get you some tissues." The woman almost strong-armed Elise into a chair and ran off to fetch the tissues.

"My husband will be out in just a minute. He's been waiting for you to come in."

It slowly dawned on Elise that she was the V.I.P., she had never heard herself referred to in that way before, but it did make her feel slightly less embarrassed about emptying Mrs Forbes's rather posh box of tissues.

"Do you think I could just have a minute?" asked Elise. She really needed to pull herself together before meeting "Dear Mr Forbes", then a worrying notion struck her. "Did his wife know that he had been sending very expensive flowers to her grandmother every week for the past twenty years?" If Mr Forbes had been around the same age as her grandfather, who was five years older than her grandmother, he had to be at least ninety, and this woman only looked to be in her fifties.

"Did you say you were Mr Forbes's daughter?" Elise ventured to ask, as the woman presented her with a glass of water.

"Goodness me, you certainly have your grandmother's grace and charm; no, I'm definitely Alex's wife."

Mrs Forbes suddenly blushed bright red and laughed.

"I think you are confusing Mr Forbes with Alex, I'm married to Alexander Forbes's son." Still smiling, she saw the door to her husband's office open.

A man who was definitely less than ninety stretched out his hand to Elise.

"Hello, lovely to meet you, I see you've been in Madame Jacobs's attic."

Elise nodded. "Yes, of course. I read the letter from the trunk. My grandmother told me to come to the office to see you."

"Yes, yes, please come in and sit down, my wife will make sure that we are not disturbed."

Elise picked up the tissues to put in the bin, and gazed at them in horror! They looked as if she had been cleaning the floor with them rather than wiping away her tears. She glanced down at her hands; they were filthy. There was a large mirror over the fire place in Mr Forbes's office, and Elise risked a quick glance. She was even more horrified at the reflection staring back at her.

No wonder poor Mrs Forbes had been heading for the door. She suddenly remembered using her jumper as a duster, and looking down saw great gobs of dust and cobwebs on her chest. "Yes, it was definitely her in the mirror." Elise didn't dare look anymore, she dreaded to think about what must be attached to her hair. Trying to hide her now flaming cheeks, she suddenly understood Alex's reference to the attic.

"Please sit down. Could I get you a brandy? I'm sure this has been a very difficult day for you. Please accept our sincere condolences, I've known your grandmother ever since she came to England, and your grandfather of course."

Elise shrank into the chair, then panicking that she was going to leave a mountain of cobwebs in her wake, she decided that it would be best to hover above the expensive-looking upholstery.

"My father and your grandparents were great friends, my father used to joke that he was the best–dressed lawyer in England. Your grandfather was an amazing craftsman, he made all my father's suits. I still have them, can't part with them. You know he made me a suit for my graduation ceremony, it was the best present I'd ever had. I'm sure it's what made Esther notice me. I'd been trying to catch her attention all through my final year, but all it took was a classy suit! She couldn't wait to marry me after that. I can't fit into it anymore, but can't part with it either."

It was strange to meet with someone who knew her grandfather; Elise started to relax, but still managed to maintain the hover.

"And of course, your magnificent grandmother, Madame Jacobs, she was the most fashionable woman in Surbiton; raised the bar for all the other ladies, let me tell you.

"My father did everything he could to help when Tom died. We lost my mother to cancer only a few months after his death, and your grandmother, even though she was suffering terribly, did everything she could to help him, and me of course. She was a wonderful cook, and always brought us the most beautiful cakes and pastries; she was a true friend to him, and to me as well. She was a truly wonderful lady.

"My poor father has dementia now, so I'm sure he won't mind me sharing his little secret. After my mother passed away, your grandmother was a constant source of comfort to him. She was always there when he needed her, she organised the funeral almost single-handedly, I was working abroad at the time, and it took a while for me to get home. My father could not face up to the fact that my mother was dying. I rang him every few days when she was first diagnosed, and was desperate to come home, but my father wouldn't hear of it, and insisted that it was nothing to worry about.

"It was a terrible shock when he rang me and told me that she had passed away. I was angry too, as I felt that he had cheated me out of the opportunity to be with her at the end and to be able to say goodbye. I managed to get home for the funeral but then had to go straight back afterwards and it was nearly two months before Esther and I moved back to England.

"It took my father a very long time to come to terms with losing mum, and I don't think he would ever have got back on his feet without your grandmother's support. He was only too delighted to be able to offer your grandmother help whenever she needed it, and they became very close. My father asked her to marry him, did you know?" Elise was so stunned that she almost sat on the chair.

"Of course, Madame Jacobs let him down gently; she said Tom was the only man for her, but they remained incredibly close over the years. I used to take my father to see her as often as I could, his face lit up when he saw her, and she was so gentle and kind, coaxing him to chat about the 'old days', and making him laugh. He almost seemed like his old self again when they were together. I haven't told him that she has passed away. His Alzheimer's is very advanced now, and I think it would break his heart if he did remember her so it's better that he doesn't know.

"My father finally gave up work entirely nearly fifteen years ago. I thought he was going to go on forever, but at the ripe old age of seventy-five, he had to admit defeat, and I took over the V.I.P clients that he had continued to keep, so that's how I came to be your grandmother's solicitor. She insisted on calling my father, Mr Forbes, for all those years, so I'm just Alex—fortunately, she has dropped the 'Little'."

Alex eventually drew breath.

"I'm so sorry I've been rambling on for ages, but I wanted to be sure that you know that you can trust me. I loved your grandmother and she put her faith in me. I promised her that I would continue to take care of you and your mother. Sorry, I'm rambling again… look, I know you have lots to do, so let me put your mind at rest, I will organise everything for your grandmother. She has left detailed instructions, and if you would like to leave me your number, I will contact you and would be honoured if you would like to go with me when I bury her ashes with Tom."

Elise nodded. "I have to get a new phone, but I'll let you have the number as soon I get it." Elise actually winced, when she had an unwelcome flashback to the last time her ancient mobile had rung; she certainly never wanted to hear that sound again.

"Don't let me keep you any longer, I have a couple of letters for you, and some special items of value, so all you have to do is sign for them, and I promise you can escape. She said that these are her last wishes and that you must follow them to the letter. I hope everything is clear." Alex opened a small cupboard at the side of his desk and handed a large bulky parcel over to Elise.

"Please don't forget to let me have your number, I would like to have your company when I carry out Madame Jacobs's last wishes, and I know she would want you to be present."

"Of course, I insist on being present. I'm going to Paris for a few days, may be longer, I'm not really sure."

"Oh, no, it takes a while, so it won't be for a least a month," Alex interrupted her.

"That's fine then, I look forward to seeing you again too. Thank you for being such a friend to my grandmother."

"It was an honour to call her my friend, and I know my father felt exactly the same. She did tell me to remind you before you leave my office that you have to do exactly as she has asked, but I'm sure that there is nothing too onerous."

Alex handed her a business card, on which he had also added his personal mobile phone number.

"Just in case you ever need me for anything, anything at all," he added, as he escorted her to the door.

Chapter Twelve

Elise walked out of the office, praying that hadn't left half the attic behind on the chair. She wedged the parcel in the top of her handbag. It was sticking out and the broken zip dangled under her armpit.

She felt like a bag lady, and was desperately worried that the handles on this particular bag were about to give way under the weight. Elise almost jogged back to the car. Before she climbed in, she risked a second quick look, this time in the wing mirror, and caught a close-up of her head. She jumped back in horror. Her hair was thick with dust; her face was grimy, with little pale lines where her tears had cut a swathe.

Elise suddenly felt very ashamed. She thought of her grandmother, always exquisitely dressed, never without matching handbag and shoes, and never a hair out of place. She had just come face to face with Grandmere's friend dressed like this.

Elise tore off the jumper and threw it into a litter bin. She climbed into her car, plonked the bag on the seat and watched everything empty out all over the floor. Elise thought of all the rude words she could and strung them together in her head as she pulled out of the car park and headed for home.

Elise was relieved to see space on either side of her little parking spot. She now had to figure out how to get the trunk and the mirror up the stairs. She walked up the steps and unlocked the door to her flat, then returned to the car, waiting for inspiration to strike.

It didn't. She relocked the car and tried to ease the mirror down via the boot.

"Hello, Miss, you are going to be late today?" Elise jumped, and turning around, saw the man from the supermarket putting out the rubbish.

"I'm sorry," she said. "What do you mean?"

"All the bargains, I was waiting for you, but you didn't come and there are none left." The man shook his head sadly as he spoke.

Elise was mortified. "It's just the time that I shop, just a coincidence, I guess."

The man did not look convinced, "Can I give you a hand?"

"Yes, please." Elise was desperate to distract him from any more conversation about the 'Bargains'. He quickly walked over and helped her to carefully ease the mirror down from the roof rack. Elise pulled off the bin bags and blankets, desperately hoping that the mirror had survived its ignominious journey.

"Wow," the man stared, "this is so beautiful, is it really yours?" Elise nodded.

"Ah, I see now… you save your money for special things," he said, nodding appreciatively at the mirror.

"Yes, yes, I do, I'm just scared it's going to get broken."

"Here let me help you." He took one end of the mirror and Elise took the other and together they managed to manoeuvre it unscathed into the kitchen.

"Thank you, you've been great, I could never have managed without your help," she said.

"See you tomorrow, usual time." He smiled and left.

"Oh, no, you won't," Elise thought, blushing with embarrassment. Her thoughts turned back to the task ahead; she now had to do battle with the dreaded trunk.

It was almost seven o'clock by the time Elise finally collapsed on her lumpy sofa. She was emotionally and physically exhausted, and feeling very hungry. Realising that she had had only half a cup of cold coffee, Elise dragged herself into her little kitchen and opened the fridge. It contained two custard tarts, three days over their 'use by date' and a carton of milk. Elise was too tired to conjure up a long enough list of swear words to make her feel better, and in a moment of madness went to the local takeaway.

Feeling rather too full of fish and chips, Elise debated whether or not to open the huge parcel from Alex. She didn't have to get up early for work, and she didn't feel like sleeping, so she reached across the table which was spread with the contents of her bag, which sadly had not survived. There were four separate envelopes, her name was on each one, with a number underneath. "Dear Grandmere; precise as ever."

She carefully prised open envelope number 'une' and swiftly realised that it was a photocopy of the letter she had found in the trunk, complete with a spare key to the padlock. "You really didn't trust mother at all," she thought. She put the letter and key back and turned to envelope number 'deux'.

"Now Elise, two things to remember, firstly, these are my final wishes, so you cannot disobey, and secondly, before you read any further open the third envelope."

Elise, obedient as ever, picked up the envelope marked 'trois'. It was more of a jiffy bag and was bulging at the seams. Elise couldn't think what it could be, but carefully undid the metal clip and lifted the flap. "Jesus, Grandmere was a bank robber!"

Elise pulled out bundle after bundle of bank notes, all neatly bound with paper bands; she couldn't believe that she had been wandering around with two envelopes bulging with cash in her handbag.

Elise was in shock, she used the last of her milk to make herself a coffee, and then returned to envelope number 'deux'. "Maybe she stole it and wants to me to return it," was all she could think of.

She had to smile as she read the next line in Grandmere's letter. "No, my dear, it is not stolen. It's all yours. I forgot to say that dear Mr Forbes ensured that your father's money went into my bank account and not your mother's, so you have him to thank for all those wonderful birthday presents." Elise hadn't thought they were that 'wonderful' at the time; first, the 'junior Cordon Bleu' summer school, then 'Art history'. She did have to admit that her seventeenth birthday present had been the best: Grandmere had presented her with a provisional driver's licence and a block booking of forty lessons. "You can have one every day and you will be able to drive before you go back to school, and it will be a real help to me too, now that I can't drive anymore."

Elise hadn't been overly optimistic, having never sat behind the wheel of a car in her life, but the thought of being able to avoid the constant teasing and bullying that she had to endure outside school every day, and to actually be of use to her grandmother, gave her an inner strength.

She was absolutely determined that failure was not an option. She immediately applied online to do her theory test. She passed first time, and having already had ten lessons, realised that she was a 'natural'. Her test was booked for the last day of August.

Her grandmother was waiting anxiously outside the gate on her return and heaved a huge sigh of relief when she saw Elise happily waving a sheet of paper.

"Now close your eyes and hold my hand."

Grandmere carefully led Elise a few yards down the road, and then said, "You can open your eyes now."

Elise saw a lovely red Golf with a pretty bow on windscreen. "A belated birthday present," she said, as she handed the keys to Elise.

Louise Jacobs arrived back from work and marched straight into the kitchen. "Why is there a car on my driveway?"

"It belongs to Elise, she passed her driving test today, isn't that wonderful?"

"Well, at least I won't have to keep giving her lifts everywhere now," she said and wandered off to her study.

Grandmere and Elise looked at each other, and both burst out laughing.

Elise had only once been given a lift by her mother. She was in agony, with terrible toothache and had an emergency appointment at the hospital. The taxi hadn't arrived and Grandmere was starting to panic. She had knocked loudly on Louise's study door.

"Louise, we have to get to the hospital, you need to take us." Elise's mother was furious.

"I'm busy; I have so much work to do, and deadlines to meet."

"No, Louise, we have to go now, just drop us off, we can get a taxi home afterwards."

Grandmere was not in the mood to be argued with and Louise, realising that she had no choice, stamped out of the house, got into her car and started revving the engine. Grandmere got into the passenger seat, and Elise crept into the back. Louise was still fuming as she pulled out of the driveway, narrowly missing the postman. Grandmere's letters flew from his hand. With great presence of mind and an impressive show of athleticism, he hurled himself into her hedge.

"Stupid man," she said and sped off down the road. The pain from Elise's tooth faded in comparison with the abject fear she felt sitting in the back of her mother's car. Grandmere was doing her best to remain calm, but even she had to remonstrate with Louise when she shot across a roundabout.

"Louise, my dear, aren't you supposed to give way to vehicles on your right?"

"Well, I got there first," was all she said. The ten-minute drive to the hospital seemed like an eternity. Louise grudgingly stopped outside the main entrance and Elise and Grandmere shot out of the car. Elise was shaking from head to foot, and Grandmere's usually immaculate chignon was looking decidedly awry. Louise screeched off, sending a cloud of dust and gravel into the air.

As they sat together waiting for the dentist, Grandmere told Elise the story behind her mother's attempts to pass her driving test.

"There was no theory test in those days, so all your mother had to do was to learn the Highway Code and pass her test. I booked blocks of six lessons with one instructor after another, but they invariably threw in the towel after two or three trips out with Louise. By the time we'd reached Zack's Driving School, she'd already had over a hundred lessons. Zack had lasted longer than most, but even he had to admit defeat.

"Whenever anyone sees your daughter behind the wheel, they pull over or turn off the road; she clears the streets quicker than a speeding fire engine complete with horns and flashing lights. She just does not have the aptitude for driving."

Louise had refused to give up, and eventually Grandmere had persuaded her to take her test in an automatic. How she passed, Grandmere would never know, but until the day of the dentist, neither she nor Elise had ever been in the car with her, and both of them silently decided that they never would again.

For her eighteenth birthday, Grandmere had sent her on a wine appreciation course, and every year after that was some something connected with booze. Elise had been introduced to wine by her grandma at a very early age, albeit very watered down.

"First, you must use your eyes, then your nose, and lastly, your mouth," she had drilled into Elise. Elise used to mimic her every move, learning how to remove the cork, pouring a small amount into a big glass and gently moving it around. "See how it coats the side of the glass," Grandmere used to say, "that is the sign of a good wine, life is too short to drink bad wine." Grandmere would purse her lips and perform an exaggerated shudder, as she smiled over her glass and winked at Elise.

Her twenty-first birthday's present had been her passport; it lay in her bedside drawer, still in the wrapping paper. Elise had never used it.

She had always wondered where Grandmere had found the money, her birthday was in August, and being busy every day had kept her out of her mother's hair, which was the only reason she had been allowed to attend. "Wasting your money again?" was all her mother would say to Grandmere as she plonked a cheap birthday card on the breakfast table, and took a sidelong glance at the glossy leaflet in Elise's hands.

Elise sighed with relief, no surreptitious visits in the dark to return ill-gotten gains then.

"Now you have calmed down, we shall begin, Elise. Let me tell you I am loving this, I haven't had as much fun in years!

Number 1: Phone my dear friend Madeleine and make an appointment. She will be waiting for your call; actually, she has been waiting to get her hands on your hair for about fifteen years! You must agree to whatever she suggests, no complaining allowed."

"Oh, no, Grandmere, how could you?" Elise had accompanied Grandmere to Madeleine's Hair and Beauty Salon in Bond Street on numerous occasions over the years, but had either sat with a magazine, or when she was old enough, wandered off to explore the local bookshops whilst Grandmere had her hair done and whatever else they did behind all those closed doors.

"Number 2: You must go to Rigby and Peller and get yourself measured for some proper underwear." Elise gaped at this one, as she never wore bras—having no bosom to speak of, she simply wore vest tops under all her clothes.

"And please do not turn up in any of your nasty concoctions. This is the only time I will allow you to wear something from my wardrobe without appropriate underpinning.

Number 3: You must open the second drawer in my trunk; you will see a red velvet bag. Don't open it yet. I want you to take it with you to look at whilst Madeleine is doing your hair.

Almost there, my dear, you may now open the curtain on my trunk, everything else that you need is there, except for a new set of luggage! You must buy only the best, I will haunt you forever if you dare to place my things in anything else.

Everything will fit you perfectly, my dear, you are exactly the same size that I used to be." Elise found that bit hard to swallow. Grandmere was so elegant and shapely, and she was convinced that her own reflection, whenever she had had the misfortune to see it, bore no resemblance to that of Madame Giselle.

"There is a fourth letter waiting for you. Alex has it and he is under strict instructions to deliver it to you only when you are in Paris. He has given me his assurance that it will arrive safely.

Now Elise, if you haven't already guessed, take your passport out of its wrapper and next stop, Paris xxxxxxx"

In the right-hand margin, Grandmere had carefully written down the phone number of the salon, and the address and directions for Rigby and Peller.

It never crossed Elise's mind to disobey her grandmother; in any case, she was already headed for Paris, and the dreaded meeting with Armand, but she needed her job, and was ever loyal to Mike, and maybe if she let Grandmere help just once, the next time Armand saw her wouldn't be quite such a disappointment, wouldn't be as traumatic.

Chapter Thirteen

It was already getting late; Elise had yet to unpack Grandmere's large suitcase and the various boxes she had loaded everything else into. The trunk would have to wait for another day. Elise didn't dare risk her grandmother's wrath by touching anything until she had showered and shampooed the cobwebs out of her hair, so she headed through the living room and into her tiny bathroom. Even Elise was shocked at the colour of the water running down the plug hole; she couldn't believe that she had walked around Surbiton with twenty years of cobwebs attached to her scalp. "Poor Mr Forbes," was all she could think of.

Twenty minutes later, Elise emerged from the shower, feeling clean at last. She wrapped a towel around the mass of well-scrubbed hair and put on her dressing gown. And felt ready to tackle the suitcase. Elise opened the bedroom door and reached an arm in to flick the light switch. The corner of her eye caught a movement. "Jesus," she screamed, whipping her arm out and slamming the door. A burglar! He must have come in whilst she was in the shower. She bolted for the kitchen, but, strangely, the envelopes bulging with wads of euros and £50.00 notes were still sitting on the kitchen table. Elise checked the door; the two bolts and the safety chain were still in place and the kitchen window was intact. There was no other way into the flat, unless he had shimmied up the shop window. She grabbed her mobile phone; should she call the police, she wondered, but then with thousands of pounds of notes on the table, she thought she might be the one leaving in handcuffs.

"Be sensible," she told herself, "no one could have got in the flat, no one is in the bedroom, just go back in there and stop being stupid." All the same Elise armed herself with a very blunt carving knife and an old rolling pin for good measure before tiptoeing back to the bedroom door. "I'm coming in," she shrieked, not really sure why, and with one swoop, she shoved open the door and jumped inside. She felt for the switch and the room lit up. "I don't fucking believe it!" was all she could think of as she caught sight of a strange figure in a very worn-out dressing gown waving a rolling pin above her head. "The bloody mirror!"

Elise collapsed in a heap on the floor. Grandmere was certainly having a laugh. "Right, what next!"

Elise opened her wardrobe door; it had definitely seen better days, and she suspected it hadn't even started out life as anything meant to last, but it came with the flat, and never turned its nose up at her outfits. Elise was in a quandary, there was no way that Grandmere's clothes would fit next to hers. With a deep sigh, Elise fetched a roll of bin liners from the kitchen and stripped the wardrobe bare. Everything went into the bin, even a few items which still had their Princess Alice 'reduced to £1.00' stickers intact. Elise was in a ruthless mood; she moved to the chest of drawers, peeled another bag from the roll and proceeded to empty every drawer.

The alarm clock woke Elise, she had forgotten to turn it off last night and was cursing at being awoken at six, when she could have still been in the Land of Nod.

She looked around her little bedroom, boxes and bin liners covered most of the floor space, and Elise groaned as she realised what was in store. At least it was Sunday, so she had one more day's grace. She got up and headed for the kitchen.

"Black coffee it is then," she said to herself, spying the empty milk carton in the bin. Not even Elise could face four-day-old baked custards for breakfast, so feeling a bit like Mother Hubbard, she wandered back into the bedroom nursing her coffee. She pulled open a drawer, and stared at the faded lining paper. "Oops, a bit over-zealous there, my girl," she thought, the idea of going for milk in her dressing gown didn't seem to fly. She set down the coffee and started on the first box, containing Grandmere's cashmere sweaters. The thought of placing them on the nasty lining paper was enough to conjure up Grandmere's wagging finger in front of her eyes.

"Take good care of your clothes," she used to say as she carefully hand-washed her sweaters and laid them flat to dry. She always folded them around tissue paper before placing them back in the drawer.

"Why does it matter, Grandmere? Clothes don't make you prettier."

"Now Elise," Grandmere had said, wagging her finger, "making an effort, and ensuring that your clothes are appropriate to the occasion is what matters. If I were to spend hours preparing a special dinner for people, how do you think I would feel if someone showed up in their pyjamas?"

Elise wasn't really sure what the problem with pyjamas was, especially if they were nice ones.

"No," Grandmere had continued, "taking the time to dress properly shows that you have respect for yourself, and demonstrates to others that you are someone who pays attention to detail, and in turn people will show you the respect that you deserve. It is not about looking pretty, it is about self-respect. I am lucky that I could sew and make beautiful clothes for myself, but anyone can learn if they really want to, and when you find a style that suits you, stick with it. Fashion fades, style is eternal, and, I'm not saying that you cannot look stylish in your pyjamas." Grandmere had winked at Elise.

"But, my dear, only in the bedroom."

Elise rummaged around in a second box and found a beautifully embroidered pillow case. She took the old lining paper from the drawer, first dusted, then wiped the wood clean and only after placing two layers of kitchen paper on the bottom of the drawer, and then the pillowcase, did she start to refill it.

The wardrobe had to be dusted and scrubbed before Elise dared to hang up Grandmere's clothes.

The hats, gloves and handbags were placed on the shelves down the sides. Elise had had to fling out all her own shoes and boots to make room, but she was convinced that Grandmere's belongings would not rest easily at the side of her "tat" and there was no other option.

After three long hours and several cups of nasty coffee, Elise's stomach was beginning to rumble. There was only one thing on her mind and that was to purchase a new phone.

Elise ran down to the rubbish skip in the car park and placed three bulging bin liners on the top; it was almost full. Elise hesitated for a moment, fear was beginning to take its grip. "Oh, no, you don't," she said to herself, as she saw her hand trying to retrieve the bag of shoes. Throwing caution to the winds, Elise reached into the skip and pulled out last night's remains from the supermarket. Praying that no one was looking at this mad woman in her dressing gown rummaging around the rather evil-smelling bags, she emptied the contents all over the bin liners, and then for good measure, pulled the lid shut.

"The end," she said to herself and ran in before anyone called the police.

Chapter Fourteen

After another long shower, Elise headed back to the bedroom. She had dried her feet on the dressing gown, then mopped the floor with it, and finally covered it with a squirt of bleach just for the sheer hell of it.

"What now!" Other than putting on Grandmere's clothes, her only option was a faded towel. She hadn't yet touched the trunk. "One thing at a time," she told herself. "Just pretend it's the sale rail," she told herself. "Bloody grab something." Elise closed her eyes and put her hand inside the wardrobe. It closed around a cashmere skirt. "That's the one then." Elise had left one tiny drawer containing her knickers and vest tops untouched. She heard herself apologising out loud to Grandmere. "Just this once," she said.

Elise risked a glance into the cheval; up until this point she had purposefully stepped behind it on entering and leaving her room, but now there was no going back. She was truly shocked at what she saw.

For the first time in a very long time, Elise lifted her head, straightened her shoulders and stood tall, a brief childhood memory of herself dutifully following Grandmere around the kitchen whilst both were balancing books on their heads, made her smile. Grandmere's never moved, Elise was sure that she had glued it in place. "Stand tall, my dear, and glide." Even Elise had had to giggle, but after having almost worn a trench in the kitchen floor, she could glide almost as well as Grandmere.

Elise had for many years walked around with her head down and shoulders hunched. She had even mastered moving with a slight bend in her knees to make herself appear shorter, much to the growing despair of her grandmother.

"Stand tall and be proud, remember how I taught you to walk. You are not Quasimodo." But Elise had found it a terrible struggle, she hated being tall, it made it that much more difficult to hide.

Now with her bare feet encased in her grandmother's beautiful grey court shoes—she wasn't quite ready to tackle Grandmere's stockings—she pulled out a charcoal cashmere skirt and a rose-coloured silk sweater. (Elise didn't know jumpers came in silk and had had to read the label twice, before daring to put it on). She couldn't really believe that it was her in the mirror. She stepped forward and peered into it. The bed behind seemed to disappear, and then as clear as day she heard Grandmere's voice.

"You see, my dear, I told you so," was all she heard as a sudden wave of nausea and dizziness overcame her, and she collapsed onto her bed. A few moments passed before Elise opened her eyes. She still felt dizzy, but she made herself sit up. "That's what you get from too much coffee and no breakfast," she told herself. She took the grey handbag out of its dust jacket, and headed for the kitchen. She picked up her keys, took one of the wads of notes from the envelope and marched out of the door.

"Do you want to keep your number?" asked the man in the phone shop.

"No, absolutely not… no, I need a new one." Elise spoke with such passion that he took a step backwards.

"Now, are you thinking Windows or Apple?" Elise searched his face, trying to decide which choice he would prefer.

"I don't really mind, I just need a straightforward phone." The man handed her a phone the size of a brick. "This one has the best camera, the operating system is…" Elise was beginning to feel lost, but the idea of a camera appealed.

"Yes, that sounds fine," she said, feeling relieved that the ordeal was actually over.

"Are you looking for a contract?"

Elise was losing the will to live, she still hadn't eaten, and had not realised that buying a phone was this painful. After what appeared to be an age, she left, clutching her Apple phone, and immediately regretting the forty pounds a month that she had agreed to pay. Apparently, she could use it anywhere, had unlimited everything and was fully insured, she wasn't really sure against what. But once it was charged, the man had assured her, she would never look back.

Next stop was breakfast. Usually Elise would have headed straight for the supermarket for supplies. But not today. She headed for the nearest Costa and ordered a large 'Flat White' with a breakfast panini. She resisted the urge to apologise as it was definitely way past breakfast. Elise paid at the counter, handing over a brand new twenty-pound note, and headed for a table in the corner. She even had the audacity to pick up a complimentary newspaper before sitting down.

The waitress appeared at her side with the panini. "All the girls are admiring your sweater, where is it from?" Elise was stumped for a response. She had never ever received a compliment about her clothes before. Grandmere came to her rescue.

"Remember, my dear, never insult the person who is paying you a compliment by being dismissive; a gracious smile and a 'thank you' is all that is required." Elise tried this, but the waitress wasn't moving.

"It's vintage," she added, and the waitress, looking slightly disappointed sidled away.

Feeling better after eating the panini, which had taken longer than usual as Elise took great care to ensure that not a single crumb went anywhere near her clothes, she stood up and headed for the door. The bent knee walk was proving impossible in heels; she had no choice but to straighten her legs, and relive her days in the kitchen with Grandmere telling her to walk as if she were squeezing a lemon between the cheeks of her bottom.

Elise resisted the urge to check behind her, she imagined a whole basket of lemons bouncing down the street. She also realised that lemons and hunched shoulders did not work either, so she pushed back her shoulders and was slightly embarrassed to see her chest pop out. "Soldier on, girl," she said to herself. She wasn't really sure where she was going. She had the house brick in her bag, that needed charging up and she definitely needed to buy milk, so she headed for the supermarket.

"Afternoon, Miss," called out the supermarket assistant, nodding across the shop to her. "You are a bit early today."

Elise had the grace to blush. "Not at work today," she called back, and grabbing a basket, she started to peruse the aisles. Elise filled her basket with granary bread, butter, camembert, and she even added a jar of green olives, and, heaven forbid, sun-dried tomatoes. Ground coffee and milk and a box of muesli followed. The basket was starting to get heavy, Elise was worried that it might be rubbing against her skirt and placed it on the shop floor. The assistant appeared beside her.

"You look very smart today," he said. "Shall I bring you a trolley?"

Elise with a trolley! Yet another first.

"Yes, please, oh, and thank you," she answered, at least a trolley would not be in danger of marking her skirt. She decided to ignore the 'smart' comment, three firsts in one day were way too many to cope with. She added some fresh fruit and salad and a cheeky bottle of red, then, with great presence of mind, a box of 'Dreft' before heading for the checkout.

The assistant at the till infuriatingly turned all of Elise's goodies upside down and back to front before scanning them. "He's checking for the reduced tags," Elise realised and felt her shoulders starting to sag.

"Don't you dare," she scolded herself. Elise paid, bundled her shopping back into the trolley and was about to make a run for the door when she remembered not only Grandmere's heels, but also her thoughts on running.

"You do not run unless you are wearing running shoes and heading for the finishing line." Elise forced herself to walk slowly to the exit, keeping the lemon firmly in place, shoulders back and chest out.

Chapter Fifteen

Elise had a sudden thought, it was Sunday, and Amy would be expecting her. Elise trotted back to her flat laden with shopping. She and Amy always talked on Sundays.

Amy had been her best, well only (if she was honest), friend all through school and Sixth Form, and they never lost the bond between them. Amy was round and short whereas Elise was stick-thin and tall, which had made for much merriment amongst the other girls. "Here comes Laurel and Hardy," was one of the less nasty comments, or 'Little and Large' or even 'Del Boy and Rodney', but Amy and Elise, recognising in and sympathising with a fellow victim clung to each other for both comfort and support and soon became firm friends.

They didn't really have much in common; well, in fairness they had absolutely nothing in common other than being the target of every bully in the school.

Amy's parents were considerably older and a lot poorer than those of her classmates; she actually had a niece who was older than she was which had confused the hell out of Elise.

She also had a vast array of siblings, the youngest of whom had been ten when Amy was born. Amy had been a 'mistake' according to her mother, so at least they had that in common! Elise had met three of Amy's four brothers when the two girls had had to wait outside the school gates for one of them to grudgingly appear to walk her home. Amy had only one sister, Angela. Elise had been in awe of her since their first meeting and the two had become good friends over the following years.

After one particularly nasty encounter with the bullies at the school gates, Amy had gone home with a split lip, and Elise with a torn cardigan. The next day Elise was dreading the walk home, but Amy was in surprisingly good spirits. "Don't you worry, Ells, it's sorted."

As the two girls walked outside the school gates, their tormentors started circling.

"What are you staring at, Fat Arse?" the ring leader had shouted at Amy. The other girls taking this as the signal for attack, like a pack of hyenas, started moving in for the kill.

From nowhere a young woman sporting blue hair that would have put a smurf to shame, piercings in both eyebrows and an arm full of tattoos, firmly grabbed the girl by the throat and rammed her head into the railings.

"Touch my sister or her mate again and you won't walk for a fucking month."

A teacher came running across the playground to see what the commotion was, but on seeing Angela, she carefully dropped her handkerchief and made herself busy picking it up.

Angela linked arms with Elise and Amy.

"Anyone else want a smack?" she said to the girls who were nervously backing off.

"No, thought not." Angela grinned and they casually walked away.

Elise couldn't help staring at Angela. The hair, and the piercings were eye-catching, but it was the tattoos that she found most amazing. "Do you like my sleeve?" Angela had asked, catching Elise's gaze.

"Oh, is it a sleeve? I thought they were on your skin!" said Elise, feeling somewhat relieved. Angela and Amy burst into peals of laughter.

"Ells, you are priceless!" spluttered Amy. Angela treated them both to a milkshake on the way home and Elise thought she was in heaven. After that the bullying dwindled to little more that snide comments, but Elise never really felt safe unless Amy was at her side.

Once, when her mother was away on one of her many business trips, Elise had been allowed to visit Amy's home for afternoon tea.

Two weeks previously, Elise had handed a school letter to Grandmere informing her of a hastily arranged 'Teacher Training Day'. Elise had seen that she looked upset when she read the letter, the worried look on her face remained there throughout the evening.

"What's wrong, Grandmere?" Elise asked.

"I'm just not sure what to do, my dear, you see I have to go to a very important meeting on that day, and it's not going to be possible to reschedule it now." Elise was very impressed; she had always assumed that her grandmother spent every school day in the kitchen waiting for Elise to return home.

"I could ask Amy if I could go to her house, she's always inviting me and well, mum's away so she doesn't need to know, and then you could go to your very important meeting and not have to worry about me." Elise had waited with baited breath.

Grandmere shook her head. "Well, I don't know if that would be acceptable, I have never had the pleasure of being introduced to the lady." Amy always walked to and from school on her own, or on occasion with one of her older brothers, so even Elise had not met her mum.

"Perhaps you could write a note and ask her if it's all right. We could always invite Amy over the week after, because that would be good manners, wouldn't it?" Elise thought there might be light at the end of the tunnel, but was cautious not to push Grandmere too far.

"It certainly would be extremely kind of Amy's mother, and it would be a great help to me."

Grandmere considered her options for a few seconds longer and then said, "Very well, Elise, could you run upstairs and fetch my writing case."

Elise walked out of the kitchen as casually as she could manage, but once the door had closed behind her she bolted down the hallway and sprinted up the stairs, feeling that any delay may cause Grandmere to change her mind.

Elise paused outside the kitchen door on her return; she didn't want to get back too quickly in case Grandmere smelt a rat, but on the other hand, time was of the essence. She carefully opened the door and laid the red leather writing case on the kitchen table in front of her.

"You'll have to write in English, you know."

Grandmere put on her glasses and gazed over the silver frames at Elise. "Yes, my dear, I realise that."

Grandmere had dropped Elise off at Amy's door, expecting Amy's mother to be waiting for her in order that the requisite greetings and expressions of appreciation to be exchanged.

But it was Amy who opened it, still in her dressing gown. "Hello, Mrs Jacobs," she said, dragging Elise into the house.

"Blimey, you're early. I've still got me jammys on and Mum's in bed, snoring like a pig."

Grandmere couldn't quite catch what Amy had said, so Elise took the opportunity to translate.

"Amy's mother is on the telephone, it's a very important call," she added, to try and consolidate her case. "They will bring me home at six o'clock."

Grandmere was still slightly confused and hesitated on the doorstep.

"Everything is fine, Grandmere, please don't worry. I don't want you to be late for your meeting."

Mrs Jacobs, who was never late for anything, gave Elise a quick kiss on the cheek and hurried off back to her car.

Amy and Elise had the time of their lives; Amy's parents didn't seem to mind what she did as long as she kept out from 'under their feet'.

Amy made their lunch, consisting of slabs of sliced bread slathered in peanut butter and bananas, with as many packets of crisps as they could eat. Elise had never eaten anything like it in her life, but later that evening dinner proved to be in a class of its own.

Mrs Macey didn't like cooking, but as Amy had a friend over, she decided to make an effort and heated up a tin of steak and kidney pudding.

She took it out of the oven and plonked it on the table still sitting in its tin.

"Hurry up," she shouted, "don't let it get cold."

Elise wasn't sure what to do; she couldn't see any serving spoons. There were no drinking glasses on the table, no napkins and not a knife or fork in sight. She watched Amy, hoping for a clue as to how to progress. Amy simply picked up what Elise had taken to be a dessert spoon and plunged it into the pie. She was happily heaping it on to her plate, when her mother grabbed the spoon out of her hand and started transferring some to Elise's plate.

"Amy! Don't be such a greedy bugger," she shouted, whacking Amy's hand with the spoon.

"Leave some for your guest; she looks like she could do with a decent meal!" Elise's face turned scarlet, but Mrs Macey didn't appear to notice.

"Oh, mum, don't go on about her being skinny, she don't like it," protested Amy.

"Well, she should eat a few more pies then, shouldn't she?" retorted Mrs Macey and after hastily dropping two cans of lemonade on the table, she wandered off into the back yard to smoke what she considered to be a well-deserved fag.

Chapter Sixteen

Mrs Jacobs sent a beautifully written note to Mrs Macey, thanking her for her kindness and inviting Amy for tea the following week. Amy proudly read the letter to her mother, simplifying any tricky bits. Mrs Macey always maintained that she had lost her glasses, when anything needed reading. Amy had once told Elise that her mother wasn't too hot with the old ABC's, adding with a wicked grin, that she didn't seem to have progressed beyond the letter A, which explained why the entire brood had names beginning with that letter.

Elise was beside herself with excitement, she had never been allowed to invite anyone to her house before.

"Looks just like a bleeding chocolate box," exclaimed Amy as Elise opened the little white gate which led through the garden to the cottage.

"I'm sorry, my dear, I didn't quite hear what you said." Amy was about to repeat herself with great gusto when Elise silenced her with a nudge.

"She said what a beautiful cottage we have, Grandmere."

Grandmere had at first been impressed, and then frankly horrified by Amy's capacity for cake. She had watched transfixed as Amy proceeded to demolish everything on the beautifully laid table. First, the finger rolls, then the vol au vents, and eventually, once Amy had felt that she had shown due appreciation for the savoury side of life, whole plates of lovingly–prepared éclairs, delicately iced buns and an array of tiny Swiss rolls followed in hot pursuit. When, to top it off, Amy, eschewing the silver cake slice, had used her as yet untouched fork and spoon to manoeuvre three quarters of the black forest gateau onto her plate, Grandmere had finally given up and removed the remains from the table fearing that an ambulance and stomach pump would be required at any moment.

Elise, who never had much of an appetite, hadn't really taken much notice, apart from being slightly taken aback when Amy blew her nose into the napkin.

Much to Grandmere's relief they went into the living room to play Scrabble for the remainder of the evening. Elise had the presence of mind to knock the board over when her grandma popped her head around the door to see how they were getting on. Amy's vocabulary was certainly far too colourful to meet with Grandmere's approval.

One of Amy's brothers arrived to collect her.

Amy's mother had tried to read the beautifully crafted letter from Mrs Jacobs and had eventually, after much head scratching and several adjustments to her glasses, given up and handed it to Alfie.

"Ere, Alfie, I can't make head nor tale of this, what is she on about?"

Alfie, had obligingly taken a quick look over his mother's shoulder.

"Blimey, our Amy's movin' up in the world, ain't she! It says her house, six o'clock. You'd better get your skates on."

"Not with my bleedin' legs, off you go, Alfie, and mind you wipe your feet if you 'ave to go inside."

"Thank you for tea, Mrs Jacobs, it was really lovely, please could I take some cake home for my mum?" Grandmere had carefully boxed up what remained of the gateau, and having first tied the lid on carefully with an elaborate bow, silently handed it to Amy. Amy had the ribbon off and her hands in the cake before they had reached the end of the drive.

Grandmere, watching through the window, shook her head and shuddered.

"Never again," was all she had said to Elise, who was left wondering whether or not Grandmere had mistaken Amy's 'trackie bottoms' for pyjamas.

Amy had managed to get a place through clearing at University.

"I'm going to Aberdeen," she told Elise.

"Why Aberdeen, I didn't think they did the course you were looking for?" Elise was puzzled, and horrified at the thought of her best friend moving so far away.

"No, they don't," Amy replied.

"But it's the furthest place away from this dump that I could find!"

Amy had graduated four years ago, and was enjoying life in Scotland; she had a nice job and a lovely boyfriend, named Charlie, who Elise had met via her ancient laptop camera.

"You should get yourself on Facebook, Elise," she teased. "Stop living in the bloody dark ages." Elise had steadfastly refused, even the name filled her with dread, she could not imagine anything worse than having a photo of herself out there for all the world to see! Amy didn't seem to give a shit about anything; she had grown in confidence after escaping the school bullies, and was more than happy to have photos of herself and Charlie out there. She felt frustrated by Elise's shyness and constantly tried to get her to come out of her shell and start having a social life.

"You've got a lovely face and a smashing figure, you need to get it out there, girl. You'll die a bloody virgin if you're not careful."

The geographical distance had not dampened their friendship, and the Sunday evening call, complete with camera was sacrosanct. They always talked for hours about anything and everything. Amy was always formulating plans for doing away with the 'Vile Alice' and had offered on several occasions to either come down herself or send Angela to 'give her a good kicking'. Thankfully, Elise's tiny flat was incapable of accommodating Amy who certainly wouldn't go anywhere without Charlie, and she was sure that Angela was far too sensible to get involved. So, for the time being at least, Alice was safe.

Elise rested her laptop on the kitchen table; it had been state-of-the-art when Grandmere gave it to her as a present for doing so well in her GCSE's but even Elise had to admit, it had seen better days. She waited an age for the thing to 'warm up' before skyping Amy.

"You're late, you old tart, I was beginning to get worried."

Elise found herself unable to speak for a few seconds, and then the heavens opened.

"Oh, God, Elise, I'm so, so sorry. When's the funeral?"

"Amy, there isn't going to be one."

Elise was trying hard to talk, but Amy's genuine sympathy and support was almost more than she could bear.

"Why, did she have Ebola or something?" Amy had never heard of anyone not having a funeral and had already got Charlie on his laptop checking out the train timetable.

"No, it's what mum wants, and anyway, I'm leaving for Paris on Friday."

"Really?" Amy did a 'thumbs up' at the camera.

"Well, you've waited long enough to do that. Are you sure you don't want us to come down? We can be there tomorrow if you need us. Angela is only down the road, she can be over in a few minutes if you need some company. Have you told her?"

"No. I haven't really spoken to anyone, but, honestly Amy, Grandma's left me a list of things to do and she's left me loads of money and all her clothes, so I'm going to Paris at last."

"What do you mean – all her clothes? You mean she wants you to take them back to Paris or something?"

"No, you div, she wants me to wear them."

"Elise, you are having a laugh, you can't be serious, you can't be walking around with your granny's stuff flapping round your bloody ankles. Mind you, she wasn't half classy as I recall."

"She definitely was classy and her clothes actually fit me; they aren't that long on me anyway, I'm about six inches taller than she was, and they look nice; so yes, I am kind of taking them back to Paris."

"Jesus, get yourself to Topshop, or even Warehouse, if you've got the cash. I get my stuff from Asos, it's great, and Boohoo lets you return everything, no probs if you don't like it. Seriously, Elise, you've been wearing shit clothes for years, and get your bleeding hair cut at one of those snotty London salons while you're at it. Show me that fringe."

Elise obediently lowered her head so Amy could check out her fringe.

"I knew it! You're still sticking the pudding basin on your bonce and don't bloody deny it."

"I promise, Amy, anyway it's on Grandma's list along with a visit to Rigby and Peller."

"Who the hell are they? No wait, aren't they those two magicians on the telly?"

"No, you silly cow," shouted Charlie, "that's Penn and Teller."

"They make posh undies, I've got to go all the way to Bond Street."

"Nah," said Amy. "You want to go to Ann Summers, they have brilliant stuff in there. Well, if you can fit in it," she added mournfully.

"Listen, Amy, I've got a new phone, let me give you the number before I go."

"A new phone, you mean you got one from the pawn shop, hope it doesn't turn out to be nicked!"

"No, I swear it's an eye phone 5 or something, it's so big I can hardly get my hand round it, but I want to take loads of photos in Paris, and I've got it on contract, you know free minutes and everything."

"My God, Elise, what has happened to you, girl? Are you shitting me? Show me, I don't believe a word."

Elise grabbed her phone and thrust it at the camera perched on the laptop.

"No shit."

"Charlie, you've got to see this," Amy shouted.

Charlie's face obligingly appeared over Amy's shoulder and he nodded his approval at the phone. "Hey, Els, we've got some news too, go on, Amy, show her."

Amy's plump finger filled the screen. "He's finally done it, Elise, and before you start arguing, you're my chief bridesmaid. It's going to be next June, we haven't fixed the date yet, and you'd better not try turning up in Granny's gear!"

When Elise finally ended the call, she felt better. Amy always helped, she was such a down-to-earth person; Elise couldn't imagine life without her.

Chapter Seventeen

Elise checked her watch. It was just past six o'clock, her panini was a distant memory and she was beginning to feel in need of another coffee. She walked into her bedroom, the trunk stood in the centre of the room, still waiting to be unpacked. "Food first," she decided, and with great pleasure took off her grandmother's clothes and placed them back on a hanger. Grandmere's satin dressing gown was a work of art and definitely would not do as an apron. She searched through the drawers and found a nightdress that would have to do for the time being. She slipped it over her head and went in search of the fridge.

Feeling better, after a meal that would have met with Grandmere's approval, Elise took the key from the kitchen table and went to open the trunk. She opened the second drawer and carefully lifted out the red bag, which she placed on her chest of drawers. She hesitated before unzipping the curtain, and wondered whether or not she should check the other three larger drawers on the left. She tried to remember if Grandmere had left any further instructions about the order in which everything should be done, but nothing sprang to mind. She decided that the drawers looked slightly less scary and opened the third drawer. Inside lay a beautiful leather-bound folder. Yet another one of Grandmere's notes was attached by a ribbon to the cover.

"You must take this with you to Paris; there is a small vintage clothes shop, you will find the address in my address book. Show this folder to the owner. I think that it will be of interest to him."

Elise wasn't sure whether or not she was allowed to open the folder before arriving in Paris and decided to err on the side of caution and leave it until she got on the train. That way Grandmere wouldn't know whether she was in France or England, so she should be safe.

Underneath the folder was a large and very ancient chocolate box tied with an equally ancient ribbon. Elise placed the box on her bed and lifted the lid. She gasped in surprise; it contained two rows of beautiful brooches, and below them were two rows of earrings. The fifth row, which was larger, contained bracelets of every shape and colour and the last row consisted of five stunning necklaces, each neatly held in place by pins.

Elise could not remember ever seeing her grandmother wearing any of these items, but she had never really worn costume jewellery, other than a string of pearls. Grandmere always placed her earrings and bracelets in small leather pouches, which she attached to the hanger of the outfit she wore them with. Elise had seen the pouches still in place yesterday. She placed the box on a shelf in her wardrobe.

The bottom drawer contained yet another box, which was full of photographs. Elise immediately recognised her grandparents, albeit very much younger, standing outside the Moulin Rouge. The photograph brought an unexpected lump to her throat, and Elise decided that she wasn't ready to face them. "Paris," she decided and placed the box in the bottom of her wardrobe. Elise still had no idea what she was going to do with the trunk once she had emptied it. She certainly had no intentions of ever parting with it, but wasn't really sure where it would go. "One thing at a time," she said to herself, and slowly unzipped the curtain.

It was designed like a miniature wardrobe, complete with a hanging rail. Elise counted eight padded hangers, and one by one she removed them from the trunk. Seven hangers contained the loveliest dresses that Elise had ever set her eyes on. They were all similar styles, with a fitted bodice and a full skirt, but in different fabrics; three were in stiff, shiny cotton, two were in taffeta, and the final two were in chiffon silk. Each dress had an accompanying jacket with a V neck, they ended just below the waist and were fastened with a single large button.

The eighth hanger was slightly different; it was larger and made of wood and held a full-length coat. Elise took it from the trunk and simply stared at it. The coat was sky blue, with large lapels and one large jewelled button at the waist. It was made of the softest cashmere and like the dresses, looked as if it had never been worn. Elise couldn't resist slipping it on over her nightdress. There was a small hook and eye on the inside of the coat; she fastened that first and then fastened the button on the outside. Taking a deep breath, she closed her eyes as she stepped in front of the mirror for a second time.

She pulled her shoulders back and slowly opened her eyes. The coat was breathtakingly beautiful, giving her a shape that she never knew she possessed.

"You see, my dear, I told you they would fit you perfectly."

Elise peered into the mirror. "Grandmere, is that you?" Elise could see nothing other than her own reflection, but she couldn't mistake Grandmere's voice, and who else would be speaking to her in French? Besides, it was almost comforting to hear her voice again.

"It's just wishful thinking, my imagination playing tricks on me," she decided. She took another peek in the mirror, but heard nothing, and feeling slightly disappointed, she looked away.

"You are one silly cow," she told herself crossly. All this unpacking was just stirring up her grief all over again. She undid the button and put the coat back on the hanger. She then put it in her wardrobe and did the same with each of the seven dresses. The right-hand side of the trunk was now completely empty.

"I can't cope with anything else today," she decided, and instead, opened her laptop and checked the timetable for Eurostar. Elise was relieved to see that there was no shortage of trains or seats to Paris. She was tempted to book her ticket then and there, but thought it would be better to sort out her appointment with the dreaded Madeleine first. She decided, instead, to search out a suitable hotel.

Chapter Eighteen

Elise woke early the next morning. Monday, she needed to get organised, the quicker she could carry out Grandmere's wishes, the quicker she could be on the Eurostar. Now that going to Paris had turned from a dream to a reality, she could not wait to board the train. She knew that Madeleine's beauty salon didn't open on Mondays from her trips years ago with her grandmother, but decided to call the number just in case. She grabbed her new phone and tapped in the number. After a couple of rings someone picked up.

"Hello?" said the voice.

Elise hadn't been expecting anyone to actually answer, and was vaguely hoping that they wouldn't.

"Hello, my name is Elise Jacobs, I was wondering if I could possibly make an appointment with Madeleine?"

"Elise, is that really you? It's Madeleine speaking."

There was a very long pause; Elise wondered if she had accidentally put the call on hold.

"Is it Madame Giselle? Has she …" Madeleine's voice drained away and Elise could have kicked herself.

"Oh, Madeleine, yes, I'm so very sorry to have to tell you, but Grandmere passed away last Friday. It was very peaceful," she added. She should have realised that her mother would not have thought to let any of Grandmere's friends know.

"Oh, my dear, I am so very, very sorry. Madame Giselle was a wonderful lady. I hadn't had a letter from her in a while, and then she wrote and asked me for my mobile number, she said she had a little plan for you, and that I was part of it. So, I'm guessing she has managed to persuade you to let me do your hair."

"Yes, she's left me a long 'to do' list and you are right at the top." Elise tried to keep a positive tone in her voice.

"Well, then what are we waiting for, shall we say eleven?"

"Today?" Elise definitely hadn't been expecting that.

"No time like the present and we wouldn't want to upset Madame in any way," answered Madeleine.

Elise checked her watch. "Yes, I can be there at eleven."

"Brilliant, see you then; again, please accept my condolences. I can't wait to see you, it's been far too long."

Elise put down the phone. She would need to leave in forty-five minutes to get the train. Usually getting ready took about ten minutes. Knowing that she had to go through the trauma of actually selecting an outfit rather than throwing on whatever was to hand was giving her butterflies. She dived into the shower, and almost succeeded in keeping her hair dry, then flew into her bedroom and opened the wardrobe door. Grandmere's style tips were buzzing around in her head; 'echo', 'complement' and 'statement' were Grandmere's 'Mantra'. Elise stared at the clothes and tried to fix on something. "Grey must never be worn with black, only with other shades of grey."

Elise pulled out the grey skirt she had worn yesterday, and went to the drawer to find a grey jumper. She remembered as a child triumphantly pulling out a grey sweater for her grandmother that exactly matched the skirt that Grandmere had selected.

"No, my dear," Grandmere had said, shaking her head. "We are looking for sisters, not twins!" Elise had dived back into the drawer and found a paler grey.

"Perfect, my dear, you see the shades complement each other, now all we need is a statement piece. I think a silk scarf, don't you?" Elise knew where the scarves were kept and started searching through them. "The eyes should be drawn to the statement, everything else should complement it, not overshadow." Elise had found a dark grey scarf with beautiful pink roses all over it.

"You are learning, my dear, the grey echoes the skirt and tones with the jumper and the pink is the perfect statement." Grandmere did look wonderful and Elise was left feeling very proud.

She now hunted for the jumper, and then quickly moved to the shelf of scarves. The rose scarf was sitting waiting for her. Elise slipped on the grey courts, and took the matching handbag from its dust jacket. It was quite a big bag, and would hold everything safely. She picked up the red bag, reached under her bed and took out an old hold-all that held her cash stash. Elise had no idea what hairdressers charged, but decided that she had better go prepared. She quickly dragged a brush through her hair, picked up her phone and left the flat.

Once on the train, Elise texted Alex with her new phone number. If she managed to get to Rigby and Peller, there was no reason why she couldn't leave for Paris tomorrow. Then she remembered the luggage issue. "Well, I'm going to be in Bond Street," she thought to herself. "How hard can it be?"

Elise arrived at the salon at ten thirty; she was never late, and was usually embarrassingly early for anything, but Madeleine was waiting by the door. She gave Elise a bear hug and pulled her into the shop.

Madeleine had Elise in a gown and chair before she had time to breathe. "The girls have all come in especially for you," she said, nodding into the mirror. Elise suddenly saw a sea of faces, all beaming at her as she sat rigid in the chair.

"Right, coffee first, whilst I'm thinking. Hannah has the wax on, and Emily can do your nails and eyebrows whilst your hair is drying so we won't keep you here all day."

Elise was still blinking about the wax, when her coffee arrived. Madeleine had carefully brushed through her hair, and had asked her to stand up whilst she checked the ends.

"Wow, definitely virgin!" she said, smiling at Elise in the mirror.

Elise felt her cheeks burning. "How could she tell?" Elise couldn't think of a suitable response, and sighed with relief, when Madeleine added:

"Your grandmother was always complaining about how you neglected your 'Crowning Glory'. It's such a rarity these days to see any hair as untouched as this."

The next minute she was whisked out of the chair and into the eager hands of Hannah and her melting wax. Twenty minutes later, Elise, with cheeks even redder than before staggered back to Madeleine.

"I was so very sorry to hear about Madame Giselle," said Madeleine, as she combed through Elise's mass of hair. "Did she ever tell you that she was my first ever client?"

Elise shook her head at the mirror.

"She came in with Mrs Forbes, who I'd been told was a bit snooty. It was my first day in the salon. The manager asked Mrs Forbes if she would let me shampoo her hair, but she just wrinkled up her nose and said, 'I don't think so, no, thank you'. I was all flustered and just stood there holding the towel like an idiot.

"Your grandmother realised that I was about to blub and immediately asked me if I could shampoo her instead. Well, she had loads of hair, and I was so busy trying to remember what to do and when, that I absolutely soaked her. She never said a word to anyone. I'd put a dry towel round her shoulders when she got up from the basin so the stylist had no idea.

"When she left, she walked over to me and said, 'Thank you, you did a wonderful job' and gave my first ever tip. When I got home, I put it in a little box and it's been there ever since. She was such a lovely, kind lady. Now, before we both end up in floods of tears, let's get started on that 'To do' list."

"I'm going to need at least three boxes of easy-meche for this." Madeleine got busy, and Elise kept her head down, as she did not dare look in the mirror. She suddenly remembered the red velvet bag and the letter that Grandmere had left for her. She bent down to pick up her bag and heard Madeleine's comb clatter to the floor.

"Sorry," said Elise, "I've got a special bag to open and look at whilst you are doing my hair. Is it something to do with you?"

"No, I don't think so," said Madeleine, picking up a new comb.

Elise opened the red velvet bag. Inside was an envelope addressed to her and a large square leather box. Elise took out the envelope and opened another letter from Grandmere.

"My dear Elise,

Hopefully, you are sitting comfortably. This is quite a difficult letter to write, but I owe it to my parents to let you know how brave and wonderful they were. You know I hate talking about the War, but this will have great bearing on your future, and you should know all the facts. I am telling the story exactly as I remember it, and from things that my mother told me, so I hope that you can make sense of it all.

When I was growing up, we had a wonderful neighbour, Monsieur Lehrmann. He and his wife had what you would call a pawn shop. It was a tiny shop just a few doors down from ours, and I loved to go in and look at all the things they had. I would sometimes go there quite early if my parents were very busy and have breakfast with them. They had no children of their own and Mrs Lehrmann always made a fuss of me. I used to hide behind the door when customers came in; occasionally some young man would come in with big rough-looking men on either side of him, and hand over his cufflinks and rings, and watch, whatever he had of value, for Mr Lehrmann to buy. Mrs Lehrmann would never serve them, she told me that they were just silly young men with too much money and not enough brains who had managed to lose everything at the casinos in La Pigalle, and that the men would not leave until the cash from Mr Lehrmann had been handed over. She was always grumbling about her husband and his 'silly ways', but they still seemed to be very fond of each other. Mr Lehrmann had a huge cellar, just like ours, but his was full of all sorts of strange things. He was a bit of a hoarder, and often bought things just for the fun of having them. He had a real skeleton on a stand that some medical students had stolen from the university. Mrs Lehrmann hated it and made him keep it out of sight. So, it was kept right at the back of the cellar.

Poor Mrs Lehrmann sadly passed away in 1939, and my parents took great care of Mr Lehrmann; my mother would send me round most evenings with a plate of food for him, saying she had cooked too much, and I helped with the housework and of course in the shop whenever I could. Mr Lehrmann didn't seem to smile as much as before, but he busied himself with his shop and seemed determined to carry on as best he could.

As you know, the Nazis took over Paris in June 1940. I was twelve years old. Food became scarce, because the Germans took most of it. They put curfews in place, so no one could have any lights on in case the bombers came, and we were not allowed out. To be fair, the curfew was not as strict in Paris; the German soldiers liked to have a good time, as I said, and the Pigalle was always bustling.

The Jewish people suffered terribly. Our dearest friend and neighbour, Mr Lehrmann, had been born in France, but still he was not safe; he was forced to wear a big yellow star on his coat and one was placed on his shop window with 'Juif' written across it. His windows were smashed and things were stolen. No one dared to be seen entering a Jewish person's shop, so poor Mr Lehrmann found himself struggling to survive.

The German soldiers often came to our shop to buy silk scarves and handkerchiefs, and whatever, for their 'lady friends' as mother used to call them. The soldiers were laughing one day saying how a synagogue had been turned into a brothel. I heard my parents whispering together later that evening, and I knew that things were bad.

Jewish people were being rounded up and taken to a horrible camp in Drancy; I know now that it was a staging post before they were taken to Auschwitz, but at the time no one really knew what was happening. My parents knew it was just a matter of time before they came for Mr Lehrmann.

One evening in early August, 1942, my father and mother sent me out of the room. They were huddled together, whispering, so I stood outside the door. I remember being full of fear, worrying over what was going on.

My mother called me back into the room. 'Giselle,' she whispered. 'You must be a very brave girl tonight. I will wake you when it is time and you must stand by the basement door. Keep it open just a tiny bit, you must not light any lamp, everything must be very dark. When you hear me whisper your name, you must open the door a tiny bit, without making any noise, and let us in. You must never tell anyone about this. All our lives will be in danger if you do, do you understand?'

I didn't really, but I would do whatever they asked. Mother got me out of bed, and dressed me completely in black, and then she and father picked up a large black sack and hurried out of the house.

I was so frightened; I had never been in the house alone before. It was a big place, with a cellar, a basement, the shop on the ground floor, the salon on the first floor, which my parents used to fit clothes on their clients. We lived on the top two floors.

Everywhere was so dark because of the blackout, but I didn't move from the door, and had my hand keeping it from closing all the time they were gone. I don't know how long I stood there, but at last I heard my mother whispering my name. I opened the door, just a fraction and she and my father came in. Except it wasn't my father, it was Mr Lehrmann.

Mother put her hand across my mouth to make sure I didn't make a sound, and told me to stay holding the door. She then disappeared with him down into the cellar. A few minutes later, I heard my father whisper my name. I opened the door, just a little and he came in. He closed and barred the door and told me to go back to my room. A few minutes later, I heard a huge bang and thought that we were being bombed. I looked out of my window and could see flames leaping high into the air. I ran downstairs, my parents were sitting at the kitchen table. There was no sign of Mr Lehrmann.

My father ran outside to help put out the fire, and after a few minutes, mother told me to put on a nightdress. She did the same and we both went out to see what had happened.

Mr Lehrmann's shop was ablaze, flames were shooting out of the top of the house, and German soldiers were alongside our neighbours trying to dampen down the flames.

No one could get inside.

For over three years, Mr Lehrmann lived safely in our cellars. They were huge and only my father had the keys. Everyone thought he had perished in the flames. A couple of men had gone in a few days later, probably to try to find anything of value and said that his body was in the bedroom and had been burned to nothing.

After the war was over, Mr Lehrmann stayed with us; he was old and sick and had nowhere else to go. He and my father often talked about that night.

My father had heard that there was to be a final 'round-up' scheduled to take place on the 17th of August. He and my mother hatched a plan to save Mr Lehrmann, they saved every piece of tallow, anything that would burn, and hid it in that black sack. They went to his shop and dressed the skeleton in a pair of Mr Lehrmann's pyjamas, then poured tallow and pig fat all over the pyjamas. Once my mother and Mr Lehrmann left, my father had used the rest of the fuel to set fire to the skeleton which he had placed under the covers on the bed.

Everyone assumed that he had died in the fire. My father had insisted that Mr Lehrmann take nothing from the shop. 'Looters will go in and will be suspicious if things are missing,' he had said. Mr Lehrmann took only two things that he said no one knew about anyway. One was the big box containing his wife's jewellery, which you will have found in the trunk, and the other was the box that is with this letter. It contains some papers and an old watch.

Before he died, he gave the jewellery to my mother and the watch to my father. He said he would never be able to repay them for risking their lives to save his own, but the watch and the jewellery meant a great deal to him and he wanted my parents to have them.

My mother gave me the jewellery box on my wedding day. When my father died, my mother gave me the watch as well. It belongs to you now; obviously, it's a man's watch, so it won't be of any use to you, but there is a shop that deals in old watches not far from Rigby and Peller, the address is 155 Regent Street. Please take it in and show it to someone there. It may have some historical value, and I want you to sell it."

Chapter Nineteen

Elise read the letter through and then read it again. She felt overwhelmed at the enormity of what her great grandparents had done, and that her own grandmother had been part of it all.

Elise felt ashamed of herself, here she was stressing about Madeleine putting strange plastic envelopes all over her head, when her own forebears had acted with such bravery.

"Time to get this lot off now, Elise," piped up Madeleine; Elise obediently followed her to the sink, and tried to get her neck comfortable whilst all the envelopes were removed. After what seemed like an age, Elise was propelled back to her chair.

She had had to put down her letter earlier when Emily had come over to paint her nails and tackle the eyebrows: "Are you trying for a Cara Delevingne look?" Emily had asked, wearing a vacant smile. Elise had no idea that eyebrows had a 'look' and stared blankly at Emily.

"Only they look a bit more Jo Jonas at the mo." Emily had set to work with great gusto, it didn't take too long but it wasn't exactly a pleasant experience. At least her finger nails didn't hurt, and she had to admit that they were now looking wonderful; the varnish perfectly matched her scarf. Not all bad then.

Her eyebrows had stopped stinging and her head had finally stopped itching. Madeleine was still huffing and puffing in her efforts to repair the damage Elise had done with her most recent hacking job on her fringe.

Eventually, she stepped back.

"Voila! Have a look, Elise, you are all finished."

Elise looked in the mirror. Her hair looked like smooth shiny gold; she leaned forward and stared even harder. "Is that really my hair?" she asked.

"It most certainly is," said Madeleine. "Now, off you go and show it off!" Elise walked over to the counter, and took out her old purse. "How much do I owe you?" she asked.

"Absolutely nothing, I enjoyed every minute and I promised your grandmother that I would do you proud. I hope you like it."

"I do, it's really amazing, thank you so much. I didn't realise that my hair was so blond."

"That's because it wasn't," replied Madeleine with a grin. She then handed Elise a bag. "Now, don't you dare use anything but this shampoo and conditioner. It will help keep your hair looking beautiful."

Elise took the bag. "I promise," she said with a huge smile, "and thank you all so very much."

Elise took out three twenty-pound notes, and handed them to Madeleine. "Please give these to Emily and Hannah, and say thank you for me, and I've got to rush; still got lots of things on my list."

"Thanks, Elise, and please don't leave it so long next time."

Elise left the salon, feeling as if she were walking on air. She couldn't help but steal a glance at her reflection in a shop window as she passed. Her hair looked amazing! Whatever Madeleine had put in those envelopes had certainly done a wonderful job.

Elise soon found Rigby and Peller. With her new-found confidence, she pushed open the door and went over to the counter. The lady behind it smiled at her.

"Good morning, Madame, how may I be of assistance?"

"I'm in need of some new underwear, I wonder if there would be anyone available to help me?" said Elise.

A lady appeared at her side as if by magic. "Perhaps I could escort you into one of our changing rooms, so I can get an idea of your size," she said.

Elise didn't realise that she would need to be measured and was slightly disconcerted.

"It won't take long; is Madame in a hurry?"

"No, I mean, that's absolutely fine," said Elise and obediently trotted behind the lady who was already removing her tape measure from around her neck.

"Thirty-two B," said the lady, staring at her tape. "I think we could do with a little help."

Elise still with a faint blush on her cheeks nodded her head in agreement, not wanting to admit that she had absolutely no idea what size she was. She had noticed the woman shaking her head at the sight of Elise's vest top;

"Gravity, my dear," she said sagely. "We must not forget it; it catches up with us all in the end." Elise nodded again, she didn't understand a word the woman was saying but decided that she would definitely not be wearing her vest on the way out.

One hour later, Elise left Rigby and Peller with a rather large and very swish-looking carrier bag on her arm, full of a selection of stockings and tights and the most beautiful underwear that she had ever seen. Minus the one set that she had actually had the audacity to put on, after the assistant had obligingly cut the price tags off. She had been shocked by how much everything had cost, but had to admit they were definitely works of art, and well, Grandmere had insisted, hadn't she?

Elise walked along the street; she knew the watch shop was not far away. It was certainly impossible to miss; 'Watches of Switzerland' was emblazoned across a huge glass-fronted building; it looked amazing. Elise suddenly felt incredibly nervous, and wasn't sure she was going to be able to pull this off.

What if they laughed at her, or even threw her out of the shop for wasting their time? Elise almost giggled at her

143

unintended pun and decided to steel herself with mocha before going in. Fortunately, there was no shortage of coffee shops, and cradling the oversized cup so as not to spill any down Grandmere's skirt, she sat down on the nearest chair.

"I have to carry out her wishes, so I have no choice, I can just explain that she wasn't well, and was a little confused, or something like that," she thought and immediately felt like a terrible coward, willing to pretend Grandmere had dementia to get herself out of an embarrassing situation. "The worst they can do is throw me out, and I'm not ever going to come back, so it doesn't matter; it won't be the first time I've made a laughing stock out of myself, so I can handle it."

Elise drank her coffee and left the shop. "Onwards and upwards," she said to herself and marched through the big glass doors. Two security guards were standing to attention in immaculate uniforms on either side of the entrance. Elise stared straight ahead. There were rows of counters. She eventually spotted a young man standing behind one of them, and taking a deep breath, she headed over towards him.

"Good morning, Madame," he said. He was so obviously French that Elise, without thinking, replied in French. "Oh, Madame is also French, I am Michel, it is a pleasure to meet with a fellow Parisian. What can I do for you today?" Elise didn't bother to correct him, she had missed her French conversations over the last few days and speaking in French made her feel a bit more relaxed.

"Well," she began, "my grandmother died recently and she left me a watch which belonged to my great grandfather. She asked me to bring it here to see if it would be something that you would be interested in buying."

"We don't normally deal in pre-owned watches in this store," he said, shaking his head. "But for you, Madame, maybe I could take a look and see if it would be something that one of our other stores may be interested in?" Elise was slightly alarmed; she had already decided to leave for Paris the next day, and hadn't planned on having to make any detours.

"It probably isn't worth anything," Elise added, apologetically, "I haven't actually looked at it, and I really wouldn't like to waste your time."

"Certainly not, Madame, I assure you it would be my pleasure."

Elise sighed, and placed the bag on the counter. "There is a letter with it, but I haven't read that either."

The assistant slipped the box out of the bag and opened the lid. He stared at the contents for a moment, and then took out a pair of white cotton gloves, which he proceeded to put on. Elise was mortified.

"The watch must be filthy!" She had a sudden flashback to her jumper after the visit to the attic. Perhaps the spider was in there as well!

The assistant hadn't looked up. Elise assumed that he was too embarrassed, and was trying to think of something nice to say. She saw him press a button on the side of the counter, and suddenly the two security guards appeared on either side of her.

Elise felt her cheeks burning, she had been right; they were going to throw her out.

"Well, I'm not leaving without the bloody watch, however crap it is," she thought.

Another older man had now appeared at the side of the assistant, and was peering at the watch through some sort of eyeglass. To Elise's ever-growing shame, she noticed that he had also felt obliged to protect his hands. She could feel the breath of one of the guards on her neck, and fought the urge to run.

The older man looked up. "Bonjour, Madam, a Patek Philippe."

Elise's nerves were starting to take hold, and her stomach doing its usual knot twist. She hadn't really caught what he had said, she was beginning to feel a surge of anger. "Bloody cheek, he's the one who's 'pathetic'. How dare he insult my poor Grandmere."

Elise reached out for the box. "I'm sorry to have taken up so much of your time," she replied, this time in English; she didn't think they deserved her French.

"My assistant tells me that you are interested in selling this?" the man said, looking at her. Elise nodded.

"Yes, it was my grandmother's last wish, I'm sorry to have troubled you and Michel."

"Madame, please believe me, it is no trouble at all. Did you have a figure in mind?"

Elise stared blankly at him. "If it was that dirty and pathetic, why was he asking? Maybe it was a joke."

The security guards were still hovering at her shoulders, and she was beginning to feel claustrophobic. Maybe the box itself was of some value, she knew it was certainly very old. Elise was quite good at bargaining over crates of wine, but didn't know where to start when it came to dusty old watches. "Perhaps you could let me know what you would be prepared to pay for it," she said.

The two men huddled and whispered. The older man then took out the letter that was in the box. "You are Miss. Elise Jacobs?" Elise was stunned, how the hell had he worked that out? She nodded. "And of course you have identification?" Elise thought she was about to be arrested, but couldn't think what for. She dived into her bag, pulled out her driver's licence, and meekly placed it in his white-gloved hand.

The two men were still huddled as Michel, still wearing the gloves, lifted the lining from the box and pulled two other folded pieces of paper. One was yellow and looked like some sort of receipt and the other was a sheet of very ancient-looking paper. Both were unfolded with great caution by the older man.

Elise craned her neck to see if she could read anything. The writing was very faded, but her heart jumped when she recognised the word 'Lehrmann' at the top of the yellow receipt. The writing on the second sheet was barely visible; it was difficult to make anything out. She thrust out a hand to turn the letter to face her, but Michel immediately put his gloved hand over the letter.

"No, Madame, please do not touch them without gloves."

Elise resisted the urge to slap his silly glove, but given the proximity of the two 'heavies', she decided it would not be a good move.

Eventually, the older man turned his gaze back to her. "Well, Madame, all the documentation is in order, I see that the watch was gifted to you in 2000 by Madame Giselle Jacobs, and we have here the notarised letter from her solicitor. It is simply fascinating; we have here the receipt for the purchase of the watch from a Monsieur Villancourt to Mr Franz Lehrmann. Here we have a letter signed by Monsieur Lehrmann to a Monsieur Charles Meunier gifting the watch to him.

"This is a wonderful piece of history. If Madame is really sure that she wishes to part with this, then we would be delighted to take over ownership. I just need to make a quick phone to confer with a colleague of mine. Would Madame like to wait somewhere more private?"

"No, thank you, Madame is fine," snapped Elise, who was getting a wee bitty pissed off by the length of time all this was taking.

The man bustled off clutching the watch in his gloved hands. He returned a few minutes later with beads of sweat visible on his brow. "We can offer you two hundred and fifty, if that would be acceptable?"

Elise was shocked; two hundred and fifty pounds was beyond her wildest dreams. Trying not to look too eager, she nodded. "Yes, that would be fine."

"How would Madame wish to be paid?" asked Michel.

Elise resisted the urge to say, "Quickly", and not wanting to have to faff about with a cheque, said, "cash would be fine." The older man blinked rapidly, and Michel also had a stunned expression on his face. Then both started to laugh.

"Madame has a sense of humour!"

Elise was starting to fume; they really were taking the piss. "No, seriously, I would just rather have the cash, and of course I would like the letter to my great grandfather back, if possible."

"But of course, Madame, and of course, cash can be arranged if you could come back later. We would normally suggest an electronic transfer into an account of your choice."

"Well, if it would be quicker," said Elise, pulling out her debit card. "Can you pay it into this account?"

"Yes, of course, if Madame would like to wait just a moment, I will deal with this directly and bring you the receipt."

The two men disappeared with the watch, and Elise heaved a sigh of relief, as the two uniformed guards slowly retreated.

A few minutes later, the two men reappeared. Michel, still wearing his little white gloves, placed the letter back inside the red bag, as the older man handed her a large folded sheet of paper. "This is a great moment for us, Madame, a real piece of history, we are so grateful that you bestowed the honour of bringing this to us. Your receipt, Madame."

Elise looked down at the paper, the room suddenly started to spin and she felt her knees giving way. Luckily, her two new 'bezzies' managed to break her fall and placed her in a chair that Michel had whisked into place behind her.

"Are you all right?" he asked in French, and the older man appeared at her other side with a glass of water and wafted the guards back to their post. "It is an emotional moment for all of us," he said. Elise gulped the water and stared back at the sheet of paper.

"This says two hundred and fifty thousand pounds," she said weakly, wondering which one of them was going mad.

"Yes, Madame, was that not what we agreed?"

Elise started to feel woozy again.

"That little watch is really worth all this?" she gasped.

"But of course, Madame, it is an extremely rare Patek Philippe, a magnificent time piece, sought after the world over. As far as we knew, there were only two of these in existence. We could not be more delighted to find that we were wrong."

Elise's heart was thumping loudly, she could not believe what she was hearing. "Grandmere must have known all along that this was really special." Elise still not wanting to risk getting out of the chair, turned to Michel, "Did you say that the watch was gifted to me in 2000?"

"Yes, it would have been done to avoid any complications with the tax. Your grandmother must have been a very astute woman."

Elise nodded, and tried to get up from the chair. Her legs weren't quite ready, and she flopped back down. A few moments later, her effort to stand was more successful.

"Yes, she certainly was," Elise answered, and picking up the bag from the counter, she tried to glide as gracefully as possible out of the shop.

Chapter Twenty

"Definitely in need of another mocha," she decided and staggered back to the coffee shop.

Elise settled herself into a corner, with a coffee and a croissant in front of her. She had toyed with the idea of a 'Danish', but overcome by a fierce sense of loyalty, she settled for the croissant. Her knees were knocking together and her hands were shaking. She couldn't deal with the enormity of what had just happened. That huge sum of money was actually in her account. She had not only the deposit for a flat; she could probably buy one outright!

Elise firmly decided that she did not have time for a meltdown over the watch as she still needed to buy a suitcase to use for Paris. She gobbled down the croissant, and gulped down the coffee—she hadn't realised how hungry she was—and quickly checked her watch, nearly four o'clock. No wonder she was starving. "Never mind, I'll have something nice when I get home," she said to herself and headed back into the street.

Elise realised that she didn't have a clue about what constituted the best when it came to suitcases, and pondering her options when she noticed a very smartly-dressed man walking towards her pulling a very posh suitcase behind him. In a moment of either boldness or desperation, she waited until they were about to collide, and said, "Excuse me, I know this may sound a little strange, but I need to buy a large suitcase, and your case is exactly what I'm looking for. Could you tell me where you got it?"

The man, after initially looking a little startled, smiled at Elise and said,

"Yes, of course, it's a 'Samsonite'. I think it's called a 'Pop Fresh'. I'm sure they will have them in House of Fraser on Oxford Street."

"Really! Oh, thank you so much, you are very kind."

The man smiled again. "No, it's been a pleasure, I always like to help a lady in distress!" Elise smiled back. She couldn't quite believe that she had just harangued a perfect stranger.

"What the hell," she thought, and drawing herself up to her full five feet eight inches (well, ten, if she added on the heels on Grandmere's courts) and squeezing as hard as she could on the lemon, she started to glide towards Oxford Street.

Elise left the House of Fraser proudly pulling a beautiful black Samsonite 'Pop Fresh'. She had carefully placed her carrier bag of undies inside and not wanting to risk scratching the case in the scrimmage of the rush hour on the tubes, she hailed a cab all the way to Waterloo.

It was nearly seven o'clock by the time she reached her flat. She quickly carried the case up the steps and dived head first into the fridge.

Elise made herself a salad, with the ingredients left over from yesterday's shopping trip, followed by a bowl of fresh fruit and muesli. "Well, I did miss breakfast!" she thought.

Still managing to keep her meltdown in check, she cranked up her laptop and logged on to Eurostar. Using her company credit card, she booked a seat on the afternoon train, and booked three nights at the Citadines Republic Hotel. Elise thought that any more than three nights on the company credit card might just be taking the piss, and decided that she could chose a different hotel whilst she was there. She wasn't really sure how long she wanted to stay and booked an open return.

She then quickly rattled off two emails, one to Gerry to let him know that she was actually going and one to Armand to let him know that she was actually coming on the one o'clock train. She also sent her new phone number to Armand. She certainly had no intentions of carting her ancient laptop to Paris. The stress of the journey would probably kill it off.

Once all the important stuff was done, Elise changed into her nightgown and charged around the flat singing loudly a song that she made up as she went along, the main gist of the lyrics being "I'm going to Paris, I've got a deposit. I'm buying a flat."

Meltdown over, she grabbed her phone, texted Alex with the dates of her trip and the name of her hotel, and then poured herself a very generous glass of wine.

Having drunk enough to calm her nerves, she rang Amy.

"This is a bit of a special, isn't it? You do know it's only Monday," shouted Amy.

"Yes, I know, I'm sorry, but I forgot to tell you loads yesterday, and you wouldn't believe what happened today."

"Tell me you got your hair cut, please?" begged Amy.

"Yes, I did, and had a colour put in it and spent four hundred pounds on undies."

Elise was speaking so fast that Amy had trouble keeping up.

"Have you gone nuts? You must have cleared out the whole of Marks and Sparks."

"No, I went to the posh one I told you about, and I took an old watch of my grandfather's and sold it for loads of money."

"Wow, and you went and spent it all on knickers?"

Elise suddenly felt embarrassed about the money. It didn't seem real. She needed to talk to Alex Forbes to make sure that she wasn't dreaming before she told anyone else.

"Oh, and Amy, I forgot to tell you that I found out who my dad is!"

"Not Prince Andrew, then?" asked Amy with a giggle.

"'Fraid not, just some Danish bloke, who didn't want anything to do with my mum, and obviously has never wanted anything to do with me."

"Well, you can hardly blame him for not wanting anything to do with your mum, she is a bit nuts." Amy never felt the need to shrink from the truth.

"What do you mean 'Nuts'?" asked Elise. "She just didn't like me very much. I always thought it was because my dad ran off, but my grandma left me a letter explaining what had happened between him and mum. She was very young, and he sounded like a real arsehole, so I do feel a bit sorry for her now."

"How can you feel sorry for that nasty bitch? I mean, I know my mum was a lazy cow, but she was an old fart when she had me, and I know she loved me, even if she didn't show it very often. Honestly, Elise, I know your mum wasn't right in the head after you were born, because my mum had the same midwife, and seen as mum had just about kept her in business, with all the sprogs she had, they were always gossiping about stuff.

"Mum mentioned it once that day I came to your house for tea. She suddenly twigged who your mum was. She said they only let you go home from the hospital because your grandma was there to take care of you. Maybe she just had that 'post-navel' depression or something."

Elise heard a groan from Charlie in the background "It's post-natal, you daft cow, how the hell did you ever get a degree?"

Amy laughed, she never took offence at Charlie, "Since when do you have to be that Stephen Hawkins bloke to get a degree in Media Studies?"

"In any case, Elise did most of my essays. Actually Ells, I think you did all of 'em if I remember rightly."

"It's Hawking," screamed Charlie. "We only saw the bloody film last month. Can't you remember anything?"

"Oh, shut up, Charlie, you can't half be a right pompous git sometimes," yelled Amy.

"Listen, Amy, I'd better go. I'm off to Paris tomorrow, and I've still got my packing to do."

"Well, don't forget the naughty knickers, it's about time you got yourself a bloke, so go and do something really bad with your Airman, and don't forget to send me a bloody postcard."

Elise put her phone on the table, next to the half-drunk glass of wine. She knew she should be getting her stuff ready for Paris, but Amy's comment about her mother bothered her.

Chapter Twenty-One

Elise wandered into her bedroom. Her lovely new suitcase lay open on the bed. Elise unpacked her posh underwear and put the sets together in the case. She carefully wrapped the large folder in tissue paper and placed that in a separate compartment on the front of the case along with the box of photographs.

Those were the easy bits, now she had to figure out the clothes.

Elise laid out all the beautiful dresses and jackets, and carefully placed them in the case. The weather was warm, but she couldn't resist packing the coat as well. She would have preferred to travel in a pair of trousers, but unfortunately, Grandmere had never owned a pair, and given the height difference, even Elise might have blenched at wearing them. She managed to pack twelve outfits, plus shoes, scarves and toiletries, and was very impressed with the capacity of her case. When she felt sure that everything she needed was in there, she sat down and cast her mind back to her conversation with Amy.

Elise couldn't get the conversation about her mother out of her head. It was the first she had ever heard of her mother suffering from post-natal depression. She decided on reflection that it was quite conceivable that her mother would have had some issues given all the trauma that she had been through. Knowing Grandmere, she would have spared no expense at getting the right help, so her mother presumably made a quick recovery.

Her mother had held down a high-powered job in the city ever since she could remember, it wasn't likely that any company would employ her in such a role if she had had anything wrong with her.

Elise had once asked her grandma why her mother had to travel so much. Grandmere had been late returning from dropping her off at Heathrow and Elise had been getting worried. Grandmere had immediately set about preparing dinner for the two of them and simply said that she was not allowed to discuss it, as Mother's work was secret. Elise was filled with excitement when she heard that, "What, you mean like James Bond?"

"A bit like that, yes," Grandmere had replied, and Elise didn't mention it again. She loved all the James Bond films and realised that she could be 'putting everyone's life and, maybe even the whole country in danger' if she ever breathed a word.

It had been the norm growing up that many things were not 'talked about' and Elise simply accepted that her mother working for MI5, was one of them.

After a couple of exhausting hours, Elise was satisfied that she had everything that she needed. She stashed some of the euros in the suitcase and took two thousand pounds out of Grandmere's envelope. She didn't know how much hotels cost, and although she was sure that she could find a cheaper one than the Citadines, she didn't want to run out of cash. She put another thousand pounds in and decided that that would be more than enough.

Elise debated whether or not to ring Alex about the watch, but decided that she couldn't take any more traumas for one day, so she placed her phone on charge and crawled under the duvet. Five minutes later, she jumped out of bed to check that she had put her passport in her handbag. She suddenly remembered Grandmere's address book and put that in with the passport. Five minutes after that, she jumped out again to copy the reference code for her travel bookings into her diary, just in case her phone broke. Five minutes later, she got up and had another bowl of muesli. "It will save me time in the morning if I have my breakfast now," she thought.

Chapter Twenty-Two

Elise arrived at St. Pancras International, feeling very impressed with the outfit she had put together, and trying not to swish her hair around too much, she went to check in for her train.

"Your train doesn't leave for two hours," said the guard. "Plenty of time for shopping," he said with a smile.

"Do I always have to be so bloody early," she said to herself crossly. Unfortunately, Elise possessed the 'early' gene and no matter how hard she fought it, she always found herself arriving everywhere at least an hour before she needed to.

"Never mind, I can have a leisurely lunch," she decided. There were certainly plenty of places to choose from and everywhere looked glamorous and exciting. Elise still couldn't quite believe she was here, but with everything else that had happened since Friday, travelling to Paris seemed to be 'small change'. Elise hadn't yet plumped up the courage to phone Alex about the watch. "A huge shop like that was hardly likely to have made a mistake," she told herself, and if they had, it was their fault; they had agreed the price and when she checked her bank account on the way to the station, the money was in it.

She hadn't been able to resist printing off a mini statement, but she still had to look at it every few minutes to convince herself that it was real. The company credit card had finally arrived that morning, and Elise was beginning to feel extremely rich!

Then a voice came out of nowhere and interrupted her thoughts. "Excuse me, Madame, please allow me to tell you about the special complimentary makeover that we are offering all our clients today." Elise turned and saw the voice was actually coming from a young girl, wearing a large sash and a strange belt full of brushes.

"Sorry," said Elise, "I was miles away."

"Well, I'm guessing you will be soon," said the girl, pointing at Elise's case.

"Yes, I'm off to Paris, but I got here a bit early, so I'm just going to have a walk around."

"Why don't you come in and let me give you a 'makeover', not that you need one, but it's my first day and if I don't find a willing victim soon, I think they'll probably sack me."

"Oh, I'm sure they won't," Elise answered, not sure whether she was joking or not, and beginning to feel a little flustered.

Elise's mother hated make-up and had been furious, when Elise's grandmother had allowed her to try on some lipstick.

"Why do you want to put that cack on your lips?" she shrieked, and actually wiped Elise's lips with her hand. "Are you really that desperate to attract a man? They are all vile, and you will end up in a terrible mess, so don't go looking like a slapper, unless you're determined to spend your life being bloody miserable."

Grandmere had placed a protective arm around Elise. "It's only a bit of fun, she was just trying on one of mine, please don't upset yourself, Louise."

"I'm just looking out for her, that's all, she's inviting trouble and you know it."

Elise had run upstairs and washed off the lipstick; it was the one and only time she had ever worn make-up. And now she felt torn, she knew what it was like to feel nervous, and wanted to help the girl, whose name was Annie, according to her badge. Plus, she did have a long time to wait.

"I'll tell you what, Annie, what if I let you give me a make-over or whatever, as long as you promise to clean it off, afterwards."

Annie looked a bit dubious, but decided any customer, however weird, was better than standing in the doorway feeling like a twit, so she readily agreed, and grabbed Elise's case before she had time to change her mind.

Annie couldn't believe that this tall elegantly-dressed woman had agreed to let her loose on her, but she made sure that all her colleagues 'clocked' the two of them as they made their way to her station via the 'scenic route'.

"You have amazing skin," said Annie, as she was laying out her various pots and pencils, "what do you use?"

"Er, soap and water?" answered Elise, wondering if this was a trick question. Annie roared with laughter.

"No, really, I mean, I bet you have a religious cleansing, toning and moisturising routine."

"Don't we all?" answered Elise, whose only routine was to buy whatever soap was on special offer at Superdrug, when she needed new supplies.

"Well, it's certainly working, now I'll just go for a light day look as you are travelling, just a light foundation, and something to make those eyes pop even more."

Elise sighed and closed her eyes; Annie seemed like a genuinely nice person, and she really couldn't spend two hours sitting in a coffee bar, so she persuaded herself it was a win-win situation.

"All done, what do you think?" said Annie.

Elise opened her eyes, and quickly closed them again; the next time she opened only one eye at a time. Elise couldn't accept that the reflection in the mirror was actually her. It was only when Annie's smiling face appeared alongside it that she knew it was definitely her face looking back.

"I knew you would look amazing," Annie said happily, smiling in satisfaction as she noticed a few of her colleagues taking sneaky peeks.

"Hold on a moment whilst I get some tissues," said Annie and went away leaving Elise still gazing into the mirror. Annie returned with a bowl and some cotton wool.

"It seems such a shame," she said, dipping the cotton wool into the bowl.

"What do you mean?" asked Elise.

"Well, you know, taking it all off again, but a deal's a deal!" Elise jumped up out of the chair.

"Oh, God, no, Annie, I was only joking." Elise realised that she had inadvertently grabbed hold of Annie's arm, and quickly let it go.

"No, really, you've done a wonderful job. How long will it last?"

"Well, until you take it off, all our products have wonderful staying power."

Elise had been hoping that she would say, "At least three days."

"Don't forget our special deal; you get thirty percent off, if you purchase any of the products that I've used on you today."

"I'll have them all," said Elise. "Oh, and could you write down for me what you put where?"

"Of course, I'll make up a card for you to take." Annie was on cloud nine, her first customer was going to buy the entire kit.

She bent down and whispered into Elise's ear. "Thank you so much. Some of the girls here can be a bit well, snotty, you know. You don't know how much this means to me."

Elise shook her hair back into place, and carefully straightened her skirt before following Annie to the counter. She didn't even blench at the bill, and said in a very loud voice, "Thank you, Annie, you've done an amazing job, absolutely wonderful."

Annie smiled in satisfaction as a few more heads turned her way. "I've put in some samples of our eye-and-face-make-up removers, please do try them, I'm you will find them preferable to your usual brand." Elise nodded; the thought of scrubbing at her eyelashes with soap didn't seem very appealing.

"Yes, I will, thank you."

She then slipped Annie a ten-pound note. "Thanks, Annie, you've just made my day as well."

Chapter Twenty-Three

Elise walked out of MAC with a jaunty step. She still had an hour left before boarding commenced. She saw a 'Boots' and wandered in. She needed to stock up on cotton wool, tissues and a bigger tub of something to remove make-up. Meanwhile, Annie was pretending not to notice her colleagues whispering together and staring at her. Eventually, one of the girls came over to her.

"Who was your client?" she asked, trying to adopt a casual tone.

"Oh, didn't you recognise her?" asked Annie, trying to pull off a casually surprised expression.

"She just popped in to try and evade the paparazzi, and decided to try a new look. I can't believe you don't know who she is, but I promised her I'd keep her visit quiet, so obviously, I can't break my promise."

With that, Annie marched back to the front of the store. She glanced back and caught sight of the snotty girl grabbing a bunch of fashion magazines and starting frantically flicking through them.

Elise bought some food to take on the train, and after worrying about smudging her lipstick, treated herself to a tiny mirror, so she could reapply it. "After all, lipstick must be easy enough," she told herself.

Elise had to admit she was beginning to enjoy herself; she had caught people giving her second glances as she walked around the shops, and whereas before she would have put her head down and fled into the nearest dark corner, she now kept her head up and smiled back. "Maybe Grandmere had been right after all."

At last it was time; Elise walked along the platform and climbed into the nearest carriage. She had no intention of allowing her suitcase out of her sight and sat herself directly behind one of the luggage spaces so she could keep her eye on it.

Before anyone else entered the carriage, Elise took out the leather-bound folder and the box containing the photographs and set them down on the seat next to her.

Luckily, the carriage was only half full, and the seat next to Elise remained empty. Once the train pulled out of the station, she turned her attention to the folder. She placed the unfolded tissue paper on her knee and carefully untied the ribbon on the side.

Inside Elise found the most amazing drawings, in pencil and ink, on sheets of parchment. Each sheet had two or three sketches showing outlines of women wearing wonderful outfits. Each drawing was annotated in tiny handwriting with numbers and arrows pointing to different parts of the outfit. The writing was very faded, but she still made out a few of the words. Some were references to fabric, and she read several references to lace scattered about the pages.

There were signatures at the foot of each page, but Elise couldn't make them out. She knew her great grandmother's name was Elouise Meunier, but the squiggles didn't seem to match.

Intrigued at why Grandmere had wanted her to bring them to Paris, she wondered if they belonged to someone else, maybe the man at the Vintage shop. Perhaps her grandmother had borrowed them, and when the accident happened, she had forgotten to give them back. She decided that the mystery would be solved, once she found the shop and carefully repacked the folder.

She then picked up the box of photographs. They weren't in any sort of order. Some were very old, and looked like the kind of photographs that were taken in a studio. Others were more recent; she immediately recognised her grandmother and guessed that the man who appeared at her side on many of the pictures must be her grandfather.

Many of the sights in the photos were familiar to Elise; the 'Moulin Rouge' featured as a backdrop to many, and there was one of a beautiful sculpture in a graveyard. "Must be the famous 'Nijinsky' in the Cimetiere de Montmartre."

Elise took out her diary, she decided to make a list of all the places on the photographs and visit them all. She could buy herself a little street map, and to find all the places that had meant so much to her grandmother; she may even be able to find her great grandmother's little shop. Some of the photographs had names and dates on the back, but very few identified the location. Elise took out her new phone, and took a new photograph of each picture in the box. She didn't want to run the risk of damaging them by carrying them around with her. There were lots of photos and it took a long time.

Elise placed the photographs back in the box and took out her sandwich. She had only managed two bites, when she heard the guard announce that they would soon be arriving in the Gare du Nord. Elise quickly gobbled down the rest of her lunch and pulled out her suitcase. She stowed the box of photos safely away, and then took out her new mirror. Annie had been right. Her lipstick looked exactly as it had when she had applied. Elise thankfully put the mirror back in her bag. She had decided that trying to apply lipstick on a moving train was definitely not for the faint-hearted.

Elise stood by the carriage doors; she still had to keep pinching herself to believe that she had actually made it all the way to Paris on her own. She was bubbling over with excitement. All she had to do now was to find the hotel, which was less than a mile away and her adventure could begin.

She made her way through the passport control and stepped out excitedly onto French soil.

She stood still, and gazed around—for that moment no one else existed. She let go of her suitcase and clasped her hands.

"I'm here, Grandmere, I'm finally here." Elise didn't realise that she had spoken aloud, and for once, she would not have cared. This was the moment that she had been waiting for, for as long as she could remember.

She looked around, trying to decide which way to go, when she heard someone call her name. Elise stopped for a moment, then carried on walking. "You aren't the only Elise in Paris, you silly cow." But she heard her name again, and saw a man rushing towards her. Elise stared and realised it was Armand.

She stopped in her tracks and frantically looked around for somewhere to hide, but it was too late; he was heading straight for her. Elise felt her stomach flip and her hands shook. She had no option but to put on the bravest face she could manage. After all, she had harangued a complete stranger in Bond Street, how hard could it be to remain calm and say a polite "hello" to the man she had been dreaming about for years.

"How did you know what time I would be arriving?" she asked, confused as Armand gave her a hug and planted a quick kiss on each cheek.

"Elise, it's wonderful to see you, and you told me what train you were getting. Did you forget? I was so worried about you, but you look wonderful." Armand stood back and gazed admiringly at Elise. "Please, would you do me the honour of allowing me to escort you to your hotel?"

They set off together on the short walk to the Citadines. Elise wished she had booked one slightly further away.

"I have to go back to my office for a while, but I would love to take you out for a special dinner to celebrate your arrival here in my beautiful city," Armand announced as they entered the hotel lobby.

Elise was taken aback. Armand meeting her at the station had been a big enough shock, and now he was actually offering to take her to dinner.

"Oh, no, please Armand, you've been so kind already, I really couldn't trouble you any further."

"Of course, I should have realised that you have already made plans," said Armand, bowing his head slightly.

"No, no I don't have any plans at all; you are the only person that I know here."

"In that case, I shall meet you here; is seven o'clock okay? It's a little early for dinner, I know, and believe me, Elise, it is no trouble at all."

Chapter Twenty-Four

Armand left and a porter took her suitcase and showed her to her room. It was big and airy, and the windows opened enough for her to stick her head out and look out on the streets below. Elise noticed a beautiful bouquet of flowers and a box of chocolates lying on the bed. She was very impressed, did all hotels do that? She picked up the envelope that was on top of the chocolate box and opened it.

Elise realised that the hotel hadn't done it. The chocolates and flowers were from a very contrite Jean-Pierre, who, with much laboured rhetoric, apologised effusively and wholeheartedly for the 'accident' in Clapham and begged her forgiveness.

Elise was reasonably sure that Armand had had a very large hand in this, but she didn't care. No one had ever bought her a bunch of flowers before, and these were beyond spectacular. Elise looked around for something to put them in, when there was a knock at the door. The hotel porter stood there holding a vase that was almost as lovely as the flowers. "For your flowers, Madame," he said, nodding his head towards the bouquet.

Elise grabbed her bag and handed him a ten euro note. "Thank you," she said, as he bowed his head and left. "Sorry, Gerry," she said to herself. "Definitely no receipt for that."

Elise unpacked her case and hung everything neatly in the wardrobe. She placed the folder, photos, and Grandmere's address book on the dressing table and took out her phone. The battery was flashing, Elise pulled the charger from her bag, but realised that it wouldn't fit into the French socket. "Never mind," she thought, "it can wait until tomorrow."

She treated herself to a long luxurious soak in the bath, definitely a step up from her poky little shower; she had fastened her hair up out of reach of the water and prayed that her make up wouldn't melt. Elise picked out one of the dresses from the trunk. The weather was warm and sunny, and she wanted to look her best for her first ever date.

Just before seven o'clock, Elise made her way down to the lobby. She was so excited about going out for dinner that she had been sitting on the armchair in her room for the past forty minutes, but had forced herself to hang on till the last minute, determined not to look too desperate.

Armand was already there; he gave her a quick hug, and then stood back and stared at her. Elise felt her cheeks going red, but she had checked carefully in the mirror and knew there was no smudge on her nose, and that the dress fitted her perfectly. She waited in silence.

"Elise, you look even more beautiful than before. I can see that I shall be the envy of every man in Paris. Now please tell me where you would like to go for dinner?"

Elise, blushing redder than before, shook her head. "It's my first night in Paris. As long as it is somewhere French, I don't mind."

Armand laughed. "You are in Paris, Elise, everything is French. Do me the honour of taking my arm, and I will take you to my favourite restaurant. Are you up for a walk?"

Elise thought that this would possibly be the best evening of her life. She was actually here, in Paris, going out to dinner with Armand.

They sat together outside a beautiful little French restaurant, with a wonderful view of the Place de l'Opéra. Armand ordered and as they sat together enjoying a very nice glass of wine, Armand leaned into her and said, "I'm so very sorry that I had to leave you last week, but I was so angry and just wanted to deliver that vile boy back to his parents as soon as possible. Arek promised me that he would get you home safely, but still it was not very gallant of me to leave you like that."

Elise was cringing, trying not to revisit the scene of herself astride the plant pot.

"Oh, no, please, Armand, don't even think about it. Arek and Dave drove me back to my flat. Everything was fine, no harm done."

"There was plenty of harm done," answered Armand, shaking his head. "Jean-Pierre's parents were furious with him. They've whisked him off on holiday for the month, but I got the feeling that he wasn't going to have such a good time, especially now they have confiscated his laptop and his phone."

"Please, Armand, don't worry about it, and please promise me that you won't cancel your contract with us. We are depending on you. I don't think the company will survive if we lose all the customers who buy your wines."

Armand shook his head again. "Surely, you do not want to work there anymore? How can you bear to even look at that disgusting girl, and the stupid Mr Gerry! When I called him, he had the nerve to tell me that you had had too much to drink!"

Elise was shocked to hear that Gerry had tried to blame her. But it had never crossed her mind to work anywhere else, and the thought of losing her job terrified her. "I love my job," she protested. "Please, Armand, can't we forget about all this and carry on as if it never happened?"

"I would not wish to cause you any distress, Elise, and of course if that is what you want, then I will agree to renew our contract. As long as I never have to deal with Gerry again. I have emailed Mike and his business partner with every last detail of what transpired, and forwarded all the ridiculous messages between that dreadful girl and Jean-Pierre. So, I will leave it up to them to put their own house in order." Elise heaved a huge sigh of relief, and smiled happily as the waiter brought over their food. Now she could stop worrying and really enjoy her holiday. She couldn't help but smile at the thought of how much this short conversation had cost Gerry.

Elise looked across the rows of tables at the other diners eating and chatting together, and suddenly felt conscious that people were looking at her and Armand. She felt her face redden and put her head down quickly.

"Armand," she whispered, "everyone is staring at us."

Armand laughed.

"They are not staring at us," he answered. "They are staring at you."

Elise glanced up, horrified. "What am I doing wrong?" she asked him.

"Absolutely nothing," Armand answered in a surprised tone.

"You are a beautiful woman, and here in Paris, we love to admire things of beauty!"

Elise wasn't sure whether he was joking, but decided to keep her attention fixed firmly on her plate.

"I have to go into the office tomorrow, but I could meet you in the evening and take you sightseeing if you would like," said Armand, as they finished dinner.

"Oh, yes, I would love that. Do you think we could go to the Cimetiere de Montmartre?"

"I was thinking more of the Louvre, or the Tour Eiffel, but we could definitely go to the Cimetiere, and afterwards, the Sacré Coeur, if you wish?"

Elise nodded; she couldn't wait to visit the place that had meant so much to her grandmother.

"I have some shopping and things to do tomorrow, but that would be lovely, thank you."

"I guess you'll be heading straight for the Boulevard Haussmann first thing in the morning then?" Armand said, as he took her arm. They walked together as darkness fell. The streets were bright and still bustling with people. Elise kept having to pinch herself. She was still finding it hard to believe that she was actually here, whilst trying to remember the Boulevard Haussmann for the morning.

Armand left Elise in the foyer of her hotel. "Have fun tomorrow," he said, and gave her a quick kiss on the cheek. "I'll be here at seven, don't go anywhere without me!" he said with a smile as he headed for the door.

Chapter Twenty-Five

Elise watched him disappear into the night and then went up to her room. She lay down on her bed, feeling exhausted. Too much had happened in too short a space of time, she felt as if she needed a few minutes to let her brain catch up!

After a quick shower, Elise carefully spread out her MAC purchases and started with a heavy heart to remove her make-up. Tomorrow she would head out to find a MAC shop in Paris to buy some brushes and try to figure out how to do it on her own.

Once Elise was reassured that her old face had returned, she carefully opened the safe, hidden in the wardrobe. The envelope containing Gerry's euros was on one side, along with the credit card and her passport and Grandmere's bulging envelope was on the other.

Elise looked with distaste at the euros; she made a mental note to replace the note that she had tipped the porter with and took out one of the bundles of English pounds. Elise stared at the money; she had never seen as much cash as that in her life.

After paying her rent and bills and setting aside money to run her aging car, she didn't have much left over.

Apart from the extravagance of buying coffee at Freddie's, Elise watched every penny. She berated herself for her coffee habit, but even on the most awful of days, Freddie always managed to bring a smile to her face. The other assistants always gave her a smile, but never attempted to take her order. As soon as she entered the café, Freddie would appear as if by magic and they would enjoy a few minutes of small talk whilst he prepared her drink. Elise was already imagining how excited she was going to be to tell him all about Paris.

She placed one thousand pounds in her purse and tucked it away in her handbag. Tomorrow, she could exchange them for euros. She needed to buy some brushes and some shoes to wear to visit the cemetery and to do some serious walking. Elise didn't want to risk scuffing Grandmere's beautiful court shoes; they needed to be saved for shorter, more delicate activities.

Elise was up bright and early. This was her first full day in Paris and she was determined not to waste a moment. After a quick croissant and coffee, Elise headed back to the Gare du Nord and purchased tickets for the metro.

She managed to find the right line to the Boulevard Haussmann and nervously waited on the crowded platform. There were screens with sliding doors along the platform edge. An electronic notice hung over the platform showing which train was about to arrive.

As the train pulled in everyone made for the doors. A loud buzzer sounded as the train doors opened and everyone made a rush for the train. People were trying to get off as others pushed their way on. Elise, who had been waiting patiently on the platform, felt herself being shoved into an already packed carriage just as another buzzer sounded and the doors closed.

She grabbed a pole in the centre of the carriage and refused to budge. There was a map of the train line above the doors and a light above each station lit up as the train pulled in. Elise was thankful that she was only a few stops to go, as it was getting very hard to breathe.

She hugged her bag tightly under her arm, and as soon as the Boulevard Haussmann light started flashing on the map, she started to push through the crowd to get near the door. Elise felt herself being carried off the train by the impatient passengers behind her. The doors did not stay open for long, and it appeared that Parisians had not discovered the art of forming an orderly queue.

Elise followed the exit signs. There were large glass doors with green arrows on blocking the exit. Elise looked around for somewhere to put her ticket, but couldn't find anything. She heard a terrific bang on her left, and saw a young man kick open the doors and run through. The lady waiting behind him simply walked up to the doors and pushed them open. Elise gave up with the ticket and pushed the door in front of her which opened without a fight. Slightly puzzled, she walked through, climbed the stone steps and walked out into the sunshine.

Elise saw the huge sign for 'Printemps' and looked up to see a ceiling of beautiful pink flowers running the length of the street. Satisfied that she was in the right place, she crossed the road and went into the first bank she saw and armed herself with a bag full of euros. Crossing back, Elise boldly walked through a set of 'Printemps' double doors and to her amazement, found herself in the cosmetics department. There was a huge MAC counter, and filled with relief, Elise headed straight to the counter.

A young man hurried over to her. He was dressed from head to toe in black and was wearing the same brush-filled bag around his waist that Elise had seen on Annie. She fervently hoped that she wouldn't be needing all of those.

"May I help you?" he asked. Elise nodded. He had the most beautiful eyes that she had ever seen, and eyelashes that were almost as long as the strange caterpillars that Alice went in for. Elise was sure, however, that with this man, there was definitely no glue involved! The man stood patiently whilst Elise tried to decide what she wanted when she caught sight of a card on the counter, stating that one-hour make-up lessons were available. She pointed to the sign.

"I'd like a make-up lesson. Do you have any time free now?

The man consulted his watch. "Yes, actually, I do," he said.

Elise nodded again. "Only, I think, I might have to book a double session," she said, as she sat down in front of the mirror.

Two long hours passed before Henri stepped back from the mirror, looking exhausted but very proud. "You see, you can do it! Perfect."

Elise looked in the mirror, and had to agree, that both sides of her face now matched perfectly.

"It just takes a bit of practice," said Henri, "but you have done a brilliant job, you look stunning."

Elise peered into the mirror again; she looked at her reflection. It didn't seem like her, and she felt like a fraud.

Henri noticed her expression. "What's wrong? Don't you like it?"

"Well, I do, but it's not really me, is it?"

Henri glanced over both shoulders and then smiled into the mirror. "Well, there is no one else here, so it must be you."

"It just doesn't look like the 'me' I'm used to," said Elise.

"Maybe the 'you' you were used to wasn't really you'. Perhaps this is the real you. In any case, make-up doesn't really change anyone; it just gives them a bit of self-confidence, that's all."

Elise got up from the chair, and went with Henri to purchase the brushes. She gave him a very generous tip and thanked him profusely. He would probably need a lie down after all that effort.

Elise left the shop and went in search of lunch. She saw a Starbucks down a side street and went in. Clutching a sandwich, and a takeaway cappuccino, she started walking along the road, looking for somewhere to sit and think. Elise saw a sign for the Louvre and followed the directions. She soon found herself gazing at the magnificent building with its giant glass pyramid filling up the square in front of her.

Elise sat down on one of the seats in the square and took the lid off her coffee. Here she was sitting outside on of the most famous and beautiful buildings in Paris, maybe even the world, but all she could think about was Henri's comment about the 'you'. Elise couldn't really sort it out. Was the old 'her' the real 'her', or was it as Grandmere had said, a 'you' that had been created by her mother?

Elise had had time to digest the information in the letters from her grandmother and was beginning to understand why her mother had treated her the way she had. Elise realised that her grandmother had been right. It was nothing to do with her. Her mother would have resented and loathed any child who messed up her life. Maybe Elise didn't know who she was because she saw herself only through her mother's eyes.

An image of Amy's sister, Angela, suddenly appeared before her. Angela's hair changed colour weekly. Her sleeve of tattoos had seemed to stretch over most of her body the last time Elise had seen her.

It was as if Angela had thought long and hard about whom she really was and had changed herself to fit her image of herself.

Maybe that was what Elise needed to do. She really had no idea of who she really was, and how she fitted into the world. At least her father was now no longer a mystery. It wasn't the ending that she had hoped for, but at least it explained a lot.

Chapter Twenty-Six

The hours passed as Elise sat in the sunshine, oblivious to everything around her. She tried to conjure up in front of her all the people who had influenced her life: Her loving grandma, her beloved Amy, and the evil Alice. Had they made her who she was?

Elise tried to think of any decisions that she had actually made for herself through the course of her twenty-four years. It took her a while, but she could only come up with finding her flat. Every other decision had been made for her by someone else. "I'm nearly twenty-five; I've spent my life doing what other people have told me to do, no wonder I don't know who I am," she thought. "I've tried my best to please everyone else, just so that they might like me, or at least not be unkind, but I've never really been kind to myself."

Elise's head was banging, she heaved herself up from the little seat and wandered back towards the shops. Her brain was too tired to deal with anymore deep thoughts and she mentally folded up all the ideas flying around in her head and firmly locked them away for later. Elise had set her heart on visiting 'Grandmere's cemetery' and she needed some suitable footwear.

Elise saw a small boutique and walked towards it. Annoyingly, the 'lock' was not securely fastened, and images kept flooding back into her mind. Gerry suddenly loomed up before her, with his outlandishly trendy designer suits, ridiculously pointy-toed shoes and his shiny black hair. Gerry, a man who was so full of charm and self-adoration that he only had to learn someone's name to assume that they were best pals.

His brimming self-confidence, his assiduous attention to his appearance and his 'posh' accent opened lots of doors for him, but Elise had realised very early on in their working relationship that there wasn't much inside to back it up.

Elise knew that Gerry despised her. He could never understand why she made no effort to 'look the part', as he called it. He had given up trying after a few months, and just let her get on with it. She had always been happy to remain hidden in the background, quietly taking care of everything whilst he loudly took all the credit. She suddenly felt furious that she had allowed him to treat her the way he did. All the crap about coming to Paris, all he cared about was not losing face in front of Mike; he wouldn't have given a shit about Alice's antics, if Armand hadn't been involved.

"Fuck him," she said to herself as she walked into the shop.

Racks of clothes were laid out artfully in the shop. Elise stood still, not knowing where to head; a young girl approached her. "Can I help?"

"Yes please, I need some comfortable walking shoes, and maybe some casual jumpers and jeans."

The girl ushered Elise to a comfy-looking chair. "Can I get you coffee or anything whilst I put some things together for you?" Elise nodded thankfully; the thought of ploughing through all those rails was too much!

Whilst Elise drank her coffee, the assistant put together a selection of jeans and chinos with co-ordinating t-shirts and jumpers. The only thing she asked of Elise was her shoe size. Elise walked over to the rail.

"What would you like to try first?" asked the assistant.

Elise was taken aback. Apart from the embarrassing episode in Rigby and Peller, she had never ever tried anything on before buying it.

"Do I need to do that, they all look as if they will fit."

The girl smiled. "Well, you probably get your clothes fitted for the shows and things, but we can't really do alterations here, so it might be safer to try at least the trousers."

Elise was puzzled "What shows?" she asked.

"Oh, I assumed you were a model."

Elise shook her head. "No, why would you think that?"

The girl blushed. "Well, you just look like one, that's all. I mean, you're the perfect height, the perfect size, and well, your clothes are amazing."

Elise blushed. "You are very kind, but no, I'm definitely not a model. Maybe you are right, I should try on a few things."

Elise left the shop with bulging carrier bags. She headed back to Starbucks, this time more desperate for the loo than the latte. Feeling morally obliged to buy a coffee after visiting the 'ladies', she sat outside, nursing another café au lait. It was nearly four o'clock. Elise decided to walk the short distance back to her hotel rather than face 'certain death' on the metro.

Having had to ask for directions at least twenty times, Elise decided that 'certain death' on the metro would have been preferable. At last she reached the doors of her hotel. She had booked only three nights and knew she would have to start looking for somewhere else to stay tomorrow.

Elise nodded to the porter and made her way up to her room. Her head was still buzzing, and she needed time to think. She almost regretted agreeing to dinner again with Armand; she had to sort through all this chaos in her mind, and needed some space. Elise ended up nodding off on her bed and awoke with a jump. She had exactly twenty minutes to get changed and get ready to meet Armand.

Chapter Twenty-Seven

Elise opened her shopping bags and pulled out a pair of jeans, a t-shirt and a sweater. She took her new walking shoes out of the box and realised with horror that she didn't have any socks. "Shit, shit, shit," was all she had time to come up with. Never mind, she would just have to go commando and hope for the best. She certainly wasn't up for risking Grandmere's wrath by trekking round a muddy cemetery in grey suede courts.

Elise unplugged her phone from the charger. She was looking forward to taking some photographs that evening. As she put it in her bag, she noticed that she had a missed call from Alex. Armand would probably be waiting, so she decided to call him back tomorrow.

Armand was in the lobby; he had a taxi waiting outside to take them up to Montmartre, and apparently, he wasn't too keen on the metro either.

The taxi driver took them along through the back streets, and dropped them off on the top of a bridge. Elise was confused. She couldn't see any signs of a church, let alone a graveyard. "It's under the bridge," he said, as he paid the cab fare. Elise saw some huge green gates, but they were firmly locked. Armand led her over the bridge and down some steep narrow steps. There in front of them was the entrance to the cemetery.

It was like a different world! The bustle of the Paris streets just a few metres away was gone. Elise felt an overwhelming sense of peace and tranquillity overtaking her as she looked around. This was like no cemetery she had ever seen before. There were no mounds of earth with uniform headstones. Instead there were tiny stone-built mausoleums surrounding her. All different, some with wrought iron doors, some with stained-glass windows. Each had a stone above the doorway with the name of the family carved out.

There were no muddy paths. The cemetery was laid out like a tiny village, complete with cobbled streets and signposts. Elise stood in silence for a few moments, taking everything in. Armand lightly touched her arm. He pointed to a larger signpost just under the bridge.

"There is a map of the graves over there, if you are looking for one in particular."

Elise nodded. "Yes, I'd like to see Nijinsky's grave please." Armand led her over to a map.

The graves were listed in alphabetical order. "There, it's on the Rue Samson," said Armand, and taking Elise's arm they walked briskly along the cobbled streets. The sun was beginning to set, and there were few people around. Suddenly, Elise caught sight of a large more modern-looking tomb. She recognised the name engraved in huge gold lettering from one of the letters from her grandmother.

"Look, Armand," she said, pointing at the black marble slab. "Paul Derval, from the Folies, my grandmother knew him. She talked about him in one of her letters to me."

Armand walked with her to the tomb and they both read the inscription. Elise could hardly believe that her grandmother and great grandparents had known this man.

Elise would have liked to stay a little longer, but Armand seemed impatient to move on, so they walked on until they arrived at a short set of steps which led down to the Rue Samson, and there on the left Elise saw the tomb of Nijinsky, complete with the beautiful sculpture of him as the puppet Petrushka, sitting on top of the tomb. Elise hurried over to take a closer look. It was unbelievably captivating. She took out her phone and took a photo.

"I can't believe I'm really standing here," she whispered to Armand. "This is like another world down here."

"We are in an old gypsum quarry," explained Armand. "They turned it into a graveyard over a hundred years ago. It is an amazing place," he added.

Elise nodded again; she had a feeling that Armand wasn't quite as entranced by the place as she was, and decided that she would come back alone the next day to spend more time there.

Armand led her quickly back to the stone steps.

"There are lots of places to eat around here, but I had planned to take you somewhere really special for dinner. I'm just not sure we have time now. If you like, we could go up to have a look at the Sacré Coeur, and get a cab after that."

"Yes, please," said Elise. She was falling in love with this place. She could come back in the morning and find a hotel somewhere in Montmartre to book into for the rest of her stay.

The Sacré Coeur was a short, extremely steep, walk away; it was packed with tourists, but the view over the city below was spectacular. Elise leaned over the railings and stared out over the vast the vast and stunning panorama of Parisian architecture her. People were sitting having a picnic on the large expanse of grass beneath the railings. Elise would have liked to have sat there too, but she sensed Armand probably wasn't into picnics.

They wandered down the cobbled streets, which were still heaving with people. There were street artists and buskers entertaining the evening crowds. Elise saw a tiny Italian pizza restaurant, complete with outside tables; it was brightly painted in yellow and orange and had hanging baskets everywhere.

"Could we eat there?" she asked.

Armand followed her gaze. "Are you sure?" he said. "I'm not sure how good the food will be."

"Well, it's pretty hard to spoil a pizza!" said Elise, "and I would love to sit outside at one of those pretty little tables."

Armand, shaking his head, grudgingly agreed. "If you insist," he said.

Elise leapt for one of the tables, making sure that no one else got in there first! The busker was in full swing and an artist seated with his back to her was sketching a Japanese tourist. Elise had a perfect view of his work and was enjoying watching his progress.

The pizzas arrived. Elise set to work devouring hers. It was absolutely the best pizza she had ever eaten. Glancing up occasionally for air, she noticed that Armand was hardly touching his. Instead, he was just prodding the delicious toppings suspiciously with his fork, as if probing for land mines.

"Don't you like yours?" she asked.

"Not really," answered Armand. "Pizza is not really my kind of food."

Elise felt slightly irritated; she finished every scrap of hers, and as the waiter appeared at her side, she gave him a beaming smile. "That was absolutely wonderful!" and then just to piss Armand off, she asked for the dessert menu. Whilst she was checking out the delicious sounding puddings, Elise asked the waiter if he lived in Montmartre. When he nodded, she asked if he had heard of the Rue Legendre.

"But of course," he replied. "It's about a twenty minutes' walk from here, but it is a very long road."

Armand, who had pushed away his uneaten pizza, seemed quite miffed that Elise had asked the waiter instead of him.

"I'm going to come over tomorrow and have a look around," Elise continued chatting to the waiter. "Do you know what the nearest metro station is?"

"It depends which end you want to be at," he said. "Guy Môquet is probably the best one, it's at one end, so you can't go wrong; just cross the road and you will be on the Rue Legendre. You can just follow it right to the other end."

"Thanks, that's really helpful, and could I please have that one?" Elise said, pointing to a very opulent-looking ice cream dessert.

She could almost hear Armand groaning in the background. "Oh, and a café au lait as well please. Armand, would you like anything else?" Armand shook his head. "In that case, could I have the bill as well please?" Armand looked even more shocked. Elise insisted on paying for dinner.

"It's only fair, it was my choice and you paid yesterday," she said, as he tried to argue.

"As long as you allow me to choose tomorrow." Elise felt another wave of irritation. She had been so excited about meeting Armand, but now, shockingly felt like she could do with a night off.

The waiter soon returned with Elise's ice cream. "Would you like an extra spoon?" he asked. Armand shook his head, and Elise thankfully dug in, she didn't feel like sharing.

As she devoured her dessert, Elise thought back to the times when she and Amy and occasionally Angela had scraped together enough money to go to the local pizzeria. The evening always began with muffled giggles as the waitress who had got to know them all well, simply used to walk over and say "The usual, Ladies?" and then with a grin at Amy would add, "Yes, I will tell the chef not to be so mean with the pepperoni!"

The meal always ended with gales of laughter as the three 'ladies' would all dig into their one dessert and fight over who got the best bits. Pizza was meant to be fun; Armand was acting as if he rather be sticking pins in his eyes.

Elise slowly drank her coffee, and wished she hadn't scoffed all the ice cream, but it was definitely too delicious to leave. She paid the bill despite Armand's protestations and added a generous tip for the waiter.

"I can't wait to take you out tomorrow and let you sample the very best French cuisine," said Armand, as they got up to leave.

"You're forgetting that I had a French grandmother who was a wonderful cook," retorted Elise. "I grew up on French cuisine." Armand looked slightly crestfallen, but soon conjured up a smile, and actually patted Elise on the head as if she were some wayward child.

"I'm sure she was, but this will be the real thing. I just know you will love it," he said.

Elise was stunned. "Did he think her grandmother was some kind of stunt double?" She fought off a sudden urge to kick him on the shin as they set off back to the main road to hail a cab.

Chapter Twenty-Eight

At last Elise closed her bedroom door and kicked off the shoes, which had been rubbing her bare heels raw and making her toes cry for most of the evening. It wasn't really their fault, she reasoned, they were definitely meant to be worn with socks.

After a soak in the bath, she lay on her bed and started making plans for the morning. Elise got her grandmother's address book out and checked under 'V', sure enough there was the address for the vintage shop, and much to her surprise, she saw that it too was on the Rue Legendre. She had been planning to return to the cemetery for another walk around, and then find a hotel in Montmartre. Now she would be able to carry out her grandmother's wishes and take the sketches with her at the same time.

She also needed to return Alex's call, but decided she would do that after she had found somewhere to stay, so she could let him know the address.

Elise finally closed her eyes and tried to sleep, but she couldn't help reliving the evening with Armand. All these years, she had imagined how wonderful it would be to actually meet this 'man of her dreams'. Now she had, she was quite shocked at her feelings. She couldn't understand why she wasn't as overwhelmed with joy as she had expected to be.

Armand, on the other hand, seemed to really enjoy her company; he was keen to spend all his free time with her and was desperate to show off his beloved city. Elise had actually felt relieved to see the back of him when they returned to her hotel that evening. She couldn't understand why she felt this way. Surely, not being passionate about pizza was not a crime! She wanted to compare notes with Amy, and wondered if it was too late. She checked her watch. It definitely was. That would have to go on her 'to do' list for tomorrow. Right at the very top!

Elise woke just after seven the next morning. She was feeling slightly anxious about the day ahead; there were just too many things to do. She tried to calm herself, and focus her mind on finding something suitable to wear to visit the vintage shop with the sketches. Her feet were still aching from her 'sockless' evening out, so she delved into her underwear drawer and fished out a packet of 'hold ups' that the lady at Rigby and Peller had told her were a must.

Elise didn't dare to admit that she had no idea what they were, but having read the instructions on the packet she decided that they would at least give her feet a bit of a rest. She looked through the wardrobe and picked out one of the beautiful dresses from the trunk. The sun was already shining and it would be a perfect choice for the shop. She picked out a pair of her grandmother's pale blue court shoes; she had brought them to go with the wonderful coat, but that sadly would have to wait for a slightly less sunny day. Her eyes suddenly glimpsed a cream-coloured short waisted jacket and realised that the lining exactly matched her dress.

The shoes looked nice with the dress and jacket; she found the matching handbag and quickly put in her phone and some cash. The sketch book was far too big to go in the bag, so she used the carrier bag from yesterday's shopping expedition. All she needed now was some breakfast.

Elise dived into the lift and hit the ground, running for the café across the road. She ordered a large coffee, which she had discovered equalled only a 'small' one at Freddie's, with a croissant. As she gulped down the coffee, she pulled out her phone and checked the time; it was eight forty-five, which meant it was only seven forty-five in England, so hopefully she would catch Amy before she left for work.

"Hiya." Amy shouted down the phone.

"Hope I haven't caught you at a bad time," said Elise anxiously. "I just needed a catch-up."

"No, course not," said Amy cheerfully. "I'm just having a wee." Elise heard the toilet flush in the background.

"Amy, seriously, you take your phone with you into the bathroom?"

"Of course, doesn't everybody? Anyway spill the beans, I just know this is going to be the guilt trip of a lifetime, 'cos you got down and dirty with old Airman. I want all the juicy details, and don't you dare spare me any blushes." Amy giggled.

"Oh, no, I mean, God no, nothing like that, really," spluttered Elise, blushing into her croissant and checking around to see if anyone could possibly have overheard.

"Crikey, what are you waiting for? You can't seriously not have shagged him by now?" Amy sounded disappointed.

"Not even close," admitted Elise.

Elise quickly filled Amy in on the pizza and head-patting incident.

"Am I being silly?" she asked.

"God no, you mean he actually left the pizza?"

Amy was beyond shocked; suddenly, a thought came into her head.

"No, wait, did it have those vile hairy fish on it, 'cos, you know, maybe he didn't realise when he ordered it and then was too embarrassed to say: They are fucking disgusting. I had to pick them off mine once, and it was still bloody foul."

"No, Amy, no anchovies, he was just being a bit of a snob, and then when he patted me on the head, it just really bothered me."

"He's probably just a twat then," said Amy. "Don't worry, there are plenty more frogs in the pond; just ditch him quick. You can't afford to waste any time with a snobby git like that, and what does he think you are, his bloody dog?"

189

"Amy, do you think wearing make-up changes people?" asked Elise.

"God, this is a bit heavy for eight o'clock in the morning," said Amy.

"I haven't even had my Weetabix yet. Now, let me see, in answer to your question, no, of course not, you silly cow. Just gives you a bit of confidence and covers up the odd zit, that's all, doesn't change who you are. Think about that stupid bitch at work. Do you think she would be nice if she washed all the cack off her face? Would you be nasty if you actually put some on? It's just like a bit of armour, that's all, you know you always say that you can be confident and whatever on the phone, because no one is judging you on the way you look." Amy paused for breath, and then started off again.

"Just think of it like a phone, you will always be you, and thank God, 'cos you are perfect and don't you dare change!"

It was quite a long speech for Amy, but underneath her cheery tone, she was beginning to feel quite anxious about her friend.

"I've got some leave owing. Do you want me to come over to Paris? Just say the word and I'll jump on the next plane!"

"Oh, no, Amy, you are so kind, but I'll be all right; it's just all a bit overwhelming at the moment. I've been rushing round trying to do everything, I think I'm just a bit tired."

"You've just lost your grandma, and you haven't given yourself five minutes," said Amy.

"You're on your holidays, just put your feet up and have a rest for once."

Elise nodded at the phone. "I will, I've just got a couple of things left to do and then I promise I will. Thanks, Amy, hope I haven't made you late for work."

"No, you silly cow, this is a bloody mobile. I'm walking up the steps to the office as we speak. Please, Elise, give yourself a break and get shot of the pizza dodger."

Elise put her phone back in her bag, and ordered a second cup of coffee. Amy was right as always; she was tying herself

190

in knots, worrying about stupid things, and of course, the make-up thing was true, she did act differently with the make-up on, but she was beginning to realise that people actually treated her differently when she wore nice clothes and had her hair and make-up done.

She was slowly shedding her invisibility cloak. Maybe people were shallow, but could she blame them? Elise recalled Mrs Forbes's look of horror when she had walked into the office and asked to see Alex. To be fair, she had even given herself a fright when she had caught sight of her reflection, so she could hardly blame other people for the way they had looked at her.

Her grandmother's words floated back into her head, and she understood for the first time, what her grandmother was trying to teach her about self-respect. Grandmere was right; Elise had never had any respect for herself, so why should she have been sad when other people did not respect her? She wasn't really becoming a different person because she had changed her clothes and had her hair done, she had just given herself a bit of respect, which in turn had given her the confidence to stand up straight and smile, which made other people react towards her in a more positive way.

There was no great mystery! Elise downed her second coffee, and felt her head clear a little bit. She saw a salon a little way down the road, and as she hadn't actually dared to wash her hair, since Madeleine had attacked it four days earlier, she decided a wash and blow dry was long overdue.

The stylist was delighted to see Elise standing in the otherwise deserted reception area.

"Please don't worry, I'm very experienced, it's just that August is a quiet month for us."

Elise watched with strained attention as the woman deftly sectioned and then proceeded to blow dry her hair. "Could you show me how you do that? I really would like to be able to do it myself, only I haven't a clue where to start!"

"Well, you definitely need the right tools to start with and you do have a lot of hair."

The woman talked Elise through every step and even handed her the hairdryer to make sure she got the technique right. Elise left the salon an hour later, clutching a piece of paper with the names of the brushes the stylist had used, and feeling slightly more confident in attacking her hair. If all else failed, she was still a whiz at creating a perfect chignon!

Chapter Twenty-Nine

Elise got on the metro; it was quite a few stops to Guy Moquet, but the carriage wasn't packed and she actually managed to squeeze into a seat.

Elise ran up the steps at Guy Moquet and felt relieved to be back in the fresh air.

A signpost directed her to the Rue Legendre, but it was split into numbers pointing in two opposite directions. It certainly appeared to be a very long road. Elise checked the number on the address for the Vintage Shop and started to head up the road. She kept her eyes peeled for a hotel as she walked. There were plenty of smaller ones dotted along the road, but Elise needed a room with a safe to stash all her cash.

Elise caught sight of a sign for the Art Hotel Batignolles, which had a four-star rating and looked perfect. She walked purposefully up to the desk and waited for the receptionist to look up from the desk.

"I need to reserve a room from tomorrow, but I'm not sure exactly how long I'll be staying, possibly until the 28th of August. Oh, and I'd like to settle my bill in cash?"

The receptionist looked quite surprised. "Yes, but we would need to take a credit card from you whilst you are a guest here."

Elise was a bit surprised as well.

"I could leave my company credit card details with you as long as you are sure that I don't have to use it to pay."

The receptionist seemed to think that that would be okay. Elise began to feel a little happier; at least she had somewhere to stay. She wandered back out into the sunshine and sat down outside the nearest café. Once her coffee arrived, she took out her phone and called Alex.

"Hi, Elise, how are you, is everything okay?"

"Yes, Alex, everything's fine, I just wanted to give you the address of my new hotel. I know Grandmere wants you to deliver a letter to me here. Oh, did you know about that watch?"

"I'll bet that was a bit of a shock for you, I did want to warn you, but Madame Giselle wouldn't let me. She knew it was quite valuable, but had no idea of what it would be worth in today's market. Actually, I wasn't very sure either, but I knew that Patek Philippe is a very famous brand."

"They gave me two hundred and fifty thousand pounds," whispered Elise; she was still finding it hard to believe.

"Wow, I expected it to be about fifty grand, I didn't really get a good look at it, crouching in that awful attic, but your grandmother wouldn't let me bring it downstairs. Now, don't forget to ring or text me if you need any advice, or anything at all. I promised your grandmother that I would look after you and I have absolutely no intention of letting her down. Now, when are you thinking of returning to good old Blighty?"

"I'm thinking of coming back on the 28th," said Elise.

"Right, I'll make sure you have the letter in your hand before then. Don't forget, any time, just ring me."

"I will," she replied. "And thank you for everything." She put the phone back into her bag and sat back to enjoy yet another coffee and a delicious-looking sandwich. Next stop would be the Vintage Shop, which according to the street numbers shouldn't be too far from here.

It wasn't too hard to find. Elise stood outside for a few minutes; the window display was beautiful, with a backdrop of the Champs Elysees and elegant mannequins, in languid poses, dressed in amazing ensembles that would have impressed even Grandmere!

An old-fashioned bell rang loudly as Elise pushed open the door. The shop was like a treasure trove, full of knickknacks and circular clothes rails, all labelled with the era they were from. There was an old bicycle, complete with a flower-laden basket, propped up against an ancient lamppost and amazing posters on the walls, promoting Hollywood films from long ago. There appeared to be no one in the shop. Elise was so entranced by the place that she could have stayed there the whole day.

"Bonjour Madame." Elise jumped, as a man appeared from a back room. "Can I be of assistance?" Elise was lost for words; the man was dressed as if he had just stepped off the stage in a magnificent dinner suit, circa 1930 and straight out of Hollywood! His hair was parted down the centre and shone. His moustache, equally shiny was twirled at the ends, and looked as if it was held in place with invisible thread.

Elise stepped out from behind a circular rail of clothes and started to walk towards him.

"Stop! Madame, do not move!" he shouted. Elise stopped in her tracks, and looked down at her feet, expecting to see an open trapdoor in the middle of the floor!

The man fished in his pocket and pulled out a pair of ultra-modern and definitely designer glasses.

"Sorry," he said. "I know they ruin my image, but I am, alas, blind without them!" The man bowed his head theatrically.

"Laurent Mercier, at your service, Madame." He took a step closer to Elise, and reached out his hand. Elise extended hers, but he ignored it, reaching for the cuff of her jacket sleeve instead.

"It cannot be?" he said, as he touched the fabric.

"Madame, where did you get this wonderful ensemble? Please tell me it is not a copy?"

"I don't think so, I think it was made by either my grandmother, or my great grandmother, or maybe both, I'm not sure."

"But, please, come into my little office, and take a seat, I am in awe!"

"My grandmother was Giselle Jacobs, and my great grandmother was Elouise Meunier. She had a shop here on the Rue Legendre. My grandmother passed away only last week, and she asked me to come here to bring you something to look at, if you would be interested?"

"I don't believe this," Laurent said, shaking his head. "My family have owned this shop for many years. My grandfather knew both your great grandparents. My great grandparents opened the shop; they would purchase anything and everything and would recommend that their customers took their purchases to your family to carry out any alterations. They all did a roaring trade, and I, of course, knew Giselle. I am so sorry to hear that she has gone. I often visit the grave of Charles and Elouise. They were wonderful, courageous people, and their actions during the war were not forgotten. My grandfather never tired of telling me the story of how they saved the life of one of their neighbours."

"My grandmother left me a letter, telling me about how they hid Mr Lehrmann," said Elise. "I am so proud, to think that I am related to people who acted so bravely. Are my great grandparents buried near here then?" she asked.

"But of course, Madame, they are in the Cimetiere de Montmartre. I would be honoured to escort you, if you wish."

Elise couldn't believe her ears. "But I was there yesterday," she said. "My grandmother told me about Nijinsky's grave and I went to see it."

"Well, you were not very far away from Monsieur and Madame Meunier, they too are buried on the Rue Samson, you probably walked past their grave."

Elise was ecstatic. "I would absolutely love to go back with you, when you have time," she said.

Realising she hadn't actually introduced herself, she bent down and pulled out the folder of sketches and placed them on the desk in front of Laurent.

"I'm sorry, I forgot to tell you my name. I'm Elise; I received a letter that my grandmother had left for me to open after her death and in it she asked if I could bring these to you, so please do have a look at them. To be honest, I'm not really sure what they are, perhaps you could tell me?"

Laurent pushed his glasses firmly onto his nose and sitting opposite Elise at his small wooden desk, he began, with shaking hands, to slowly turn the pieces of parchment. At one point, he opened a drawer and removed a large magnifying glass to focus on the faded letters. Elise sat patiently in silence as Laurent, with lots of sighs and gasps along the way, finally reached the last page. As he went to close the leather-bound cover, a tiny corner of paper sticking out from a panel in the leather caught his eye.

He looked up at Elise. "May I?" he asked. Elise had not noticed the panel before, let alone the tiny slip of paper.

"Of course," she said.

Laurent reached back into his drawer and pulled out a large pair of tweezers. He carefully grasped the paper and eased it out from the panel. Elise looked over to try to see what it was. Laurent laid the paper on the desk. Elise could now see that it was a small envelope, bearing her great grandmother's name and address in the Rue Legendre. He handed the envelope to Elise.

"I think that you should be the one to open this," he said.

Elise looked at the envelope; it had been opened before, but the letter was still in place. She pulled it out, and opened it.

The sheet of paper was of the highest quality and was bordered in black ink. There was a name in bold copper plate across the top and the letter was dated March, 1947. Elise read the letter out loud.

"Dear Madame Meunier,

Thank you so much for your kindness in expressing your condolences.

The last few weeks have been so difficult for me, but I am starting to get used to being alone.

I very much hope that you will do me the honour of accepting this trunk and the clothes that you worked so hard to create for my beloved wife. It was her last wish that I gift them to you. Isabel was very fond of you and so appreciative of your skills and artistry. She would have hated these to go to anyone else, so I very much hope that you will find some use for them.

Yours sincerely,

Paul Chabert"

Elise looked up at Laurent. "That's all," she said simply. "I guess it explains the trunk and all the outfits."

"You have the actual trunk, and the collection? Your dress is from this trunk?" Laurent almost jumped out of the chair.

"Madame Elise, please could I look inside your jacket?" Elise obligingly took off the jacket and handed it over to Laurent.

"I knew it, I absolutely knew it," he said, shaking his head. "Do you realise what you have here?"

"Apparently not," Elise answered, looking nervously at Laurent who was now bright red and puffing like an old steam engine. "Please tell me," she added, hoping that he might calm down a little.

Laurent handed back the jacket. "Look at the label, here," he said, pointing with his finger. Elise looked, and saw for the first time the name 'Christian Dior' in the back panel of the jacket.

"Well, I'm sure I've heard that name before," she said.

Laurent looked up from the jacket. "Not just Christian Dior, my dear; these clothes, the ones you have in the trunk must be part of his famous New Look, from his February 1947 collection. This lady must have ordered straight from the show and your great grandmother who was known throughout the fashion world for her skills in sewing would have been tasked with fitting them personally on the client. When Isabel Chabert died, her husband must have bundled the whole lot into her cabin trunk and sent them back to Madame Meunier. What a find, I can hardly believe it."

Chapter Thirty

Laurent pushed at his glasses again and stared critically at Elise. "Of course, they would have been much longer on Madame Chabert. The new look was meant to almost sweep the ankles, but you have much longer legs. You have a short waist, so the jacket and dress fit perfectly everywhere else," he added quickly.

"My grandmother said in her letter that she knew they would fit. I can't believe that they are more than sixty years old, they are all so perfect." Elise didn't really know how she felt about wearing the clothes of a long-deceased individual and was beginning to feel slightly uncomfortable.

"I doubt that they have ever been worn." Laurent shook his head. "They would have been designed to be worn in the summer. And this letter is dated March. The poor lady probably died before she had a chance to wear any of them."

Elise felt a little better. "My grandmother brought the trunk back to England with her after my great grandmother passed away. I think she packed all her mother's special things in it and I don't think it has been touched since she put it in the attic after my grandfather died."

"Oh, yes, I remember that, it was a dreadful, dreadful accident. We were all so horrified by what happened and your poor grandmother and the little girl, truly, truly terrible." Laurent shook his head, and sat back down in his chair.

"That would have been my mother, the little girl, I mean," Elise said. "I didn't know anything about how my grandfather had died until I read her letter. It did sound awful."

"Yes, your grandmother never returned to Paris after that. Perhaps it would have been too much for her; that is why we tend the grave, as a way of showing our respect for her parents and a mark of respect for poor Mr Jacobs. He was incredibly brave, his actions saved others as well as your mother and grandmother, you know." Laurent looked at his watch. "I have a couple of young ladies coming in from 'Vogue'; they want to borrow some pieces for a shoot they are doing on the steps this afternoon. They should be here in a few minutes. If you aren't in a hurry, would you let me take you for lunch?"

"I would love that, I'm not in a hurry at all." Laurent handed the folder back to Elise.

"These sketches are wonderful. Do you know what they are?"

"No, I haven't a clue; I was hoping that you could tell me; I thought they might belong to you, actually."

"No, sadly they do not; I got so carried away with the letter. I should have explained the sketches. Never mind, we can talk over lunch."

Elise heard the shop door open and two young women ran in. They greeted Laurent with great enthusiasm, and handed over a list of items. Laurent glanced down and nodded. "Yes, everything is ready, all in boxes for you, apart from the bicycle. Please don't try to ride it, ladies, I don't think it has any brakes!"

Laurent bowed stiffly at Elise. "Please excuse me a moment, I have to change." He hurried back into the shop. Elise sat quietly at the desk, the sketches lay forgotten as she pondered Laurent's words about the bravery of her grandfather. How was it that she could have great grandparents and a grandfather noted for their courage, and yet she was such a coward? Was her father a coward? He had certainly left her mother in the lurch, yet he had supported her financially all those years.

Her mother was more a bully than a coward, so genetically they should have cancelled each other out. Elise had a feeling that genetics were not really that simple! Anyway, was she such a coward? She had obeyed every one of her grandmother's wishes, however daunting they had seemed; she still cringed over the watch incident. She had got herself to Paris all by herself, and had (with little effort, she had to admit) managed to persuade Armand not to abandon the company. Maybe she wasn't such a coward after all.

Elise didn't have time for any more deep thoughts, as Laurent suddenly appeared in front of her. This time he was in a lounge suit, and sporting a panama hat. His moustache had disappeared and he looked about twenty years younger.

"Wow!" said Elise. "Paul Henreid, straight from 'Now Voyager'."

Laurent laughed appreciatively. "You love the old Hollywood films as well!"

"Not as much as my grandmother, she loved Paul Henreid, and that was her favourite film."

"Well, my dear, I am very flattered to be compared with Monsieur Henreid, but you are far too beautiful to be Bette Davis! Now, the girls are waiting, shall we join them?" Laurent escorted Elise from the shop and locked the door behind them. There was a large car outside the shop, the driver was still fighting with the bicycle as Laurent and Elise jumped in.

"It's part of the deal," whispered Laurent, "I lend them all the props they need for the shoot and I get a 'walk-on' part in the ad." The driver jumped in and they set off down the street.

The girl sitting in a single seat in front of Elise and Laurent turned her head. "We were wondering, if you are not tied in to an exclusive contract, would you like to have a 'walk-on' part with Laurent? Christine and I love your outfit, and it would go perfectly with our 'Homage to the fifties' theme."

Elise was stunned. "I'm on holiday, I don't have a contract with anyone," she said.

Laurent chimed in. "Bravo, you girls are going to do well in this industry," he said. "Madame Elise is wearing vintage

Christian Dior, and I'm sure she won't mind playing my leading lady!"

The girls were overjoyed. "We will have to ask the director and the photographer, but we are sure that they will be thrilled."

Elise wasn't feeling quite as thrilled; she suddenly felt an attack of nerves coming on.

"I thought we were going for lunch?" she whispered.

Laurent nodded. "These things take ages to set up, and there's a lovely café, just at the top of the steps, so we will have lots of time to eat. Please don't disappoint me, in my youth I dreamt of being an actor. However, after only managing a few 'walk-on roles', I soon realised that I was no Gerard Depardieu!"

Elise laughed. "No, you are certainly far too handsome to ever be mistaken for Monsieur Depardieu and besides, you still look very youthful to me."

Laurent grinned. "You are very kind, my dear! I offer my goods for the magazines and occasional films and in return, I have a tiny moment of glory. It would be wonderful if you could share it with me today."

Chapter Thirty-One

The car pulled up to the kerb on a cobbled street. To her surprise and delight, Elise realised that they were outside her 'favourite' pizza café. The driver and the girls jumped out and started unloading the props from the car and taking them over to a long steep flight of stone steps. The steps were already a hive of artistic activity, with people rushing about arranging large pots of flowering plants on the landings and a bistro table and chairs under a lamp post. The bicycle was now parked against the railings half way up the steep stone steps. There was a small white tent, just to the right of the steps. "That's where they do the hair and make-up for the models and store the clothes for them to change into," said Laurent.

Christine came galloping back towards Elise and Laurent. "Would you mind if the make-up artist had a quick look at you both? The photographer is keen to get started because of the light."

Christine ushered Elise into the tent first. Two girls were seated in little canvas chairs having the finishing touches done to their hair. Christine rushed over to the make-up artist, and said, "It's just going to be a back and profile of her leaning over the railings." Christine plonked Elise in another canvas chair and quickly ushered the two models over to the clothes rail. One of the girls shot Elise a vicious glare, and began speaking in English. "Who is that bitch, and why did they give her that outfit? I'm sure it was on my rail."

The other girl nodded. "She arrived with that idiot 'has-been'. I haven't seen her before; she's not with our agency.

She must have run over and grabbed it whilst we were in make-up."

Elise couldn't believe what she was hearing. The girls' English was so laughably bad; they obviously assumed she was French and that they wouldn't be understood. It was bad enough that she had been accused of stealing her own clothes, but insulting poor Laurent was going too far. Elise was filled with uncharacteristic feelings of indignation. Normally, any accusation made against her of wrong-doing would drive her into panic-mode, stricken with a sense of guilt and failure.

Elise had grown up with the need to apologise profusely even when she knew she was innocent. This would be followed by her doing her utmost to rectify whatever was wrong.

Her brain infuriatingly refused to allow her to forget these accusations; they would creep back into her mind, usually when she turned out the lights and got into bed. She would be forced to relive every single moment during long, anxiety-filled sleepless nights.

Something was very different today. Elise felt as if she were having some sort of 'out of body experience'; she had the sensation that she was floating up to the ceiling, with a bird's eye view of everyone, including herself below. Now comfortably seated on one of the poles supporting the tent roof, she watched with baited breath to see what this strange new Elise was going to do next. She didn't have to wait too long.

Elise got up from the canvas chair and strode over to the whispering girls.

"Hello, ladies, sorry we haven't been introduced, I'm Elise. I couldn't help overhearing you complimenting my dress. It's part of my personal collection of vintage Dior, and the girls are dying to get it into the shot. Oh, and by the way, your English is really very good, I understood every word!"

Elise turned swiftly around and marched back to the somewhat bemused make-up artist.

"Sorry, I was forgetting my manners," she said and plonked herself back in the chair. Her out of body spirit settled back into the chair with her. Elise wasn't sure who this strange new version of herself was, but she definitely liked her. The make-up artist who spoke no English, simply shrugged her shoulders and got to work sticking tissues all round Elise's neck and a large sheet over her clothes. She deftly applied a bright red lipstick, eyebrow pencil and eye liner and finished off with a quick blast of powder.

"I haven't seen you around before, are you new?" she asked.

"Oh, no, I'm just being Bette Davis," Elise answered. She jumped out of the chair and rushed off in search of 'Paul Henreid' and pizza.

Laurent was waiting outside the café. "Sorry, I didn't know what you wanted. I'm just going to do my hair and make-up. Can you order me a mushroom pizza, and I'll be back in a minute?"

The waiter recognised Elise from the previous evening. "You found your road okay?" he asked.

"Yes, I did, thank you."

Laurent returned, looking even more handsome than before; as far as Elise was concerned Laurent definitely kicked Paul Henreid to the kerb! Pizzas, sparkling water, and coffee quickly appeared, and between mouthfuls, Elise asked 'Paul' about the accident.

"You said my grandfather saved other lives as well in that accident, my grandmother only mentioned that he saved her and my mother. Could you tell me any more about it?"

Laurent nodded. "Probably your grandmother could not bear to talk too much about it. I can tell you what I know; obviously, I wasn't even born when it happened, but it was talked about for a long time afterwards. We often used to cut up through the Rue Lepic and, of course I saw the plaque and asked my grandfather about it; he and my grandmother were there at the café and saw everything."

"Wait," said Elise, "what do you mean, 'plaque'?"

"Didn't your grandmother tell you?" Laurent seemed surprised. "Everyone who was there that day raised the money for a little commemorative plaque to honour your grandfather. It's there on the wall of the café where Tom grabbed the bike."

"Maybe she didn't know about it," said Elise.

Laurent didn't answer, instead, leaning forward in his seat, he clasped his hands in front him on the table and began to speak:

"It was early evening on the rue L'Epic; it was still sunny and the street was crowded with people shopping or sitting having a drink. Your grandparents had been up to the cemetery with your mum, I think they were due to return to England the next day and had arranged to meet my grandparents at the café for a drink. Our grandparents were very close friends. Madame Giselle and my grandmother had known each other all their lives.

A young man on a huge motorbike came speeding round the corner; he was trying to turn left to go down the hill, but he was going too fast and hit a pot hole or something in the road, skidded and lost control of the bike. He fell off the bike and was killed instantly, but the bike just carried on going; it was turned on its side and was heading straight for the café.

Your grandfather shoved Giselle and the little one out of the way and launched himself at the bike, to push it away from all the people. He managed to steer it away, but he got caught up in the wheel and ended up being dragged down the road under the bike. He lost his own life, but his brave actions saved many others. People talked of nothing else for days. He was so very brave. They saw the whole thing. It was a dreadful tragedy. No wonder your grandmother never wanted to come back here."

Chapter Thirty-Two

The sudden arrival of Christine ended the conversation.

"Would you like to come and watch? We'll be ready for you in a few minutes." Elise followed Laurent over to the long line of steps. They both stood behind the photographer as he tried to get a shot of the nasty model pretending to ride the bicycle. She saw Laurent and Elise and in a fit of temper stamped hard on the left pedal. Obviously not a seasoned bike rider, the girl squealed in pain as the right pedal immediately shot round and whacked her on the back of her ankle. Elise and Laurent both had to stifle giggles as the photographer groaned.

Christine magically appeared at their side. "If you go up to the second landing and start walking slowly up the steps, the camera will get you in view. When you get to the top landing, just lean over the railings, and wave as if you have spotted someone in the street below." Laurent and Elise walked down to the landing. Laurent moved to her left and smiled at Elise's not-too subtle efforts to practice her 'wave'. They were about to start the slow walk back when a wardrobe lady ran up and plonked a small hat on Elise's head. "The bag is wrong," she said, shaking her head. Christine obligingly appeared with a small silk purse and swapped it for Elise's bag. Laurent looked approvingly at the purse. "Ah, one of mine," he said and they set off up the steps.

Laurent was chatting away, and Elise forgot about the camera. He had put his arm loosely on her shoulder and guided her over to the railing at the appointed spot. As she leaned out to wave, a sudden gust of wind threatened to take the hat. Elise shrieked and almost flattened it with her hand. She then, like a true 'pro' leaned and waved with great gusto, and fervently hoped that her shriek hadn't ruined anything.

"All done," said Laurent. "Now, we can finish our pizza!"

They returned to their table, and Christine came running up to them.

"Thank you, you were brilliant, I'm sure we've earned some extra points for getting you into the shot." She handed Elise's bag back before carefully removing the hat and taking back the purse.

"Vintage Dior," said Laurent, nodding at the purse. "Perfect for your outfit!"

"Then I definitely need to buy it, if it's for sale?" Laurent pulled an exaggeratedly sad face.

"Of course, it is. It is the only downside of owning my shop, when I have to part with my beloved pieces."

Elise wasn't sure whether he was joking and took the opportunity to take the leather folder out of the carrier bag again.

Laurent once again pored over the parchment. "These date back to the nineteen twenties," he said, pointing to one of the more faded drawings. "These are originals, sketched by the designers themselves. They would then be passed on to highly skilled people like Madame Meunier to produce the lace or trim detail. You can see the little annotations here and here," he said, pointing at the faded writing. "This is the signature of the designer; this one is Paul Poiret, he was famed for his magnificent evening gowns in the 1920s.

"The fashion business was huge in those times. The designers employed thousands of women to sew their wonderful creations. Some like your great grandmother were sought after by all the great designers, because they had such amazing skill. They would actually travel with the gowns to the client's homes to do any final alterations and ensure that everything was perfect."

Laurent carefully turned the pages. "See," he said, pointing at another sketch. "This is a design by Schiaparelli, and this next one, is Christian Dior himself. This is the coat; it would have been part of the 1947 collection that your dress came from."

Elise studied the sketch. "Yes, I have it in pale blue, it's beautiful!"

Laurent nearly choked on his pizza. "My God, I just don't believe this; I have to see this collection."

"It's a good job I brought it with me, then," said Elise with a smile.

She couldn't remember a day when she had felt as happy and relaxed as she was sitting there eating pizza and poring over the contents of the folder with Laurent.

"Would you be free to visit the cemetery with me on Sunday?" he asked, after they had finished their third cups of coffee.

"Really, oh, yes, that would be perfect," answered Elise. "Sunday is actually my birthday and I couldn't think of a better way to spend it."

"In that case, maybe I could bring a picnic and we could go and sit somewhere afterwards and enjoy the sunshine. Then, end the day with a cosy dinner somewhere, if you would like?" Laurent was smiling hopefully at her.

"Absolutely perfect," she answered, with a huge smile and a faint blush on her cheeks.

It was nearly five o'clock when Elise reluctantly realised that she had better return to her hotel, and get ready to meet up with Armand.

"I'm so sorry, but I have to leave. Thank you for a really wonderful day."

"The pleasure has been all mine," said Laurent.

"I can't wait to see you on Sunday."

"I'll be at the Art Hotel Batignolles. Would we be able to see my grandfather's plaque on our way to the cemetery?"

"Yes, of course, it's not far and I love walking. I could meet you at your hotel at ten o'clock if that's not too early?"

Elise shook her head. "No, that sounds perfect. Now, I need to find a taxi."

"Allow me, Madame," said Laurent and nodded to the waiter. "Jose will call a cab for you; it will be here in a few minutes."

The cab pulled up and Laurent ran over and opened the door for her. He gave her a quick hug, and said, "Until Sunday." Elise nodded and climbed in. She turned to look back at Laurent as the car pulled away. He was still standing outside the café and was waving at her. She waved back and then sank back into the seat. She knew she was going to find it hard to wait until Sunday.

Chapter Thirty-Three

Elise ran through the lobby at the Citadines and raced up to her room. The roads had been busy and the taxi had taken longer than she had expected. Elise jumped into the shower having first bundled her hair into the swish shower cap that she had found alongside the other hotel freebies.

She carefully hung up the dress and jacket. She would need to find a good dry-cleaner's soon, before she ran out of clothes!

Elise heard her phone bleep as she sat at her dressing table trying to remove the last stubborn vestiges of make-up. There was a text from Alex, asking her if she could be at her new hotel at three p.m. on Monday to collect the last letter from her grandmother. Presumably, it was going to be delivered by hand to her. She quickly replied with a 'yes' and started redoing her face.

Elise wasn't really looking forward to another evening with Armand, but at least she would be able to make her excuses to come back to the hotel early to start packing her things ready to move out in the morning.

At exactly seven o'clock Elise stepped out of the lift. Armand was waiting for her, almost hidden behind a huge bouquet of roses. He rushed towards her and handed over the flowers.

"Elise, I'm so sorry about yesterday, I made a real idiot of myself, can you forgive me?" Elise was stunned by the apology and even more shocked by Armand's red face and his desperate expression.

"Thank you, Armand," she said, taking the flowers. "These are really beautiful, there's really no reason to apologise."

The porter appeared. "Good evening, Madame, shall I take these to your room?" Elise handed over the flowers and took Armand's outstretched hand. He really did look quite upset and she felt an overwhelming surge of sympathy for him. "Let's go for a walk, the weather is so beautiful, it seems a waste not to enjoy it."

They walked out arm in arm into the sunshine, and walked down towards the Place de l'Opéra. Elise spotted a lovely little wine bar with a few empty tables.

"Shall we go and have a glass of wine?" she asked. Armand, with a grateful expression on his face, nodded and the two sat down enjoying the last rays of sunshine.

"Elise, please I really want to explain. I had made all these plans for us and everything seemed to have gone wrong."

Elise sat quietly sipping her glass of wine. Armand, still red-faced, gulped down his drink and poured himself another, after politely trying to top up Elise's barely touched glass.

"I always dreamt of meeting you one day," he began. "It just didn't happen the way I planned it. My God, London, I still have nightmares about it." Armand actually shuddered as he spoke.

"You and me both," said Elise, trying to calm his nerves.

Armand didn't seem to hear her and carried on talking. "I really don't like travelling abroad, and I hate England, because, well, my English is so shit. Jean-Pierre's parents insisted that I came, to introduce their son to some of our English clients, so of course I was stuck with him.

"It was supposed to be a 'flying visit'. We never expected to do anything other than meet with Mike and a couple of other merchants and then shoot straight back on the train. I was so nervous when I got your message, about the train being delayed, I wanted to go straight to the station, but Jean-Pierre was having none of it and insisted that we go to the wine bar. Then I saw you, but you didn't seem as excited to see me, you looked really stressed, and of course, I had the stupid boy to deal with, and that awful girl. It just seemed to go from bad to worse."

"None of that was your fault," said Elise, feeling mortified at being reminded of the dreaded incident with the flower pot.

"Anyway, I'm sure Alice was behind all of that; poor Jean-Pierre had no chance against her. He did send me a wonderful bunch of flowers, and a box of amazing chocolates, with a long letter of apology, so he did try his best to make amends."

Armand looked surprised. "I didn't know about any of that, his parents were furious with him. Madame Duval contacted me to ask where you were going to be staying so it was probably her doing. It wasn't just that, though Elise. I had planned to arrive early at the station to meet you, with flowers and everything, then just as I was leaving the office, I got a frantic phone call from Arek, telling me that Gerry had tried to double up on their order in case I cancelled the contract and had messed up everything. It took ages to sort out and I just ran out of time.

"I was rushing about like an idiot, no flowers, no chocolates, I had to turn up empty-handed and I was so nervous about how you would feel towards me after I rushed off and left you before. Then I recognised you, and shouted your name. I started walking towards you, you looked so beautiful, everyone was staring at you, and I just wanted to run and hide. Whatever made me think that you would be interested in someone like me? I realised that you had heard me call your name, and I just had to try and act confident, and try to pull it off."

Elise was stunned, the fact that he had turned up at all had been wonderful, and the thought of him being as nervous about meeting her as she had been about meeting him, made her blush.

"It's no big deal," she said, taking his hand.

213

"You know, I'm embarrassed to admit this, but I felt just as nervous when I knew you were coming to that wine bar in London. I had had dreams about meeting you face to face and they didn't end with me smoking a joint and falling over a plant pot."

Elise felt embarrassed by her revelation, she was sure that she had gone a bit too far with that last comment, but she couldn't bear to see him in such a state. Armand was at last looking a bit less stressed. She hoped that after having downed two glasses of wine in a very short space of time, he wasn't going to end up in a flower pot as well.

"I think we should order some food," she said, picking up the menu. They both ordered steak and salad; Elise hoped there would be plenty of bread to soak up Armand's wine, failing that, at least the steak might slow down its transit! Armand however was determined not to let the matter drop and started off again.

"Yes, but then I messed up again, I had made all these plans to take you up the Tour Eiffel for cocktails and then out to an amazing restaurant. I had never thought about what you would like. I felt as if I acted like a bully trying to rush you around the cemetery so that I could impress you with my plans, and I ended up acting like a spoilt brat. I really am so sorry, I never meant to annoy you, and I know you must have thought me a dreadful snob over the pizza thing, but I really hate pizza, I just can't help it."

Elise smiled. "Well, I did a bit, but then, I love pizza, and can't imagine anyone not, but then you might have tried to make me eat Moules Marinieres; my grandmother did for years, but I'm sorry, I just can't stand them, so you see, I totally understand."

Armand smiled, at last. "You are as wonderful as I thought you would be, and a great deal more beautiful than I remembered. Please can we put the pizza and the pot behind us and start again?"

"Absolutely, of course," said Elise. "Let's do that, now eat your steak!"

Elise found herself once more enjoying Armand's company. She had been wrong about him, he wasn't a snob, just shy and nervous, and she could definitely relate to that.

His nerves were certainly getting the better of him. Elise watched in consternation as he downed a second bottle of wine before touching his meal. She could see how stressed he was, but didn't know what else she could say to calm his nerves and get him to slow down. At least he managed to eat some of the food on his plate. Elise concentrated on doing justice to her own delicious dinner and left Armand to fiddle around with his steak. "Perhaps he's just a 'picky' eater," she decided. His eating habits were beginning to get on her nerves. She picked up her own glass of wine and drank it too quickly, unfortunately, giving Armand the excuse to order a third bottle.

Conversation had dwindled to nothing as Elise helped Armand to finish the wine. He left his half-eaten steak on the plate and ordered large cognacs for them both. Elise felt herself getting irritated again. She hated cognac and was annoyed at him ordering her a drink without even asking. Armand was actually slurring his words, he kept grabbing at her hand, and Elise ended up hiding her hands in her lap under the table to avoid his clumsy clutches.

Armand's manners seemed to have 'left the building'. Seeing that Elise hadn't touched her cognac, he picked up the glass. "Don't you want it?" he asked. Elise shook her head and watched in horror as he downed it in one and ordered two more.

"He's not going to be able to stand up," thought Elise as he motored through the cognacs. She leaned forward, "Armand, slow down, you won't be able to walk if you carry on."

Armand was holding his head in his hands. "I've ruined everything, I love you so much." Now it was Elise's turn to shudder; she looked at him, and "Gross" was the only description that sprung to mind.

"Armand, I think we should get you a cab, what's your address?"

Chapter Thirty-Four

Armand didn't seem to be able to remember where he lived and Elise wanted to kill him. The waiter came over to the table and shook his head at Armand.

"You served him the bloody drinks so stop pulling faces. Can I have the bill now?" Elise snapped at the snotty waiter.

Elise had the presence of mind to speak in English, so the waiter only caught the word 'bill' and hurried off to oblige. Armand was now about to fall sideways off his chair and the waiter wanted them out of there as quickly as possible.

Elise placed enough euros on the plate to supply a generous tip and tried to get Armand on his feet.

"Come on, Armand, let's go and get some coffee." Armand managed to stand up and Elise spotted a slightly less salubrious kebab shop a few yards up the road. There were a couple of tables outside. She half-dragged the staggering Armand to the shop and unceremoniously shoved him into a chair in the corner against the wall.

The waiter appeared; he shook his head at Armand and smiled sympathetically at Elise. "This is what happens when you have a date with a beautiful woman, and your nerves get the better of you," he said.

"He needs to get over himself," said Elise, "so please could you bring us two very large black coffees and a jug of ice water?"

"You are not going to throw it at him, are you?" asked the waiter?

Elise smiled. "Well, I hadn't thought of that, but now you mention it." They both laughed and the waiter ran inside. Elise looked at Armand, she wasn't sure whether he was asleep or unconscious, and she didn't really care.

"What an arsehole," she thought.

The waiter returned with a large jug full of water and a generous helping of ice cubes and two mugs of coffee. Armand hadn't stirred. Elise had no idea what to do next. She could just walk away and leave him sitting there, but she didn't think that the waiter would be overly impressed, and Armand was to be fair, not in any state to look after himself. She called the waiter back over.

"Do you think you could be kind enough to call a cab for me, so I can get him back to my hotel?"

The waiter shook his head. "With respect, Madame, I am sorry, but I don't think any cab driver would agree to take him anywhere."

Elise was at a loss, her hotel was less than half a mile away, but she didn't have a hope of getting him there on foot. She looked around, the waiter had disappeared and the other tables were empty. She carefully scooped a handful of ice cubes from the jug. "Back or front?" Elise couldn't decide which would be more effective, she took a last look round and then eased Armand's sweater away from his neck and tipped the ice down his back. It didn't have the effect she was hoping for. Armand groaned and shuffled in his seat, but that was it. Elise scooped up another handful and plonked that down the front of his neck. This time Armand groaned more loudly and opened his eyes.

"Armand, for God's sake wake up, we have to leave," Elise hissed loudly in his ear. Armand looked up at her through glazed eyes. In desperation, she picked up the jug and emptied it over his head. This last attack got the desired effect and Armand jumped out of the chair. Elise dropped ten euros on the table and swiftly grabbed his arm.

"Come on, get moving, Armand, now!" Elise staggered down the road trying to prop him up and sagging under his weight. The hotel seemed to have moved much further away than she remembered, but Armand was at last getting the hang of his legs again, and they eventually made it back to the Citadines. Elise hustled Armand through the lobby and into the lift.

The porter made no comment, but Elise noticed his eyebrows shooting up and down as the lift moved up through the floors. He helped Elise get Armand back to her room, dumped him unceremoniously on the bed and quickly bowed his way back out into the corridor.

Elise looked at Armand in disgust. He was flat on his back and snoring loudly. She had no idea what to do next. Elise grabbed her phone and locked herself in the bathroom.

"What's up, girl?" Elise almost cried in relief when Amy's cheery voice answered on the third ring.

"Amy, thank God, hope I didn't wake you up."

"Nah," she replied, "It's only just after ten." Amy heard the tension in her friend's voice. "Elise, what's wrong, have you got yourself in a mess?"

"Bloody Armand has passed out on my bed, and I don't know what to do," Elise replied.

"God, what did you do to him? He hasn't had a heart attack in the middle of it, has he? That's what you get for waiting so long."

"Please, Amy, absolutely not; he just had too much to drink at the restaurant; it nearly killed me getting back here and now he's just lying there snoring like a pig." Elise opened the bathroom door. "There," she said. "Can you hear that?"

"Christ, he sounds just like my mum." Amy was suitably impressed by the noise.

"Why did you bring him back to your room? You should have just left him at the restaurant."

"I couldn't just leave him there, he could barely stand." Elise was feeling near to tears at this point and locked herself back in the bathroom. Amy immediately took charge.

"Listen, Elise, you can't stay in there with him. Do you have enough money to pay for another room?"

"Yes, of course," Elise replied.

"Right then, pick up the hotel phone and ring down to reception and tell them you need another room just for tonight. Do it now, I'll wait on the line." Elise obediently emerged from the bathroom and grabbed the phone.

"Yes, Madame Jacobs, how can I be of assistance?"

Elise was relieved to hear another voice. "I have a bit of a problem; do you have any rooms free, preferably on this floor, just for tonight?"

There was a slight pause as he checked the computer. It seemed like an eternity to Elise as she tried to move as far away as possible from Armand.

"Yes, Madame, we have room 547, it's just across the corridor from your room."

"Thank you, could you please send the porter up with the key, and if there is anyone else free to lend a hand, I'd be very grateful, oh, and would it be okay if I pay in cash for the room in the morning?" Elise could imagine the look on the receptionist's face, but she was past caring.

"Are you checking out of both rooms in the morning?" Even the receptionist had trouble wording that one. But diplomatic as ever, simply shrugged his shoulders at the phone and called over the porter, who was just about to leave for the night.

"Yes, please could you bring me the key?"

"It's on its way, Madame, goodnight." Elise replaced the receiver and picked up her mobile.

"I've booked another room, Amy; they're sending someone up with the key."

"Great, well, either get him out or get yourself out. I knew he was bad news, never trust a man who doesn't eat his pizza."

"It's fine, the porter's coming in a minute, he can help me get him out, the other room's not far away." Amy was relieved to hear Elise sounding a bit less stressed.

"Not exactly the night of passion you had in mind then; seriously, Elise, make sure you lock your door when he's gone."

"I will, thanks, Amy, you're a life saver."

"Life is a lot easier to save when you have plenty of dosh, now get some sleep, and I'll speak to you in the morning."

Elise put the phone back into her bag and went to wait in the corridor. Amy was right, she thought. Money did seem to make life easier.

The porter arrived, still in his coat, accompanied by the doorman. Elise opened the door to her room.

"Could you help me get him out?" she asked.

The porter walked down the corridor and used the key card to open the door of room 547. Elise followed him and held the door open whilst the two men grabbed Armand and carried him out of her room; they dropped him on his new bed and turned off the lights.

"Thank you so much, I'm really sorry, but I didn't know what else to do. Have I made you late going home?" she said, noticing the porter's coat.

He shrugged. "My wife is used to it," he said with a smile. Elise ran back into her room and grabbed Armand's still wrapped bouquet.

"Please give her these, if you think she would like them, and tell her I'm sorry." Elise handed both men twenty-euro notes. The porter took the flowers from her.

"She will love them, thank you. I will make sure to wake your friend up nice and early in the morning." Both men bowed and headed quickly back to the lift.

"He's not my bloody friend," thought Elise angrily as she slammed her door and slid the chain across for good measure. She pulled off her clothes and collapsed on the bed. Elise suddenly became aware of a cold damp patch of duvet beneath her and leapt up in horror.

Chapter Thirty-Five

"Bloody Armand," she said, and blushing slightly as she relived the 'Watergate' incident, she quickly flipped the duvet so that the wet patch was now at the bottom, and climbed under the cover.

It was nearly midnight, but Elise was too upset to sleep. Her brain insisted on conjuring up the worst bits of her dates with Armand, and she eventually dissolved into tears of disappointment and frustration. If her knight's shining armour had been slightly tarnished by the 'pizza and head-patting incident', it had now been completely oxidised after tonight's debacle, and she was left with a deep sadness and the realisation that her fairy story was not going to end the way proper fairy stories should.

Elise woke to the annoying sound of her alarm. She had set three to go off at five minute intervals and the last one had finally managed to drag her into consciousness. She forced herself to get out of bed, and dived into the shower. As she emerged, Elise heard a knock on the door. She froze in a panic. How the hell had Armand found her room?

"Madame, it's only me."

Elise recognised the porter's voice. "Is everything all right?" she called back, still not daring to move.

"Oh, yes, I just thought you might like to know that your friend has just vacated his room."

"Thank you," she said and collapsed back onto the bed. The thought of dealing with Armand before coffee was unbearable.

Elise set to work packing her suitcase; she seemed to have accumulated an awful lot of stuff over the last few days and had to resort to cramming as much as she could into the hotel laundry bag.

When she was satisfied that everything was safely stowed away, Elise opened the safe and took out her cash, credit card and passport. The porter greeted her at the lift with his usual friendly smile and helped her get everything to the reception desk.

She handed over the credit card, and stood anxiously as the clerk checked the computer.

"No extras to pay," he said, handing over her receipt.

"Yes, but I have to pay for the other room. I was told I could pay in cash, room 547."

"Ah, yes, Madame, the gentleman insisted on paying when he left this morning. So, everything has been taken care of."

"Serves him bloody right," thought Elise as she stashed the hotel invoice and credit card in her bag.

The doorman called a cab and soon she was on her way back to Montmartre.

Elise as usual arrived far too early at the Art Hotel Batignolles. She must have looked as desperate as she felt, as the hotel clerk offered to store her bags and suitcase until the room was available.

Feeling more than a little embarrassed, she handed the bulging Citadines laundry bag to the bemused clerk, added a generous tip and then ran out in search of the nearest café.

Elise couldn't believe that she had the whole day to herself, no errands to run, and no dinner dates. Just a day to relax and potter around. Elise sent a quick message to Amy, letting her know that she was okay as she waited for her coffee and croissant.

She had already guessed that the long-awaited fourth letter from her grandmother would be a check list of things to see and places to visit, so she thought she should put her 'day off' to good use by getting one step ahead, and tick off a few of the tourist traps.

Elise opened her bag to pay for her breakfast and realised to her horror that she was wandering around with around nine thousand pounds in cash on her. The thought of taking a trip to the Louvre and the Eiffel Tower with all that in her bag made her extremely nervous. She decided instead, to walk back to the hotel and see how long she would have to wait before her room was available.

"Two o'clock, Madame," said the clerk, then noticing Elise's crestfallen look, he offered her the option of an early check-in. "Madame may check in at eleven a.m. for a small charge of thirty euros."

"Oh, yes, please," she said without thinking twice.

Elise wandered through the lobby and sat in the small bar to wait the half hour until she could get into her room. "What is happening to me?" she thought. The girl who had waited in the street outside the co-op was a lifetime away, now she was willing to 'throw away' twenty-five pounds at the drop of a hat.

Elise sat in the bar and pondered her change in fortunes. In two days' time, she would be twenty-five years old. She had managed to amass savings of twenty thousand pounds over the last six years by living in a way that would have put Scrooge to shame; refusing Amy's endless requests for girly weeks away in Benidorm, and even Angela's regular invites to stay with her and her girlfriend in Brighton. Kate had, after many months of trying, eventually given up asking her out for drinks after work.

Virtually, all she did was work and sit alone in her little flat. That ancient watch had changed her life: she now had enough to probably buy a flat outright, let alone put down a deposit. Elise suddenly began to question whether her obsession with buying a flat had actually been worth the cost. She hated having to admit it, but having her hair done, and buying a few clothes actually had been fun. She was now beginning to have confidence in herself. Her crippling shyness had all but disappeared, and maybe if she had done these things years ago, her life wouldn't have been quite so empty. Elise had always thought that her sensible approach to life was the right one, but now she was beginning to question everything that she had held dear.

"I really have no friends, apart from Amy, Angela and maybe Arek," she thought to herself. She immediately felt ashamed of herself for not being friendlier towards Kate. She could hardly blame her for ending up hanging on to Alice's coat tails. Kate had been almost as lonely and shy as she was when she first moved to London and started working at First Blush, but Elise's obsession with saving money had led to her refusing all Kate's suggestions of nights out, or after-work drinks. Kate probably thought that Elise had been snubbing her. The more Elise thought about it, the more guilt she felt. She had been in that place, and she should have helped Kate.

Elise knew that Kate and the reps and probably even Alice took it in turns to pay for Kelly's coffee; her apprentice wages did not allow for splurges at Freddie's, but Elise herself had never offered.

She could feel her cheeks burning as she forced herself to scrutinise her past behaviour.

Elise thought about all the missed opportunities that her frugal lifestyle had cost her. In a nutshell, she had done nothing, been nowhere and never given herself the chance to have a boyfriend or even, for that matter go on a night out.

Amy had pleaded with her to join a dating website, or even have a look on Tinder, but Elise had refused, her laptop was too old, and her phone was far too basic to allow for any extras and the thought of dipping into her sacred savings had never even crossed her mind.

Chapter Thirty-Six

"Things are going to be different when I get home," Elise decided, and the first thing on her new list would be a weekend trip to Aberdeen to see Amy.

The porter arrived at her side and Elise got up thankfully, too much of this sort of thinking was frankly dangerous as far as she was concerned. She followed him and her luggage to the lift, cringing again at the sight of the bulging laundry bag. A posh hold-all was definitely on the shopping list, right below the socks that still eluded her feet; sticking plasters were sadly now also a must.

Elise was relieved to get into her new room, and after thanking the porter and handing him a ten-euro tip, she quickly found the safe and started stashing the cash. She still had five hundred euros left from the thousand she had changed and recklessly grabbed another thousand pounds.

"Start as you mean to go on, girl," she said to herself, and one thing she was determined to do was to buy some nice gifts for everyone at the office... well, apart from Alice. "She could go poop herself," thought Elise, unless she could find a shop selling the fake dog turds that Amy was so fond of. She would also get some presents for Amy and Charlie, and take them up to Aberdeen, and maybe give Angela a call and treat her to a fancy dinner.

Feeling inspired and energised by her new goals, Elise unpacked the rest of her belongings. She needed to find a laundrette, she thought, but then as she unpacked her Citadines bag, it dawned on her that the hotel could take care of that for her. She was, however, not willing to leave Grandmere's outfits at the mercy of the hotel laundry and decided to find a specialist dry-cleaner's to look after those.

Elise skipped out of her room, and ran down the flight of stairs and out into the sunshine.

Half an hour later, she was back outside the amazing glass pyramid, just about to check out the 'Mona Lisa', she was sure that it would probably feature on Grandmere's 'tick list'.

Elise wandered around for a while; some of the paintings were truly magnificent, and she couldn't help admiring the amazing architecture of the building itself. The famous 'Mona Lisa' was a bit of a disappointment; it was much smaller than she had imagined, and having had to wait twenty minutes for a large enough gap to appear in the crowd for her to get near enough to see, she found that the painting was actually roped off, making it even more difficult to appreciate. "Sod that," she thought, and decided that she had had enough of art for one day and needed fortifying with a large cup of coffee before heading off to the Tower.

The Tower was certainly spectacular, although she did have problems locating it which she found hard to believe. Eventually, she gave in and asked a passer-by.

He turned out to be a very helpful American tourist, and explained that it was actually just ahead of her, hiding behind some very tall buildings. Elise scurried down the road and found herself on the edge of a lovely park. Straight ahead of her, and impossible to miss, stood the Tower.

Elise waited patiently in the queue, and was grateful for the lovely sunshine. She eventually got her ticket and started up the stairs. The view was amazing and well worth the wait. She made it as far as the stairs would allow her and walked round the metal viewing balcony, staring down at the whole of Paris.

Elise reluctantly gave up her space at the railings and started back down the steps. She walked over to the Seine and crossed over the bridge. There were rows of tiny wooden stalls selling everything from tacky souvenir fridge magnets to original paintings and posters. Elise loved everything and spent ages looking at all the posters.

There was a beautiful print of the Notre Dame, which Elise couldn't resist buying.

The stall holder carefully rolled it up and placed it in a cardboard tube before handing it to her. She set off to find the Notre Dame Cathedral, which was certain to be on Grandmere's list.

Notre Dame was unbelievably beautiful. Elise lingered, admiring the amazing architecture and the magnificent stained glass windows, before heading to a Starbucks which had been calling her name for some time. She sat at an outside table, with her large coffee and panini, feeling very happy just watching the world go round.

Elise pondered what else could be on her grandmother's list; the Musée d'Orsay and the Pompidou Centre were definitely too modern to be on there, but she decided that she would like to see them anyway. Maybe the Palace of Versailles, but that was not too easy to get to. Feeling a bit tired now, she gave up on her plan and decided that she would have enough time to work her way through the list once she got it on Monday; besides, it was never a wise move to second guess Madame Giselle! Elise finished her coffee and decided to exchange some more of her cash and have a wander round the shops.

Elise wasn't the world's best shopper, apart from the socks which were easy enough, she struggled with the concept of picking some random piece of clothing off the rails and couldn't make up her mind what sort of gifts to take back. Eventually, she decided on silk scarves. She could buy some really lovely ones and then choose which person would best suit each design. She doubted that Angela was a silk scarf kind of person, but she was sure that she would be able to find something more suited to her more 'eclectic' taste.

Elise set off towards the Pompidou Centre. It was the strangest building she had ever seen; it looked as if it was inside out, with great metal pipes running up the exterior. The escalator also appeared to be on the outside and made Elise feel quite queasy. There was a sort of shallow lake on one side filled with weird brightly coloured sculptures which all seemed to have lives of their own.

"Now if only I could buy one of those for Angela!" Elise smiled at the thought of trying to pack an enormous pair of bright red lips into her suitcase and walked over to a group of traders who had their goods spread out on the ground. Most of them were selling traditionally made jewellery. Elise was delighted, and after much deliberation purchased a beautiful silver and amber necklace, with a matching bracelet and earrings. She couldn't wait to see Angela's face when she handed them over. The purchase bolstered her confidence, and with a sudden surge of energy, she set off, gliding more briskly than usual, to attack some of the local boutiques.

Elise eventually found what she was looking for and having bought six beautiful silk and cashmere scarves in an array of colours, she treated herself to a glass of orange juice and a very decadent-looking plate of waffles and ice-cream. Just as she was spooning in the last of her dessert, Elise heard her phone beep. She saw Armand's name appear on the screen and declined the call. She really couldn't be bothered to listen to any more crap from him at the moment.

Elise still hadn't got anything for her mother. For years, Elise had stressed about choosing birthday and Christmas gifts for her; Louise either didn't bother to take off the wrapping paper, saying she was too busy at the moment, or having taken off the wrapping, looked up at her daughter with a quizzical expression, and asked:

"Whatever made you think that I would like this?"

At some point during Elise's teenage years, her mother had developed a fascination for china cats and had amassed a huge collection of them in all shapes and sizes. She had bought special shelves which held them on every available wall in her study and spent ages dusting, polishing and rearranging them.

Grandmere and Elise thought they were hideous, but at least it made present buying easier. Elise remembered on one occasion freezing with horror when she realised, as her mother was taking the gift wrap off, that an identical cat was staring her straight in the eyes. Her mother however was overjoyed!

"Look, Mother, I have twins!"

"Aren't they just adorable," she said, clasping her hands with joy. Grandmere and Elise looked across at each other and shrugged. At least it had been nice to see her looking so happy. They both crept out unnoticed by Louise as she pondered on the choosing of a name.

"There must be a china cat somewhere around," Elise thought to herself, but the thought of transporting it back to England was too daunting and she decided it would be much easier simply to buy one when she got back. Elise knew the whereabouts of every 'China Cat' shop within a fifty-mile radius of Surbiton. Unsurprisingly, there weren't that many!

Her phone suddenly bleeped again. "Bloody hell," she thought, groping around in her bag, "not him again!" She was pleasantly surprised to see Laurent's name and quickly accepted the call.

"How's everything at the Art Hotel?" he asked.

"All fine," answered Elise, "I'm out doing a bit of sightseeing and shopping, how are you?"

"I just wanted to ask you, if I could make a special dinner for us on Sunday at my apartment, instead of going to a restaurant; after all, it is your birthday, and we could eat outside in my roof garden."

Elise hadn't seen any gardens anywhere in Paris and was intrigued at the idea of having one on the roof.

"That sounds like a wonderful idea. I would absolutely love it, as long as it's not too much trouble for you."

Laurent sounded delighted. "No, I love cooking, it would be my pleasure. We'll probably be tired after being out all day, I thought it would be nice just to be able to relax and enjoy a glass of wine, and look at the stars together."

Elise couldn't imagine anything better than to spend her evening having dinner and star-gazing with Laurent by her side.

"It all sounds wonderful, I can hardly wait... are you still able to meet me at ten to go up to the cemetery? I'd like to see the plaque you talked about as well, if we could."

"Yes, absolutely, of course, I'll be there, picnic and rug at the ready." Laurent sounded as enthusiastic as she felt, and Elise began to look forward even more to her birthday.

Elise got up from the chair, every trace of waffle and ice-cream had been demolished, and she was beginning to feel very tired. Her phone beeped again. Elise grabbed it, hoping that Laurent was going to suggest meeting up before Sunday, which was beginning to feel like a very long way off.

"Elise?" Too late she realised that it was sodding Armand. She debated whether or not to decline the call, but decided that it was just too rude, and to be fair, she was a little worried that he might actually change his mind about cancelling the contract if she ignored him for too long.

"Armand, I hope you are okay?" Elise thought that she had covered all her bases with that and waited for him to speak.

"Yes, I'm so sorry, I just don't know what happened, can you forgive me again?"

Elise was frankly bored by Armand's breathless apology and couldn't really think of anything to say. Armand took her silence as a positive sign and continued with his long and desperate pleas. Elise spied a metro sign just ahead, and took it as an ideal opportunity to end the conversation.

"Armand, please don't worry, it's all forgotten. Listen, I have to get on the metro, so the signal will go, I'll ring you later, and honestly everything is fine."

Elise ran down the steps and switched off her phone. She wasn't sure whether the signal would really go, but wasn't prepared to leave it to chance. She would ring him again as promised, but it would definitely be much later.

Elise eventually got back to her hotel; she was beginning to feel really tired, and decided on room service and a long soak in the bath. She realised with embarrassment that she had actually counted the hours before she would be meeting again with Laurent, like a child waiting for Christmas.

"You are one sad girl," she said to herself as she carefully opened the calendar on her phone and typed in the appointment. As if there were any chance she was going to forget!

Chapter Thirty-Seven

Elise lay on her bed; she had finished her dinner and having flicked through all the TV channels available, and found nothing remotely exciting, suddenly felt quite lonely.

The realisation that the whole of Saturday was stretching out in front of her was quite depressing. There was nothing she really wanted to do, she was fed up with shopping and sightseeing, and apart from a pedicure and manicure and locating a decent dry-cleaner's, there was absolutely nothing on the horizon. She was tempted to ring Armand, but the thought of another horrendous meeting with him made her blood curdle. She grabbed her phone and dialled Amy.

"I'm just feeling a bit lonely," she said, as Amy answered in a panic-stricken voice.

"Nothing dreadful has happened, and definitely no unconscious men in my room tonight."

"Thank God for that," answered Amy. "I'm almost beginning to dread your calls! Haven't you got anything exciting to tell me about?"

"Not really, to be honest, I just feel a bit homesick, except there's nothing much to come home to." Elise was surprised at herself, but, to be honest, she did miss her job, the daily chats with customers, and her banter with Arek.

"Well, just come home then," Amy said. "If you've done everything you wanted to do, why not?"

"I've got to wait for another letter from my grandmother, it won't arrive till Monday, and I'm going out with Laurent on Sunday. He's really nice and I'm looking forward to that, so it's not too bad. I wondered, if it's okay, if I come back a bit earlier and fly up to Aberdeen to see you and Charlie for a few days, before I go back to work."

"Absolutely, it's about time you actually met Charlie in the flesh, and I haven't seen you for at least a year. Only thing is it might be a bit crowded here," Amy added after a slight pause.

"Oh, don't worry about that, I'll book into a hotel. Is there one near your flat?"

"Yes, we live right in the centre, there's one just down the road that would be perfect for you, not too far to stagger home after a night on the piss."

"Sounds perfect," answered Elise. "Can you text me the name and I'll sort out a room when I get organised?"

"It really will be wonderful to see you, I've got loads to tell you, and don't you dare change your mind." Amy sounded so excited that Elise immediately felt much happier.

"No chance of that, I'll let you know as soon as possible."

As Elise put the phone down, Armand's name flashed up on the screen. She was feeling a bit more confident, and felt that she could deal with anything at the moment.

"Do you think we could meet for a coffee tomorrow?" Armand sounded desperate, and Elise couldn't think of a good excuse to refuse him, so she agreed. She had no intention of giving him the name of the hotel, so in a moment of uncharacteristic malice agreed to meet him at the little pizzeria. "I'm sure you can remember where it is," she added.

"Yes, of course, is eleven o'clock okay?"

"That's fine, I'll see you there." Elise put the phone down. At least it would give her something to do tomorrow. She had to admit that feeling as lonely as she did, even the prospect of coffee with Armand was something to look forward to. He was also the reason that First Blush had footed the bill for her trip, so she needed to act professionally and at least ensure that the contract was still firmly in place.

Returning to work having failed in her mission was just not an option.

Elise really was missing work; she hadn't appreciated how huge a part of her life it was. Hopefully, the horrible event with Armand would be forgotten, and there was just the tiniest chance that Alice might have been just a little bit squashed by Gerry's outburst and might actually leave her alone!

Feeling surprisingly cheerful, Elise snuggled under the duvet and fell fast asleep.

Despite her best efforts to be late, Elise managed to arrive at the pizzeria with twenty minutes to spare. She laid the blame firmly on her new phone; a newly discovered app meant that she didn't get lost even once on the walk from her hotel.

Elise's gaze darted around, there was no sign of Armand, so she busied herself looking around the little gift shops and prodding the odd scarf. Having duly prodded everything and re-read all the post cards at least twice, she ran into a newsagent's and bought herself a newspaper. Elise waved at the pizzeria waiter who obligingly waved back and pulled out a chair for her. Elise sat down, ordered a coffee and became engrossed in the paper, refusing to lift her eyes, even when the coffee arrived just in case Armand was approaching.

"Hi, Elise." Unfortunately, Elise was actually engrossed in the paper by this time and was so startled by Armand's silent approach that she jumped out of the chair and dropped her newspaper into the untouched coffee. Not really the auspicious start to the date that she had been hoping for!

The waiter rushed over and hastily disposed of the newspaper and mopped up the coffee. Armand ordered more coffee, whilst Elise tried to regain her composure.

When she did eventually look up, she was stunned to see how handsome Armand was. Her annoyance at his behaviour had somehow blurred his good looks in her memory and turned him into someone bearing a close resemblance to 'Shrek'. Here in the bright sunlight, she felt as if his brilliant blue eyes were burning holes through her.

Determined not to make a 'tit' of herself again, she took a firm grip on her coffee cup and checked for drips before raising it to her lips. Armand was sitting across from her and looking decidedly nervous. Elise felt that she could not bear another two hours of 'mea culpa' from Armand and smiled cheerfully across at him.

"Shall we do another 'Let's forget all about everything' and try and have a nice afternoon without any traumas?" she asked.

Armand smiled back. "If you can, I really promise not to do anything horrendous ever again."

They both grinned at each other and actually started to enjoy the afternoon. Every time Elise looked at Armand, she thought he got even more handsome. Armand in turn tried hard to forget that he was sitting opposite possibly the most beautiful woman he had ever met, and the conversation flowed.

Elise was getting decidedly peckish and caught the eye of her favourite waiter. As he walked over to their table, Elise leaned across to Armand.

"Would you like something to eat?" she asked, "I'm sure that there is something on the menu that you like." Elise ordered her favourite pizza and Armand went for salmon. Thankfully, everything was delicious and even lunch passed without incident.

Chapter Thirty-Eight

Elise and Armand left the restaurant arm in arm and set off for a wander. The sun was shining as usual, and Elise was delighted to explore the narrow streets around the Sacré Coeur. Armand was proving to be a wonderful companion, and the two of them walked for miles. Elise felt truly happy. The afternoon rekindled their old friendship, and as darkness fell, Armand treated Elise to a dinner that even she had to admit, was definitely in a different stratosphere to pizza!

Neither wanted the evening to end, but eventually after several nightcaps just across from the Art Hotel, Elise reluctantly got up to go. Her phone suddenly started beeping, and Elise grabbed it from her bag, wondering who could be ringing her at this time of night.

"Happy Birthday, Elise," shrieked Amy down the phone. "Hope I got the time right."

Elise couldn't help but smile.

"Yes, you did, Amy, thank you."

"Hope you aren't curled up in bed on your own being boring?" asked Amy.

"No, actually I've had a wonderful day, just having a nightcap with Armand," she answered.

"Right, well, I'm off then, don't want to be a party pooper; catch up with you in the morning, and you'd better have something exciting to tell me, love you!" Amy rang off before Elise had time to reply. Armand was looking slightly worried.

"Is everything okay?" he asked.

"Yes, of course, it was just my friend, wishing me a happy birthday."

"Is it your birthday today?" he asked.

Elise checked her phone, it was five past midnight.

"It is now," she said with a grin. "I've officially hit the quarter-century mark."

"Then we must celebrate," said Armand, summoning the waiter.

A bottle of champagne arrived at their table and Armand did the honours.

"Happy birthday, Elise," he said, as they raised their glasses. "I didn't know, I'm so sorry, I would have liked to bring you a gift."

"I've had a wonderful day, and now I'm drinking champagne. What could be better than that?" she answered simply. Armand suddenly leaned across and planted a kiss on Elise's lips. She found herself kissing him back and pulled away, as she felt her cheeks start to burn.

"Would you like to come back to my hotel?" she heard herself saying.

Armand, looking slightly stunned, stared back at her.

"Are you sure?" he asked.

Elise quickly swigged the last of her champagne.

"Well, it is my birthday!"

Chapter Thirty-Nine

Elise woke to the sound of her phone informing her of a new email.

Armand hadn't stirred, so she lay there for a few moments, luxuriating in his warmth, before carefully lifting his arm off her and tiptoeing into the bathroom.

Suddenly remembering her date with Laurent, she checked the time.

Thankfully, it was only half past eight. Leaving her emails, she jumped into the shower. Now swathed in her towel, she sat on the loo seat and read through her messages. Elise was pleased to find that her birthday had not been forgotten. Alex had sent greetings. Along with a long message from Amy demanding every detail from her date and wondering how the hell she had ended up back in the arms of the airman!

There was also a long email from Arek, who aside from hoping she was having a wonderful time, demanded to know when she was returning to work:

"Please come back soon, or I might have to kill Gerry, how do you cope with him? That man is a complete wanker."

Elise decided that Arek could wait for a reply and wandered out of the bathroom to check if Armand was back in the land of the living.

He was still fast asleep. Elise couldn't help staring at him. He was possibly the most handsome man she had ever seen, and she couldn't help blushing as she recalled the events of last night. Definitely the best birthday present she had ever had.

Elise ordered room service and hoped the smell of hot croissants and coffee would wake Armand. She opened the door to the waiter with as much noise as she could manage and tried to rattle the dishes as she pushed it into the room. Armand still did not stir. In desperation, Elise poured out the coffee and moved over to the bed and the still snoring Armand. She could not resist resting her hand on his shoulder for a few seconds.

"Wake up, Armand, your coffee's getting cold," she announced in a voice loud enough to wake the entire floor. Thankfully, it did the trick. Armand opened his eyes, stretched out his arms and grabbed Elise. The coffee sadly went cold.

The two lay wrapped in each other's arms for a while, luxuriating in the warmth of their bodies before Armand regretfully threw back the covers, kissed Elise firmly on her bottom and headed for the shower.

Elise reluctantly climbed out of bed and grabbed her dressing gown. She was suddenly starving, and was already busy munching on a delicious croissant when he returned.

Armand casually searched for his clothes whilst Elise ate, and then joined her at the little breakfast table.

"Have you got any plans for today?" Armand asked, as he devoured the remaining pastries managing at the same time to hold her hand.

"Well, yes, I have, I've arranged to meet one of my grandmother's friends, and we will be going out to dinner afterwards." Elise glanced across at Armand as she spoke, hoping that he wouldn't be too curious about her grandmother's friend.

"Maybe we could meet up on Monday evening? If you aren't busy."

Armand shook his head. "No, I've got a business meeting with one of our biggest clients and it will definitely end up with dinner and a late night, but I'm having dinner with Alain

240

on Tuesday evening. He's just got back from a business trip to the States and is very keen to meet you, why don't you join us?"

Elise was surprised; given her last encounter with his son, she thought she would be the last person Monsieur Alain would want to share his evening with.

"If you are sure?" she said.

"Absolutely, I'll meet you here at seven, if that's okay." Elise nodded, she didn't like the idea of not seeing Armand until Tuesday, as she had already made up her mind to leave for London the following morning, but it was better than nothing.

They spent a few more minutes together before Armand left to return to his apartment. Elise felt quite lost for a few minutes after his exit. Her emotions were all over the place.

Chapter Forty

She sat down on the bed and reached for her phone. Thank God, she had Amy on speed dial!

At ten o'clock Elise was already waiting in the hotel foyer. She wondered if the receptionist had mentioned her nocturnal exploits to the other staff and wondered what they would make of her new date this morning.

"Get a grip!" she told herself crossly, but still ran outside into the street when she spied Laurent approaching the doors.

"Happy Birthday, Elise," Laurent said, as he gave her a huge hug and handed over a small beautifully wrapped gift. Elise couldn't help smiling as she took the package.

"You really didn't need to bring me anything, I've been so looking forward to seeing you again, and spending the day together is the best present in the world."

"Couldn't resist it, and I need a large coffee before we start on our expedition, so you can open it whilst we have a drink."

Elise felt that she had already had enough caffeine to keep her going until suppertime, but was so happy to see him that she felt she could manage to swallow another one. She felt as if she was five years old again, and couldn't wait to rip open the present.

As they sat enjoying the sunshine on the Rue Lepic, Elise carefully unwrapped her gift. She gazed in shock at the beautiful vintage Dior purse that she had used at the photo shoot.

"Oh, Laurent, you can't. This is too much!" Elise tried to hand the purse back to him, but Laurent shook his head.

"I would never let it go to anyone else, it belongs to you, my dear, so use it and enjoy it. Your grandmother would most definitely approve."

"Yes, she would, thank you, it's beautiful." Elise rewrapped the purse and put it into her handbag. She looked at the streets bustling with people, as she drank her coffee and thought that this could possibly be her best birthday ever.

"Would you like me to show you your grandfather's memorial plaque?" asked Laurent, draining the last of his coffee.

"Yes, please." Elise stood up. "Which way is it?"

"It's just up here on the left." Laurent pointed to the steep hill.

"Do you see the alleyway over there on the right, just by the café?" Elise followed his gaze.

"Is that where the bike came from?" she asked.

Laurent nodded his head. "Yes, the people who were nearest thought that maybe he hit something in the road, but he was going so fast he came straight towards us here, then the bike went sideways alongside the pavement here. This is where your family were standing, and where your grandfather pushed them clear." Laurent pointed at the brick wall just above her head, and there she saw the small oval plaque bearing her grandfather's name and commemorating his brave act. Elise took out her phone and took a photograph.

One of the waiters approached them, pad in hand, and Laurent pointed at the plaque and at Elise. The waiter disappeared.

"Elise, come and sit down a minute," said Laurent, pulling out a chair.

"Laurent, you surely can't be in need of another coffee already?" protested Elise, but she sat down anyway. The waiter came out, this time accompanied by an elderly man who was leaning heavily on a walking stick.

Laurent stood up. "Elise, I thought you might like to meet Monsieur Montand. He has owned this café for many years, and was here when the accident happened." Elise got up and looked towards the café door.

The old man slowly made his way towards Elise and took her hand. She was stunned to see tears in his eyes, and had to catch her breath.

Monsieur Montand sat down in the chair and motioned Elise to sit next to him. "Please, sit for a moment, Mademoiselle. My grandson can fetch us some coffee."

Elise didn't dare to refuse, but the thought of another coffee was making her feel slightly nauseous! Hopefully, lunch wouldn't be too far away and would help to soak up some of the caffeine.

"You must be so very proud of your heritage, my dear girl." Monsieur Montand's voice was little more than a whisper and Elise had to lean her head close to his to hear his shaking words.

"Not only was your grandfather a hero, who saved the life of my wife, as well as others on that terrible day, but also your great grandparents who offered sanctuary to old Monsieur Lehrmann during those terrible days. They will never be forgotten." Monsieur Montand paused for a moment to take out a handkerchief and mop his eyes. He held tight to Elise's hand for a few more moments, and then beckoned his grandson to help him back indoors.

Elise's eyes filled with tears, when she realised the effort that this man had gone to come outside and meet her; it took the considerable efforts of both Laurent and his grandson to help raise the man from his chair slowly and escort him back into the building.

Laurent hurried back out a few moments later, Elise could see that he too had tears in his eyes.

"Sorry about that, Elise, I hope it didn't upset you, but when I mentioned your name to his grandson, he shot straight inside to tell Monsieur Montand."

"No, it didn't upset me at all; it's wonderful to meet people who knew my grandfather, and to know that they held him in such esteem." Elise could hear her voice shaking and was surprised at how much the encounter with the old man had affected her.

"So, everyone knew about Monsieur Lehrmann as well?" she asked as they set off again towards the cemetery.

"Of course, everyone knew everyone in those days; it was a very tight-knit community, and everyone struggled during those terrible years and very few would have been brave enough to risk the repercussions of hiding a Jewish person in their home. At the time, of course, everyone assumed that he had died, and a few thought he at least escaped the horrors of the camps; the Germans came either that day or the next and rounded up the few poor Jewish people that were left in Montmartre, they were taken away, and none ever came back."

Elise and Laurent made their way silently up towards the Cimetiere, both too filled with emotion to speak.

Elise pulled at Laurent's sleeve as they passed a florist's shop just at the entrance to the cemetery.

"Would you mind? I want to get some flowers for the grave."

Laurent shook his head. "Of course not! I'll wait here for you."

Elise disappeared into the shop and came out after a few minutes with a huge bouquet of lilies.

"I hope they like them," she said.

"Absolutely perfect." Laurent smiled and tucked his arm through hers. Together they made their way along the cobbled paths towards the Rue Samson.

Chapter Forty-One

They passed Nijinsky's tomb and Elise was shocked when Laurent stopped only a few yards further down the path.

There were two photographs etched onto beautiful oval china plaques framing the stone. Elise was startled by the one of her great grandmother. It was as if she were looking at her own mother. Elise searched hard to see if she could find any features that she shared with either of the photographs, but looked away in bitter disappointment when she realised that she bore no similarity to either of them.

She turned back to Laurent, who was standing by her side. "I don't really look like either of them," she said, shaking her head.

"You look like yourself," he answered with a smile.

"That's all that matters, anyway, you're only two letters short of her name, so you must be proud of that." Elise looked at the name on the stone and couldn't help smiling.

"Yes, you're right, we almost have the same name." Elise felt inexplicably happier knowing that her grandmother had chosen her name and that it was obviously in honour of her forebears.

Elise carefully placed the lilies on the grave, and took a photograph. She turned to Laurent. "Are you ready for lunch? I'm starving!"

"Me too, can you make it up the hill to the park?" Laurent took her arm again and they headed back along the cobbled streets and began the steep climb up to the Sacré Coeur.

The sun was shining as Laurent unfolded a blanket and laid it out on the grass under one of the trees. The view over Paris was stunning. Elise felt as if this day was one of the happiest she had ever known. To be here with Laurent sharing what was definitely one of the most delicious lunches she had ever had, complete with wine served in crystal glasses, made her feel deliriously happy.

Laurent was a wonderful companion. He had obviously taken great pains over the lunch, an array of pickles and various types of cheese and cold meat had all been packed into boxes. A small basket of fruit had taken centre stage and a delicious-looking cake packed with nuts and fruit was taking shelter under a napkin. A salad box and an assortment of bread rolls completed the lunch.

"How on earth did you fit all this into your rucksack?" she asked.

"I'm the Picnic King, or maybe Queen! Sit back and enjoy!" Elise gave up on the logistical issues and dived in.

At last, after both of them had made significant headway through the picnic and were surrounded by enough crumbs to ground a large flock of blackbirds, Laurent sighed and started to clear away the remains. The pigeons waited impatiently for the all-important shaking of the blanket and then jostled each other for the tastiest morsels.

When the blanket was more or less clean, he filled their glasses with the last of the wine and they sat together leaning against one of the huge trees to enjoy the view.

"That was the best birthday feast ever!" murmured Elise, happily rubbing her stomach. "Now, tell me all about you, and don't leave anything out."

Laurent was happy to oblige and Elise listened, entranced to his stories of a wonderfully happy childhood, surrounded by loving parents and doting grandparents.

"Mum was always waiting for me at the school gates. Every afternoon we would go to the little café on the corner. She would have her coffee and a cigarette and I would have my lemonade and tell her all about school. It was the best part of my day. Afterwards, we would walk back to the shop, my grandparents would go back upstairs and she would let me mess around with the stock, and put outfits together. They were probably horrendous, but Mum always said they were wonderful."

Laurent's father, Elise learnt, was a carpenter who had very little to do with the shop.

"My grandparents had a little cottage in Deauville, they retired there when I was about twelve and handed over the shop to Mum. I loved helping her and really got the fashion bug. I used to go with her to all the flea markets; she had a wonderful eye for fashion. I would see an old pair of faded curtains and Mum would be remodelling it in her head into some amazing gown. Your great-grandmother had taught my mum how to sew and cut patterns and she made some stunning pieces. I planned to study to become a designer, but then when I was eighteen, I got offered a modelling contract and that was the end of my plans to stay on at school."

"I didn't realise that your mother knew my great grandmother," Elise interrupted. "Did you ever meet her?"

"No, she died before I was born, but our families have known each other for many years; you know our great grandparents were very close."

"Of course, that was stupid of me," apologised Elise. "You did say that your great grandfather had told you all about that fire and poor Mr Lehrmann."

"Yes, he talked about it many times over the years; he was very humbled by the courageousness of your family."

Elise was desperate to know more, and pleaded with Laurent to tell the story again.

"I don't know that I can tell you any more than you already know. My great grandfather was one of the fire marshals that night, and I know he was the first to spot the fire and raise the alarm. By the time the rest of the men arrived, the fire had really taken hold and my great grandfather refused to allow anyone to enter the building. Everyone thought that Mr Lehrmann must have been stock-piling oil because it really was an inferno.

"Your great grandfather ran out to help and eventually they managed to douse the flames. The soldiers had arrived by then, they knew that the fire would help enemy aircraft and were determined to put it out as quickly as possible. The German officers arrived and placed guards on the door, and would not allow any of the locals to enter the building. The chance of Mr Lehrmann surviving the fire was virtually nil, but no one wanted his remains just to be left in there.

"The officers were just interested in clearing out the few valuables that were still salvageable. There had always been talk about Mr Lehrmann's wife having a fabulous collection of jewels that she had kept in an old chocolate box. The officers stripped the shop bare the next morning, so I'm guessing, that if they did exist, they would have been taken by them."

Elise's heart was thumping so loudly in her chest that she was sure that Laurent must be able to hear it. That the chocolate box, now languishing in her wardrobe in Clapham, probably housed Mrs Lehrmann's legendary collection was too much for her to take in.

She fought a desperate urge to jump on the nearest train and get home to check it. Laurent apparently hadn't been silenced by Elise's ear-splitting heart thumps and was carrying on with the story.

"To be honest, my grandfather told me that many people thought that Mr Lehrmann had probably had a merciful escape, as the SS Officers arrived the next day and rounded up every last Jewish man, woman and child. They knew that there was little hope for any of these poor souls, and very much hoped that the fire had taken place when Mr Lehrmann was asleep in his bed and that the smoke had killed him first. Your family never let on to anyone that they had found him at their door and taken him in. It was an amazing act of bravery and Mr Lehrmann never let anyone forget what they had done for him, when he emerged from hiding after the war."

Elise was puzzled. This was not how her grandmother's letter told the story. She was about to launch into her version of the events, but suddenly held her tongue. For whatever reason, her great grandparents and grandmother and even Mr Lehrmann himself had chosen not to reveal the lengths they had gone to in the elaborate scheme to save Mr Lehrmann, so what right had she to break their silence?

Laurent had by this time paused for breath.

"Your turn now: tell me about your mother; is she as fabulous and stylish as the legendary Giselle?"

Elise really hated talking about her mother, but felt that as Laurent had more or less bared his soul, she should at least offer a little in return.

"She is certainly a very beautiful woman, she looks just like the photograph of my great grandmother, but I'm not sure I could describe her as stylish. She has to dress a certain way for work, and it varies according to what case she is on, so she kind of dresses down when she's at home."

Laurent looked and sounded very intrigued. "What work does she do, is it some kind of fashion house?"

"Oh, no, nothing like that, she works for the government; don't ask me what, because she has never talked about it. It's something secret, so I think she is 'under cover' a lot of the time. Sometimes she dresses as if she has just come from a rock concert, and sometimes she looks as if she is a city lawyer, with just about everything in between."

"Weird or what, but much more exciting than owning a dress agency." Laurent laughed.

"And you really have no idea what she actually does?"

"No," replied Elise. "She always told me it was a secret and that we might be in danger if anyone found out, so we never talked about it at all."

"Blimey, sounds a bit like the secret service then. Are you sure she wasn't pulling your leg?"

Elise shook her head. "No, my mum definitely doesn't have a sense of humour, and her job just about takes over her life. It was my grandmother that brought me up and did all the mum-type things with me. My mother was always either at work or away on business trips."

"That's a bit sad really; I guess I was so lucky to have been able to spend so much time with my mother. When she became ill, I never thought twice about coming home to take care of her and run the shop. Dad tried to cope, but he had no idea about fashion. He worked when he could and between the two of us, we kept everything going. It was hard when we lost her. Mum knew Dad hated the shop, so she left the building to me and left my grandparents' cottage in Deauville to him. He'd always loved it there. He did loads of work on the place when my grandparents were alive and turned it into a lovely little place. They had always planned to retire there, and he went a few weeks after Mum died. I drive down to see him when I can and he seems to be quite happy." Laurent stopped and brushed a tear from his cheek.

"It's silly, I know, but I still get sad, when I think about Mum."

"Don't you dare apologise," scolded Elise. "It sounds like you had a wonderful childhood, and an amazing life before your mum died, you have every right to be sad."

Laurent nodded. "It's not the same anymore, I mean, I keep the shop going, but my heart is not really in it. I muddle along, supplying things for studio shoots and costume parties. The 'Agatha Christie Fan Club' keeps the wolves from the door. Their members are always in and out getting stuff for their 'Crime nights' and events; if I remember rightly, I'd just finished serving them when you arrived."

Elise couldn't recall seeing anyone else in the shop that morning, but remembering his bizarre appearance, she suddenly felt her cheeks redden.

"Oh, yes, your outfit, is that what it was?"

"Hercule Poirot, at your service," Laurent said with a theatrical wave of his hand.

"You didn't think that I dressed like that every day, did you?" Elise was stumped for a response and Laurent burst out laughing.

"I'm surprised you didn't run a mile," he said, "I was so shocked to see you standing there that I completely forgot about the costume."

Chapter Forty-Two

As the afternoon sun began to fade, Elise and Laurent reluctantly packed up their picnic. Elise was desperate to go to the loo, but didn't feel that it would be a very ladylike conversation, so she sucked in her cheeks and prayed for inspiration. It came in the form of her favourite pizzeria.

"Do you fancy a coffee?" she asked Laurent, as they approached the steps.

"Actually, I could do with a piss," said Laurent, "So if you don't mind ordering, I'll just nip inside."

Elise groaned. Her cunning plan had backfired and she wasn't sure whether she could even mention the word coffee without her bladder bursting.

Her favourite waiter approached and she threw caution to the winds.

"Could you bring us two coffees? I just need to nip to the ladies."

The waiter nodded and pointed her in the direction of the toilets.

Elise sprinted across to the door and dived into the nearest cubicle.

Feeling relieved that she had made it in time, Elise glided gracefully back across the café and joined Laurent at the table.

"Sorry, Laurent, just needed to freshen up."

"I'm amazed you weren't dying for a pee as well," said Laurent with admiration in his voice.

Elise could feel another terrible blush coming on and quickly changed the conversation.

"So, what are your plans then, if you don't want to carry on with the shop?"

"Don't laugh, but I would really like to go back to school and study fashion again. I just don't really have the money to do it right now."

"Why don't you just sell the shop, surely it must be worth enough to see you through college?"

Laurent shook his head. "I'm not sure that I could, it would be like betraying my mum and everything she worked for if I do that."

"No, it wouldn't, it would be you living your dream, just like your mum would want. I'm sure she would be so proud of you if you ended up being some famous designer."

"Maybe you're right. I really want to study in London. Dad told me to go for it, but it's a big step."

"You know what, Laurent, I've kind of been a coward all my life, never really daring to do anything; if you tried and it didn't work out, you can always come back, you'd still have your apartment here, so it's not such a big deal."

Elise was surprised at herself, what a hypocrite! For someone who had an anxiety attack over paying full price for her groceries, it was a bit rich to be advising Laurent to sell up and move to a different country!

"No, you are right. I love London, and I've got a few friends there from my modelling days, it's definitely time to move on."

"When were you last in London?" she asked.

"I came over for the Pride festival in July, and had a fantastic time, it was really buzzing!"

"I was there too," said Elise. "My friend Angie invited me, so I met up with her and her girlfriend for coffee at a little salsa bar just off Leicester Square; the atmosphere was amazing."

Elise thought back the sunny day in July when she had for once given in to Angie's demands that they meet up.

"Come on, Elise, I haven't seen you in ages, and it will be loads of fun."

Elise despite being niggled about the cost of the bus fare, had finally given in and agreed to meet Angie and her girlfriend for coffee, but it hadn't gone that well. Angie seemed to be on edge and Elise had sensed some very bad vibes between the two of them. Elise had made her excuses and left after only an hour.

Laurent looked suitably impressed. "Blimey, we might have passed like ships in the night!" He laughed.

"You are making me think about this, though, I'm definitely going to apply, and find out exactly how much it will cost. At least, I know what I'm aiming for then."

"My grandmother has left me some money, so I'm going to be buying a flat when I get home, you could always move in with me for a bit, if it would help."

"Won't you want to stay at home to help your mum for a bit?" asked Laurent.

"No, I haven't lived at home for years, I moved out when I got my job in Clapham. I would love to live back in our cottage again, but I told you, Mum and I don't really get along, and the last thing she would want would be me moving back."

Sensing that he had probably put his foot in it, Laurent stood up and placed some euros on the table. Slipping his arm through Elise's, they started heading towards the steps. "Come on, let's go, it's time I started preparing your birthday feast, and we've got a bit of a walk home first."

Laurent had turned the top floor of his building into a stunning penthouse suite. The living room doors opened out on the roof where he had created a beautiful 'Chill Zone', as he called it. He had placed high trellises down one side, and had a lawn and a beautiful little flower bed along with an amazing double lounger that hung from a metal chain.

"Go ahead, have a ride in my helicopter chair. It's great for relaxing the mind!"

Elise wasn't really sure how to get on the thing; the chain connected to a metal frame which supported the lounger, but it didn't appear to have a brake and was swinging around in the breeze.

"Just plonk yourself down in the middle of the seat, you'll be fine, honestly."

Elise obediently plonked herself down, then carefully lifted her legs up and leaned back. Laurent was right, it was very relaxing. Elise made a mental note to buy one for herself as soon as she had a back garden to put it in.

Laurent disappeared back into the kitchen to check on dinner, and returned a few moments later with two glasses of wine.

"It will just about cook itself now, so we've got time for a drink, shove over."

Elise obligingly shuffled herself over on to the side of the cushion. She was not however prepared for Laurent's weight which immediately bounced her off into his flowerbed.

"God, I'm so sorry, are you okay?" Laurent hastily dumped the wine glasses and helped pull her up. Elise was scarlet and cringing with embarrassment. Why did she always have to be such a klutz?

"No, I'm fine, really, hope I didn't kill any of your flowers," she said and suddenly gasped in horror as she realised her beautiful dress was looking less than perfect.

Laurent followed her gaze. "Don't worry, I can soon sponge that off, let me go and find you something to change into."

Laurent returned after a few moments. "I've always wanted to see what this looked like on, but I've never figured out what sort of shape it was meant to fit."

Elise looked at the pale blue jumper he was holding out. All she could think of was that it was intended for a very tall, extremely thin person with exceedingly long arms. They both burst out laughing.

"Mum bought it at a flea market. I have no idea what she intended to do with it, so please do me the honour of modelling it for me."

Elise nipped into the kitchen and slipped out of her dress. She slipped the jumper over her head. It was made of the softest cashmere and felt like silk against her skin. The sleeves stretched down to her knees, so she quickly pushed them up. The jumper ended just above her shins, and fitted like a glove. Elise glided out of the kitchen with great aplomb and received a round of applause.

"There you go, it was obviously made for you!" Laurent raced off into the kitchen to set to work on Elise's dress. She sat back down on the lounger and picked up her glass of wine.

Laurent returned after a while and sat on the grass next to her. "I get that you and your mum don't really have much of a relationship, but I've never heard you mention your dad, is he not around?"

Elise shook her head. "I've never met him, and he has never met me. My grandmother left me a letter explaining that Mum had had an affair with a married man. He was Danish and already had children. So, he dumped my mum and went back home. He supported me financially until I was eighteen, and that's when Mum kicked me out of our house. I think that I remind her of him, and that's why she has always hated being around me.

"She always made nasty comments about me being tall and thin and having blond hair. I understand now, but growing up I didn't have a clue. I just ended up feeling very different, and the kids at school picked up on me not having a dad and having a grandmother instead of a mum, so I ended up being bullied and miserable." Elise stopped suddenly. She wasn't sure where all that had come from and felt really embarrassed.

"I'm sorry; I haven't really spoken to anyone about him. I didn't mean to offload."

"Don't worry, believe me, I know all about being different, although to be fair, I was never really bullied at

257

school about it. My mum realised that I was gay before I kind of realised it myself, and my dad soon gave up trying to get me to bash nails into bits of wood. He realised that I preferred my mum's sewing machine. They both loved me and supported me, but it wasn't easy, no one wants to be different, especially when you are young. I think we all want to belong, and be accepted by our peer group, and I guess, for different reasons, you and I kind of stuck out."

Chapter Forty-Three

Laurent drank his wine and went in search of the bottle. Elise had already finished hers and was hoping that dinner wouldn't be too long as she was beginning to feel a bit light-headed.

"Dinner is ready, would you like to come inside, as I can't risk you going arse over tit with my Boeuf Bourguignon."

Elise followed Laurent back into his apartment. The table was exquisitely laid, with candles and flowers and the smell of the food was divine.

Having eaten far too much, Elise still refused to give and wedged in a slice of cheesecake before leaning back in her chair.

"You are certainly a man of many talents, Laurent; this is the nicest dinner I've ever eaten."

Laurent wandered back from the kitchen with a pot of coffee.

"So now, tell me what your plans are, and how long you are staying."

"Actually, I'm planning to go home on Wednesday. I would go sooner, but I've already agreed to go out to dinner with a work colleague on Tuesday and my dear grandma is having her last letter couriered to me tomorrow, no doubt it will be a long 'to-do' list of places she wants me to visit. To be honest, I'm panicking about something and need to get back to my flat."

The glasses of wine loosened Elise's tongue and she found herself recounting the whole story of the cabin trunk and its contents to Laurent.

He sat quietly, without even a nod of his head, listening to the story. Even when Elise mentioned the watch and the jewels, he managed with great fortitude to remain silent.

"I just don't get any of it," said Elise, when she finished.

"All this subterfuge: The letters, and the stuff in the trunk. Anything could have happened, and everything would have been lost." Her thoughts flew back to the chocolate box in her wardrobe, and her stomach started to churn again.

"I think that that is the whole point," said Laurent thoughtfully. "Your grandmother has retold the story of Mr Lehrmann. She did exactly what her parents had done, she hid everything and kept it safe until the time was right. Perhaps it was a gamble, a challenge, and she weighed up the odds. If everything had gone up in smoke, then that was a chance she was willing to take. But she did leave copies of the letters with her solicitor, so she obviously never intended you not to know about what she considered to be the most important things.

"Maybe she wanted you to succeed on your own. She and your grandfather could easily have sold that watch and the jewels when they moved to England, but they chose not to. Maybe they thought a time would come when they really needed the money."

Laurent's words kept going round and round in Elise's head. It was something that she had never considered. She was far too practical to ever even risk a pound on a lottery ticket, and had a hard time thinking of her grandmother being a gambler.

Elise glanced at her watch and realised with a shock that it was approaching midnight. "I really should get going. I don't know where the time has gone."

"You're welcome to stay here, there's plenty of room," offered Laurent.

"No, I need to get back; I'll just get a cab." Elise looked up at Laurent.

"I can't even begin to say how much I've enjoyed today; it's been my best birthday ever, and thank you for my beautiful bag."

"I think you need to keep the 'dress' too; only you could make it look that magnificent," said Laurent with a smile. "I'll put the old Dior thing in a bag for you. It's perfectly clean, no damage done."

Elise and Laurent walked out on the pavement in front of his shop, Laurent flagged down a cab and Elise climbed in. "Don't forget what I said about staying with me in London. Maybe it's time for you to take a bit of a gamble as well." Laurent bent his head in the cab and kissed Elise's cheek.

"I definitely will, and in any case, I'll be turning up on your new doorstep for a naughty weekend if nothing else."

Chapter Forty-Four

Elise woke up late the next morning. She took a leisurely shower and wandered down to the reception desk.

"I will be checking out on Wednesday morning. Could you have my bill ready please? I will be paying in cash. Oh, and someone is bringing me a letter around three o'clock, could you let them know that I will be waiting in the bar?"

The receptionist nodded. "Of course, Madame Jacobs, I will make sure everything is ready for you on Wednesday, is there anything else I can get for you?"

Elise shook her head. "No, thank you for everything." She walked outside marvelling at the bright sunshine. Hopefully, England wouldn't be too dismal.

Elise was 'on a roll' that morning, over coffee and croissants she managed to text Amy, book return flights to Aberdeen and make a reservation at the hotel, as well as confirming her Eurostar seat for Wednesday afternoon.

Her flight was booked for Friday which would leave the whole of Thursday to do something about the jewellery. Elise decided to take the box to Alex. He would know what to do, and at any rate he had a safe in his office which would definitely be better than her bottom drawer. She still had another week before returning to work, and could use that to start looking for a flat. If those jewels were real, she would probably have enough to buy her own house! Elise decided not to think too much about that, it would be better to wait and find out before getting too carried away!

Elise wandered around the shops and treated herself to another manicure and pedicure before returning to the hotel. As usual, she was hours too early for the letter. Elise headed to the reception again.

"I wonder if it's possible to get some of my clothes picked up to be dry-cleaned by a specialist company, and have them back tomorrow?" she asked.

The receptionist checked her watch. "We have a local company that deals with delicate fabrics. I could try for you. Would tomorrow evening be acceptable? They usually charge extra for the express service."

Elise nodded, and the lady made a call. "They can be here in the next forty-five minutes to collect and can return everything by five p.m. tomorrow. I will send the driver up to your room when he arrives."

The man duly arrived with a rail and carefully catalogued each of the dresses and cardigans, nodding with approval at each of them. Elise gave him a generous tip and watched her clothes disappear into the lift.

Elise treated herself to lunch in the bar. Only an hour to wait before Grandmere's final missive was due to arrive. Elise hoped the list wasn't too onerous. The deal was done now anyway, she was definitely leaving Paris in two days, so if she hadn't covered everything, she would just have to arrange a return visit.

"Madame Jacobs, the messenger is here with your package, he insists on handing it over personally. May I send him through?"

"Of course, thank you." Elise smiled at the receptionist who returned a few moments later with a man in a very smart suit.

"Elise. I presume," he said with a big smile and a very English accent.

He handed the package over to Elise. "Do you mind if we go and grab a coffee somewhere? I know Dad wants to know how you are getting on, and ordered me to take you out to dinner if you are free."

"Your Dad?" Elise looked up, feeling slightly confused.

"Sorry," said the man, "I can be such a div at times, and I'm Jim, Alex Forbes's son. Didn't he tell you that I would be bringing the letter?"

"No, he didn't, so you're not Alexander the Third then?" Elise said with a grin.

"Actually yes, but my middle name is James, so everyone calls me Jim, it makes life so much easier!"

Elise was desperate to rip open the letter, but it seemed a bit rude. She stood up. "Yes, coffee sounds good, and I don't have any plans tonight, so you have no excuse not to carry out your Dad's orders." Elise was surprised at herself for being so bold.

"Well, it would be an absolute honour; I just thought you might turn me down, if I didn't drag the formidable Alex into the equation."

"I think your Dad is lovely, and we could get coffee here if you like."

"There's a lovely little park just around the corner, why don't we sit in there? I've got some boring bits of stuff to read, and I can do that whilst you read your letter, then we can have a wander and you can fill me in on all your adventures in Paris."

Elise nodded in agreement, the bar was quite dark and she had been sitting there for far too long. Jim took her arm and they strode out into the sunlight.

A small boulangerie across the road obligingly supplied them with large coffees in paper cups and they headed for the park.

"Would it be really rude if I had a bench to myself?" said Jim. "Only I've got loads of papers and I need to spread them out a bit."

"Oh, no, that's fine, there are two empty ones over there, so we can each spread out!" answered Elise, feeling quite relieved. She wanted to be alone with her letter.

Elise sat down and Jim handed her the coffee, he then sat himself on a bench a few yards away and busied himself with his briefcase.

Chapter Forty-Five

Elise opened the manila envelope and immediately recognised her grandmother's stationery. She was surprised to find that the writing on the envelope was definitely not in her grandmother's handwriting.

Elise carefully broke the seal on the tip and took out the folded sheets of paper. The handwriting on the letter was not her grandmother's either.

Elise quickly flipped over the two sheets of paper, expecting to see a long list of 'to-do's'. Both sheets were covered in small neatly written sentences which ended with a very shaky signature that was barely recognisable as her grandmother's.

Elise took a sip of her coffee and began reading.

"My dearest Elise,

You have no doubt realised that this is not one of my usual letters. I find myself sadly unable to write, so Alex has kindly agreed to be my scribe. He doesn't trust his French, so we have agreed to him writing it in English.

I am so sad to have to tell you all this in a letter. It was always my plan to be able to sit down with you face to face and tell you everything, but, you know what they say about the best laid plans. I really didn't feel able to talk to you properly on Saturday, as I knew Louise was hovering around. I'm afraid that I have no time left. Alex begged me to call you, but Louise hasn't been coping at all well and absolutely refused to have you here.

I'm afraid there is no easy way to break this news to you, I have gone over this many times over the years, but I promised your mother that I would not tell you, and as with so many things, I have always felt unable to break my promise. I just hope that things I told you in my other letters will have given you some sort of an inkling, so that this does not come as too much of a shock."

Elise put the letter down for a moment. She glanced across at Jim; he had his nose buried in some papers, and didn't appear to be paying her any attention. She took another sip of her coffee. Elise felt afraid to read on. "Whatever could it be?"

Deciding that she had no alternative but to continue with the letter, Elise placed her coffee cup between her knees and forced her eyes back to the page.

"I'm sure that you remember when you were very little how your mother used to take to her bedroom and how quiet we had to be so as not to disturb her."

Elise did remember that certainly, Grandmere had always told her that her mother was suffering from headaches and they had tiptoed around for what felt like days on end with her grandma taking food to Louise on a tray in her room. Eventually her mother would emerge, and seem as bright as a button, but then it would happen again, and the tiptoeing around became part of their lives.

"I couldn't really find a way to explain to you that your mother was suffering from some sort of mental illness. I did tell you in my other letters that she had always been a bit different, even from being a small child, but she seemed to get better as she got older. Then when she got pregnant, it seemed to trigger everything off again.

I'm afraid that there isn't really an easy way to tell you this, so I am just going to say it: Your mother has been living her make-believe life since before you were born. She has never worked a day in her life, (as I found out that day when I went to London) but she made me promise to keep her secrets, and stupidly I agreed. I always thought that you would realise that something was amiss, and had made up my mind that if you asked, I would tell you everything, but you always accepted whatever Louise said without question and I felt honour-bound not to break my promise. I searched everywhere for a diagnosis and over the years I have taken her to one specialist after another, without ever finding out exactly what was wrong.

Medication has helped, but every so often she would refuse to take it and then have another breakdown, hence her 'business trips' as Louise used to call them.

I would take her to the hospital and she would stay there until the medication started working again and come home.

There is a day centre not far from our cottage, that provides support for people with mental health issues, and your mum would spend her days there. She convinced herself that it was her job. She never wanted you to know that there was anything wrong. In fact, I don't think she ever really realised that there was. She always thought that she was there as a member of staff, and a very senior one at that. The nurses told me that she would insist on being present at any meeting and would sit in the corner making copious notes and occasionally asking people to repeat or clarify points. Everyone went along with it, as it seemed to keep her happy.

Alex's grandfather and father have been helping me to look after her for years. We knew that she would not cope without me and everything has been put into place for her to live in a very nice home where all her needs will be taken care of.

I have left half the cottage to you, and the other half to your mother. Alex has sorted out some sort of trust for her, so she will have no financial worries. I've also given Alex a small sum of money to pay to get the cottage cleaned, and for my burial next to Tom.

I am not sure whether you would consider moving back into the cottage, or whether you would prefer to start afresh with somewhere of your own. The proceeds from the watch and Mrs Lehrmann's jewellery should have made you a very wealthy woman.

I have told Alex not to put the cottage on the market until you have decided whether or not you want to buy the other half. He will handle everything for you. The cleaning team will sort out the attic, but I have insisted that nothing be thrown away, apart from those damned cobwebs, and Tom's rusty old tools."

Chapter Forty-Six

Elise stopped reading, her hands were starting to shake uncontrollably, her knees began to knock and the coffee cup fell to the ground. Elise dropped the paper and as she bent down to try to retrieve them from the puddle of coffee, she felt Jim's arm on her shoulder.

"Are you all right?" he said, picking up the papers and placing them on the bench.

Jim sat silently on the bench with his arm around Elise to Jim sat down next to her and gently rested his hand on her shoulder. She couldn't control her emotions and gave up trying.

Elise's tears were a mixture of sadness and anger. She couldn't believe how stupid she had been. Even Amy had managed to figure out that her mother was 'Nuts', but somehow it had never crossed her mind to doubt anything that her mother and grandmother had told her. She blushed as she remembered Laurent's incredulity when she had recounted the story of her mother's 'career' and shook with disgust at her own naivete.

"I just can't believe that I never realised what was going on, and my poor mum, I could have at least tried to help, if I had known."

"Don't be so hard on yourself, Elise, when you grow up with something like this, it's just part of everyday life and you probably never questioned any of it, and to be fair, your grandmother was sworn to secrecy, so she probably made everything sound believable."

Elise shook her head. Jim was being very kind, but she cringed as she thought of the ludicrous lies she had had no problem believing.

"Your grandmother was adamant that you not be involved in any of this. She thought that you had suffered enough and was determined that you should not take on any responsibility for the care of your mother. That's why she insisted on you only getting this letter when you were in Paris; so that everything would already be sorted out. Dad has done everything to ensure that your mother is happy and receiving the best care possible, and that was what your grandmother wanted."

"Yes, but she's my mum, I can't just do nothing," replied Elise, her voice trembling as she tried to speak.

Jim quickly retrieved his papers and briefcase and returned to Elise's side. He placed his arm around her shoulder and the two sat side by side until Elise felt able to speak again.

"Do you think we could go back to my hotel?" she asked.

"Of course," said Jim, picking up the letter and the now empty coffee cup.

Elise headed straight for the bar and Jim followed her a few moments later.

"I've ordered coffee; do you think you could eat something?" Elise shook her head.

"No, I feel in a bit of a whirl at the moment, just trying to take all this in, but please, tell your dad not to sell Grandmere's cottage, I couldn't bear the thought of anyone else living there."

"You don't need to make a decision yet; Dad won't do anything until you are sure."

Elise nodded her head. "No, I'm absolutely sure, it's my home and I want to buy it, I don't care how much it is, I definitely want it."

"Okay, Elise, I'll let Dad know and he will deal with it. I heard about the watch, so I don't think you will have any problems; don't forget half of it is already yours."

"I've got a lot of jewellery as well, I thought it was just costume stuff, but apparently, it isn't, so I should have plenty of cash; at least if no one has burgled my flat!"

"Don't worry, I'm returning to England on Wednesday, I could go and retrieve it for you and take it over to Christie's if you want to sell it."

The thought of Jim entering her dingy flat was almost as frightening as the thought that burglars had been in. Elise shook her head.

"Thanks, but I'm actually going home on Wednesday as well. I've already booked my seat on the one o' clock Eurostar. I was planning to take the box to your dad for safe-keeping."

"We can travel together then," said Jim. "Dad's picking me up at St Pancras, we can drop by your flat and collect them for you. It will save you a journey and stop you worrying, you can have a chat to Dad then, and let him know about the house."

Elise shuddered at the thought of the flat again, but decided that she could quickly run in and grab them, without anyone else going in. She looked across at Jim and nodded. "Yes, that would be great."

Jim finished his coffee and got up from the chair. "Would you be up for dinner this evening? I can come back around seven, if you think you'll be hungry."

Elise shook her head. "Thank you, Jim, I really appreciate you being here today, but if you don't mind, I think I'd rather just have a bit of time to myself."

"No worries, I'll come and pick you up at eleven on Wednesday, so we can get the train together." Jim gave her a quick hug and headed out.

Elise ran for the lift and hid herself under her duvet. Everything was spinning,

In desperation, she grabbed her phone and called Amy.

Chapter Forty-Seven

After a long chat and a hot bath, Elise returned to her duvet. She didn't want to face anyone else today. "Never mind," she told herself, "You've dealt with worse shit than this." Even as she was saying she didn't quite believe it. Coming to terms with the fact that her mother was mentally ill was probably the worst thing anyone could deal with, but she had no option, so she was just going to have to. Elise switched off the light and pulled the cover over her head.

Sunshine burst uninvited into her room, and Elise shrugged off the covers.

She felt as if she had the worst hangover in the world, and struggled slowly to the bathroom.

Elise had a few jobs on her list and was determined to keep herself busy.

She pulled out the folder of sketches and placed them in a carrier bag.

After a very large coffee, she headed to Laurent's shop.

"You cannot be serious, Elise!" Laurent was shaking his head in shock as she handed him the folder.

"Absolutely, I insist, Laurent, I really think Grandmere wanted you to have them. You deserve them, and if they help you in your dream to be a fashion designer, then she would be delighted; oh, and by the way, I meant what I said about staying with me in London. I'm moving back home, so there will be plenty of room."

"I've got a little present for you, though it now pales by comparison," said Laurent as he disappeared into his office, returning a few moments later brandishing a shiny copy of Vogue.

"You're a star! Check out page 260," he said, handing over the magazine.

Elise quickly flipped to the page, and saw herself caught in flagrante flattening the vintage hat into her skull. The look of horror on her face caught Laurent by surprise and they both ended up in peals of laughter.

After a delicious lunch and lots of coffee, Laurent pulled his chair close to hers and placed his arms around her.

"This trip to Paris has been a real eye-opener for you, Elise, I'm so sorry to hear about your mum, but in fairness, from what you have told me, she has never really been a mum to you, and I think your grandmother acted out of love for you, rather than just protecting your mother. It's a terrible shock, but you're a survivor, and I know you will cope."

Elise wiped away the tears that seemed to be infuriatingly always lurking and grabbed her coffee.

"I have to get going, Laurent," she said, finishing her coffee.

"I'm leaving on Wednesday, but I really hope you will come and stay with me, even if it's only for a holiday."

Elise tucked the copy of Vogue into her handbag and with a last hug from Laurent, made her way back along the Rue Legendre.

Chapter Forty-Eight

Elise got back to her hotel and set about counting the money she had left in Grandmere's envelope. She still had seven thousand pounds left. Elise phoned reception to find out how much her bill would be. Paying in cash may be acceptable, but she was reasonably confident that they would expect euros rather than pounds.

The day stretched out ahead of her, and she wished she could just go and jump on a train now. Elise decided to get organised and opened her laptop to email Alex and tell him that she definitely wanted grandma's house. Elise had no idea how much it would cost, but with the money from the watch and her savings she felt that she couldn't be too far short. The thought of moving home filled her with a mixture of both dread and excitement.

Elise thought about their once beautiful garden and was determined to make that her first priority. The second would be the purchase of a 'helicopter chair'!

"I don't need to rush anything," Elise told herself, "I still have another week after Aberdeen to sort it all before I go back to work." Elise had tried not to think about her job. Now Armand was back on board, she was sure that all the 'crap' would be a distant memory, all she had to do was deal with the vile Alice, and she was determined to stand up to her the very next time that that nasty girl opened her mouth. Elise practised scathing comments and cutting responses in her head, she had done this countless times before, but never actually managed to say them out loud. Maybe next time would be different.

"Bollocks to her," decided Elise. "I'm still on holiday, I've got another ten days before I have to face her again, and I'm not going to waste it worrying."

With that, Elise grabbed her bag and went out for coffee. She suddenly had a mad moment and hailed a cab. Elise spent the rest of the day walking along the banks of the Seine reliving the memories of her childhood and trying to be a little more sympathetic towards her mother's bizarre behaviour.

Elise decided after a while to focus on the more positive aspects of her life.

She was going to be able to move back home, and to have enough money hopefully, to be able to enjoy life and make up for all the years she had missed. The thought that she might actually be able to look for another job and escape the constant fear of Alice also could actually be a possibility.

Elise was suddenly pulled from her reverie by an uneven paving stone which sent her sprawling. She landed flat on the ground, perilously close to the water's edge. An army of concerned citizens surrounded her and Elise found herself being lifted with great delicacy, and placed on a convenient bench by two very handsome men. An older lady, making appropriately sympathetic noises started wafting at her dress with a handkerchief, whilst another with great consternation, began rubbing the dirt from her handbag, which had taken the brunt of her fall.

Elise hardly dared to look up. Keeping her head down, to hide her glowing cheeks, she surreptitiously scanned the growing crowd of onlookers. To her surprise, no one was even trying to hide a smile, let alone giggling or pointing at her. Apparently, falling arse over tit in Paris was not considered the least bit amusing. She wasn't sure whether to be annoyed or impressed, when she realised, however, that her dress and bag were the recipients of concern, rather than herself.

Having reassured everyone that she was fine, and having carefully checked her outfit for any sign of injury, Elise arose from the bench with great panache and continued her walk; this time paying slightly more attention to the terrain.

Chapter Forty-Nine

The evening passed uneventfully, Elise ate in the bar at the hotel and then headed back to her room for another early night.

She woke early in the morning, this would be her last full day in Paris and Elise was determined not to waste it. She carefully packed her clothes after spending an inordinately long time choosing an outfit for dinner. Her mother played constantly on her mind, but she was determined not to let it spoil her last day here. She would have time on her return from Aberdeen to talk at length with Alex and would decide what to do after that.

Elise sat with her array of brushes and clips and set about drying her hair. After half an hour of struggling with errant hair and a brush that had tangled itself in an elaborate knot and refused to move, she gave up. After another shower and copious amounts of conditioner, she managed to ease the brush out. She hurriedly stuck her wet hair in a ponytail, dressed and headed back to the hairdresser's.

"I just can't get the hang of it." Elise groaned to the sympathetic stylist.

"You do have a lot of hair, why don't you just get it done in the salon?"

The thought of going to the hairdresser's every time her hair needed a wash was horrifying.

"Do people actually do that?" she asked. The look of incredulity on her face caused the stylist to burst into uncontrolled laughter.

"But of course, Madame, how do you think we stay in business! But if you do not have the time, just buy yourself a hairdryer with a brush attachment."

The woman disappeared and returned a few moments later, holding a very sleek-looking dryer. Elise looked in vain for the attachment.

"It's in the box," said the stylist with a smile.

She deftly attached and detached the brush. "See, it's really easy to use; just rough dry your hair with the dryer, and when it's nearly dry, put on some heat protector spray, stick on the brush and put the dryer on the cool setting."

The stylist handed the dryer over to Elise, who held it at arm's length, as if waiting for it to explode.

After a long lesson in drying from the extremely patient hairdresser, Elise bought the dryer and left the shop, feeling very proud of her glossy mane.

Elise was feeling at a loss. Her case was packed, (well apart from her latest purchase). She had exchanged money to pay for the hotel, and had nothing to do other than wait for dinner with Armand, and the famous Monsieur Duval.

Paris, beautiful, vibrant and exciting as it was, would have been much more fun, if she had not been alone.

Elise managed to drag lunch out for as long as she dared without incurring the wrath of the waiter, and then returned to her hotel. After a soak in the bath, she sat herself in front of the mirror and tackled her make up.

Clutching her beautiful Dior purse, and wearing her favourite rose-coloured dress and cream jacket, Elise slipped her feet into Grandmere's court shoes and headed for the lift. It was still only six o'clock, but she decided to treat herself to coffee in the bar.

Armand charged in at exactly seven o'clock, and greeted her with a bear hug and a very enthusiastic kiss.

The restaurant seemed extremely posh, so Elise walked in handbag first, hoping to reassure the Maître D' that she was a suitable candidate for dinner.

They were immediately taken to a table right in front of the window. Armand and Elise were both checking out the extensive wine menu, when Monsieur Alain arrived.

"Elise, wonderful to meet you, Armand has not stopped raving about you since you arrived. I now see that his approbation was if anything, understated."

Dinner was a delight, and all three enjoyed chatting about the wines. The sommelier spent a great deal of time at their table and Monsieur Alain managed to set up an appointment to return with some of his best wine for a special tasting event.

Elise shook her head, when presented with the dessert menu. Delicious as they sounded, she had already inadvertently jettisoned a forkful of rocket over her lap when Armand's footsies under the table extended into 'kneesies'. She was impressed by his ability to converse without missing a beat, whilst she could barely load up her fork without risking a catastrophic event. Now, with his thigh pressed hard against hers, she decided to forego any prospective mishaps, however inviting they appeared.

"Now, if I may, I would very much like to put a business proposition to you," said Monsieur Alain, fixing his gaze on Elise. She blinked, and nodded, wondering what on earth was coming next and praying that it did not involve offering Jean-Pierre work experience in London.

"As you know, my dear, we are expanding rapidly at the moment and poor Armand is struggling to keep up. So, we would be delighted if you would consider working for my company. You would be doing basically what you do now, just solely for us, dealing directly with our English customers, ensuring that we offer them the finest service, and, of course increase our presence in the UK market. I was hoping that my son could take on the task, but unfortunately, he seems to excel only in ineptitude, and I can only apologise profusely for his appalling behaviour towards you."

"Oh, no, Monsieur Alain, please do not say that about your son. His only mistake was to fall into the grasp of a very unpleasant young woman, who manages to manipulate people into behaving in a way that they would not normally dream of. She is a nasty bully, who's only excuse is that she has the brain the size of a snail! Your son wrote me a beautiful letter apologising for his behaviour and I do not hold him in any way responsible for what happened."

Elise, startled by her emotional outburst, leaned back in her chair, her cheeks glowing red and her eyes smarting with tears.

Monsieur Alain, looking equally bemused, reached out a hand and grasped hers.

"My dear, you are not only exceptionally talented and extremely beautiful, but also a kind and sensitive woman. I can see now why Armand is so captivated by you. You may rest assured that I love my son with all my heart, and have decided that he needs a few more years working beside Armand before he may safely be let loose abroad."

Elise tried to regain her composure, nodding slowly, hoping to give the impression that she was carefully mulling over Monsieur Alain's offer, as she tried to keep the offending tears at bay.

Taking her silence as a positive sign, he warmed to his theme and continued with great enthusiasm.

"Of course, we would need to spend some time discussing the finer details, and we would not expect you to make any decisions straight away, but perhaps if you could agree to let us know if it would be of interest to you within say a month, we could set up another meeting here, obviously at our expense to discuss the proposal in detail, and discuss your salary expectations. Do you think that it would be something that would be of interest to you?"

Elise was having difficulty focussing on anything other than Armand's hand which was now caressing her thigh; in desperation, she slid her hand under the table and firmly planted his hand back onto his own leg. Bracing herself, she met Monsieur Alain's gaze and nodded again.

"I'm hugely flattered by your offer, Monsieur Alain, and I promise you that I will definitely consider it. I have been thinking about moving on from First Blush, and this sounds like an amazing opportunity."

Elise decided that she had said enough. Her stomach was doing flips! This sounded too good to be true. Armand's hand had crept back onto her thigh and she didn't trust herself to say anything particularly rational at the moment.

Again, Monsieur Alain took her short response as a sign of true professionalism and nodded his approval.

"I am delighted that you are prepared to consider our proposal, I am sure that we can improve greatly on your current salary and ensure that we will put together a generous expense package for you."

After lingering over coffee and brandy, Monsieur Alain, having settled the bill, made his excuses and left the two of them at the table.

"Your place or mine?" asked Armand, leaning over to Elise, and planting a kiss on her lips."

"Definitely mine!" answered Elise.

Chapter Fifty

Lingering over an early breakfast with Armand, Elise was suddenly not looking forward to going home.

Armand also looked downcast as he held her hand across the table.

"I don't know how I will manage without you," he said with a heavy sigh.

"Promise me that you will think carefully about Alain's offer, and even if you decide not to take the job, please say that you will come back to Paris next month, to give me something to look forward to."

Elise smiled at him. "Of course, I shall, and I will definitely be back to see you, as soon as I can."

With a last lingering kiss, Armand left in a hurry for the office and Elise set about sorting out the last of her packing.

As usual, she was down in the lobby, suitcases packed and bill paid with over an hour to spare. She ordered a coffee and pulled out her precious copy of Vogue and settled down for a good read and a careful examination of the infamous photo.

"Hiya, Elise, ready to hit the road?"

Elise looked up to find Jim already grabbing her suitcases and followed him out to the waiting cab. She found herself enjoying his company and had to admit that it was much more fun to travel with a companion, especially one as nice as him.

The journey passed without incident, and they were soon back at St Pancras. Jim steered Elise out of the station where Alex was waiting in his car.

"Lovely to see you, Elise, hope you had a wonderful time?" Elise nodded into the rear-view window and they set off back to her flat.

Alex managed to squeeze his car in next to hers and she shot up the steps two at a time. The door looked exactly as she had left it, but she couldn't stop her stomach from churning as she pushed the key in the lock and bolted for the bedroom. She flung open the wardrobe door with such gusto that the whole thing nearly collapsed on top of her, and grabbed the chocolate box.

Still feeling slightly queasy, she headed back to the car. Shuddering in distaste at her dingy flat, she slammed the door shut, turned the key and skipped down the steps.

"Panic over," she said, handing the box to Jim as she fastened her seat belt.

"Wow," was all she heard as Jim examined the contents.

Alex, meanwhile, was trying to keep his eyes on the road as they drove back to his office.

Mrs Forbes was at the door, greeting her son with a huge bear hug, before turning and staring at Elise with ill-disguised astonishment.

"You look wonderful, my dear, Paris has certainly done you good," was all she could manage.

Once safe in his office, Alex pored over the box of jewels.

"I'm no expert, Elise," he said after a few minutes, "but I reckon you have some serious money in this box."

"Good," said Elise. "Does that mean that I won't have any trouble buying the other half of the cottage?"

"I think you could probably buy the entire street!" answered Alex.

"These should go to auction. If you are sure that you want to sell all of it, I can arrange that for you. Even after tax and the auctioneer's fee, you will certainly have no worries about anything."

Elise nodded. "Yes, I want to sell them, and I'd like to move back into the cottage as soon as possible."

"There is nothing to stop you moving back today, if you wish," said Alex.

"I've followed your grandmother's instructions to the letter and everything has been cleaned within an inch of its life."

"I'm going to stay with a friend for the weekend, but I would like to move back on Monday then. I still have my key; will that be okay?"

Alex nodded. "I'll take care of the paperwork, and you don't need to worry about anything."

Elise paused for a moment. She really wanted to talk to Alex about her mother, but knew that he would probably prefer to be spending some time with his son.

"Would it be okay if I popped over tomorrow to go through some things with you?" she asked.

"Of course, any time is fine, we can also set a date for the burial service for Madame Jacobs, just ask my wife to pop it in the diary, so I don't get waylaid by anyone else."

Elise got up to leave and shook her head as Jim jumped up to offer her a lift back to her flat.

"Absolutely not, I have a few things to do, and I'm sure that your mum won't be happy if you disappear again so soon after arriving."

Elise quickly arranged to come back the following afternoon and then headed down the high street to grab a cab back home.

Unpacking and packing again for her trip to Aberdeen took up the rest of the evening and Elise with only a few minutes to spare ran down to the Co-op to grab something to eat, steering well clear of the reduced for quick sale rack.

Chapter Fifty-One

Friday came and Elise arrived, as usual far too early for her flight. It would be her first time flying and she was feeling ever so slightly nervous. Putting on her best glide, she headed for the desk and checked in. As her suitcase disappeared on the belt, the ticket agent kindly directed her to the domestic flights lounge. Elise felt on top of the world. She couldn't wait to see Amy and for the first time, and had a huge list of exciting things to tell her!

Elise made herself as comfortable as she could in the aisle seat on the plane, and having eventually managed to buckle herself in, tried to take her mind off her virgin flight by reliving her meeting with Alex.

"You have nothing to worry about Elise," he had said, noticing her worried expression.

"I do need to tell you about the survey, though, the cottage needs new windows, extensive repairs to the roof, rewiring, and at the very least, a new boiler." Realising that his comments had turned Elise's worried expression into one of unmitigated horror, he had hurriedly moved on.

"You have absolutely no financial issues; the jewellery is most certainly worth far more than the purchase price of the cottage and any repairs that you wish to carry out. Even after the taxes and auctioneer's fee have been deducted, you will be a very wealthy woman. So please do not worry. Jimmy will take care of everything."

"What about Mum?" Elise had suddenly blurted out. "I don't even know where she is or what is happening to her, could you please tell me what's going on?"

Alex had told her everything, sadly leaving Elise in no doubt that her mother certainly would not welcome a visit from her.

"She has not taken the loss of your grandmother well, as we knew she wouldn't. It appears that she has reverted back to her childhood. It seems to be the only way that she can cope, and for the moment, the doctors have decided to let her be. I don't think that she would acknowledge you if you tried to visit and to be honest, it would probably be better if you leave it until she is ready."

Elise was rudely pulled back into the present as the stewardess leaned across her with coffee for the man seated next to her. Elise refused the offer of a drink; she was terrified at the thought of her knees getting in the way of the strange-looking table.

"Elise, Elise; over here!" Elise had followed all the other passengers into the arrivals area, and looking up, she immediately tried to run backwards.

A sea of multi-coloured balloons and a huge "Happy Birthday, Elise" banner was being held aloft for all the world to see; underneath she could just about make out the beaming faces of Amy, Angela and Charlie.

Amy's voice could be heard above all the clamour in the packed hall, and Elise, realising that the only way to shut her up would be to reach her as quickly as possible, set off at a fast trot taking the most direct route possible and causing other travellers to leap out of her way.

"For God's sake, Amy, shut up," she said as soon as she got within earshot.

Amy gave her a hug that squeezed every last bit of oxygen out of her lungs and then stood back to allow Angela and Charlie to move in for the kill.

"Wow," said Amy, standing back and gazing at Elise with unabashed admiration.

"You look stunning!"

Elise in turn, stared back at her friend. "You don't look so bad yourself, Amy. What have you been doing?"

Amy shrugged. "My car broke down, and I've had to bloody walk everywhere, and to be fair, I couldn't face being the fat bride with you two as my bridesmaids!"

At this, Angie blushed a very deep red that almost put her crimson hair to shame. She looked different from their last meeting at the Pride Festival, but Elise couldn't quite put her finger on what it was.

"Let's get out of here," said Charlie, taking hold of Elise's case. "We can get a cab to your hotel, and our place is just around the corner."

Amy and Angie linked arms with Elise and they headed for the taxi rank, with Charlie bringing up the rear.

The hotel, whilst not quite on a par with the Batignolles, was clean, pleasant and very handy. Charlie and Angie headed back to the flat to give Elise and Amy time to catch up.

Elise threw her suitcase on the bed and then dragged Amy off to the nearest coffee bar, for some much needed catching up. Two large cappuccinos later, Amy couldn't help but smile. "God, it's so nice to see you happy for once, Elise, I mean, I'm sorry about your mum and everything, but at least you've got no worries anymore and the airman sounds like he's got the goods, I suppose we'll just have to forgive him for the pizza and the booze! So long as you like him, that's all that really matters."

"What about you, Amy, is everything okay? You didn't tell me Angie was visiting." Elise had known Amy for too long not to realise that all was not well.

"Come on, you can tell me, it's not anything to do with Charlie, is it?"

Amy quickly shook her head. "No, me and Charlie are fine, it's just Angie's got herself into a bit of a mess. Mum's kicked her out, so she's staying with us for now, till we can sort something out."

Elise was enormously surprised, as far as she knew, Angie being at home had been a godsend to her mother. Their father had suffered a stroke some years ago, and needed a lot of care.

"Oh, you know Mum," said Amy with a sigh, "She was as happy as Larry, having Angie there, doing everything, but, well, in case you hadn't realised, Angie's pregnant, and Mum said she had enough crap to deal with looking after Dad, and wasn't up to having a baby in the house, so she just chucked her out."

Elise wasn't quite sure that she had heard properly.

"Did you just say that Angie was pregnant? How did that happen? I thought she was with Emily. I didn't think she liked men?"

"Oh, you know Angie, she's a free spirit, and goes where the fancy takes her! She's always said that she likes who she likes, and never cared whether they were men or women. I'm just shocked because I thought she was really happy with Emily and now everything has gone tits up." Amy was trying to sound quite 'matter of fact', but Elise could hear the tremor in her voice, and knew that her friend was devastated by what had happened. Amy took a deep breath and carried on with the story.

"She got off her face at one of her raves in Brighton, and ended up shagging some bloke on the pier. She swears she barely remembers any of it! Angie has no idea who the father is, so there's zero chance of him helping, so basically, we are in the shit! The baby's due in three months, and it's not going to be much fun trying to squeeze all of us into the flat."

"There's no need," said Elise, "I'm moving back into the cottage, there's loads of room for Angie and the baby, and it's only down the road from the tattoo parlour, so she will be able to carry on working if she wants."

Elise had made up her mind. For the first time in her life she was in a position to help someone, and Angela had been her hero ever since that fateful day at the school gates.

"She can come back with me on the plane if she's up for it, and we can get everything organised."

Amy was dumbfounded. "Elise, are you really sure about this? It's a hell of a commitment with a baby on the way."

"No, it's perfect, I can't wait! Let's just hope Angie agrees."

Angie was stunned. "My God, Elise, are you for real? Don't you need to think about it a bit."

"Nope, I'll go online now and book you a ticket; you can fly back with me."

Charlie had refused all invites to the pizza parlour, and despite Elise's protestations, insisted that he was taking himself to the pub to watch the footy.

"Go and have one of your girly nights," he said with a big grin. "I can do without all that natter and with three girls to deal with, I'm going to need a pint!"

Later, having fought just like old times over dessert, and over Elise's insistence on picking up the tab, the three girls sat nursing their coffees whilst Amy happily munched on the mints.

"I feel so ashamed of myself," said Elise, "I've been such a skinflint and a penny-pincher, and missed out on so much, that I feel like I've suddenly been given a chance to do something good. I don't know how I would have survived without you two in my life, so please don't begrudge me trying to repay you."

"Don't be such a silly cow, Els," snorted Amy; "I know our life wasn't exactly a bed of roses, but it was bloody paradise compared with all the shit you had to deal with. Stop beating yourself up."

Angie shook her head at Elise. "Look, I remember how upset you were when you got kicked out of the house, blimey, I'm thirty-five and I was shitting myself when mum told me to pack my bags. You were only a kid. I think you should be proud of what you've achieved. You never sat back on your arse and moaned; you just got yourself a job and a flat and got on with it."

"At least it makes a bit more sense now," added Amy. "We thought your granny was a right cow for not letting you stay, but she must have known your mum was a psycho and thought you'd be better off out of it."

Chapter Fifty-Two

Two days later, after lots of frantic kissing and hugs, Elise and Angie boarded the plane back to London.

"I can't believe this is actually happening," said Angie, as they buckled their seat belts.

"This time last week, I felt so bloody desperate; no Emily, no home and no fucking hope, and now I actually feel like I can start looking forward to my baby."

"You do want to have this baby?" Elise asked, recalling the way her grandmother had talked about her own impending birth and suddenly being overcome with fear at the thought of another child entering this world to be greeted by an unloving and bitter mother.

"God, yes, I mean, I was a bit shell-shocked when I realised, but I've always wanted a baby, just kinda never thought it was on the cards. Emily had always talked about having a family; I just don't think this was the way she had in mind. I only found out a few days before Pride, and of course I told her straight away. I thought she might be all right with it, but it was more the cheating than the baby that pissed her off. She broke up with me that evening, and we haven't spoken since."

"I'm so sorry, Angie," said Elise, "I thought things were a bit off when I met you, but well, it can't be helped and you never know, she might change her mind when the baby's here."

Angie shook her head. "No chance of that, she's met someone else. I've been stalking her on Facebook, so that's the end of it. Anyway, let's think of some decent names, and see if we can come up with a winner before we land."

"Job done!" said Angela, unbuckling her belt. "Frank if it's a boy and Giselle if it's a girl."

Elise nodded. "Definitely love both of those, now if I can just stand up without bashing my head, we'll be fine."

Elise insisted on carrying Angela's large tote bag and pulling her own as they walked out of the terminal. "No way," she said as Angie remonstrated with her.

"Come on, we need to find Jim, he's just messaged me to say he's here."

"Who's Jim? I thought your man was back in Paris?" Angie was intrigued.

"So, you've gone from no man to having two in tow, I like your style."

"No, Jim's just my friend, he's lovely, and he's going to drop us straight back to the cottage so we can start sorting everything out."

"You know, I like that name; 'Jim' ... I think that's better than 'Frank' ... now I'm torn." Angie grinned. "Blimey this name game is harder than I thought."

"Just have both, then he can choose: 'Frank James Macey'. It's got a definite ring to it."

"Done and dusted." Angie laughed. "No more 'name changing'; that's it."

She gave Frank James or maybe Giselle a gentle pat and pottered off after Elise.

Jim was waiting in the arrivals hall, and rushed over, giving Elise a quick hug and grabbing the bags. Angela was most impressed with his very posh car and commandeered the front seat.

Jim tried as hard as he could not to stare at Angie's hair or her amazing array of tattoos. He couldn't imagine for the life of him what this strange girl and Elise could possibly have in common.

"But," he thought, "it takes all sorts!"

"Dad says the house is all ready for you, the cleaners have been in and everything is done. If you like, we could sort out a time to go through all the repairs and improvements and organise some quotes."

"I just need to get settled in first and move my stuff out of the flat," said Elise. "I don't think I'm ready to cope with a load of builders just yet."

"No worries," Jim answered. At that moment, a piercing shriek filled the car. Jim almost stamped on the brakes until Angela stuck her hand in her pocket and retrieved her phone.

"Sorry, Jim, just my text alert."

"You won't believe this, Els. Jake has just sent me a message saying that I can start back at work as soon as! Apparently, they've got a great long waiting list, and he says he'll sort me out some maternity leave and everything."

"Are you really up for going back to work before the baby arrives?" asked Elise.

"God yes, I've only been away from the parlour for three weeks and I'm bored shitless! Anyway, it's only down the road from where you live, I'll be able to walk there in twenty minutes."

"You can't walk, Angela, what happened to your car?"

Angie pulled a very sad face; her beloved Morris Traveller had eventually died after a 'very long illness' and had been towed ignominiously to the nearest car graveyard. "He's dead and buried, I'm afraid, and defo no funds for a replacement," she said with a grin.

"No probs, if Alex hasn't already sold it, you can have my gran's old car, it's ancient, but it's only done about ten miles, so it should be fine to get you to work and back."

"Are you shitting me, Els? I'm beginning to feel like I've won the bleeding lottery."

Jim pulled into the driveway of the cottage and Elise walked slowly up to the door. She felt strangely nervous. The thought that this was, or at any rate was soon to be her very own, was overwhelming. Angela, however, was beside herself with excitement.

"Come on, Els, get the bloody door open!" Elise obediently unlocked the door and they piled in.

Angie insisted on checking out all the rooms on the ground and second floor, before making her way up the tiny flight of stair to the top floor. She watched as Elise opened the door to the attic.

"This place is unbelievable," shrieked Angela. "Could this be my room?" she asked, opening the door and peering into the attic. With a newly washed window and spectacularly free of cobwebs and rusty tools, the attic did look much more inviting than Elise ever remembered it.

"It's up a lot of stairs, are you sure you can cope?" she asked, staring at Angela's stomach which appeared to be growing by the day.

"No, it's absolutely perfect, it's meant for me, if you really don't mind."

"Absolutely not, if you are sure, I'm going to move into my grandma's old room, I love the view over the garden."

With the major decisions made, the two girls made their way back down the stairs to where Jim was waiting.

"I've had a quick look round, and nothing seems to be that urgent, though I suggest you get the boiler and the central heating sorted, before the baby arrives; oh, I nearly forgot, I've got some milk and coffee and stuff that Mum put in the boot for you, so you don't have to run out to the shops. I just rang Dad, the car is still in the garage, and the keys are in the kitchen drawer, so it's all yours."

Elise followed Jim out to the car and picked up the bag of goodies from Mrs Forbes. "I can't thank you enough for everything you and your dad have done for me, Jim. I still can't quite believe it all, but you've been so wonderful."

Jim smiled, giving Elise a quick hug. "No problem, Elise, I'll start getting some quotes for the heating, doesn't seem like we have much time to waste!"

Elise ran back into the house, to find Angela exploring the kitchen.

"This place just gets better and better," she said, plugging in the kettle.

"But what's with all the bin liners under the window?" Elise followed her gaze out of the kitchen window and saw a long line of very full black bags stacked up neatly next to the wheelie bin.

"It's probably all the stuff out of the attic," she said. "Alex told me that the cleaning team had been told not to throw anything away, apart from rusty tools and broken stuff."

"There must have been a lot of crap up there to fill all those bags," said Angela. "Shall we go and have a peek?"

"Yuk, I don't think so; they will be just be full of filthy cobwebs and spiders!"

Angela was already half way out the door. "You make a cuppa, and I'll go and explore, you never know, there might be something useful, and I don't give a shit about cobwebs, and the spiders will run away when they see me!"

Elise busied herself with making the tea, but couldn't help smiling as Angela worked her way down the row of bags, carefully untwisting and then re-twisting each one before moving to the next.

She returned a few minutes later, looking slightly confused.

"A couple of bags have dust and stuff in them, but all the others are filled with weird broken china; looks like someone's had a cat fight and…"

Angela stopped mid-sentence as she heard Elise's cup clatter onto the draining board and saw her run out into the garden and start tugging at the bags.

Angela appeared beside her. "Whatever is it, Elise? What's wrong?"

"They're Mum's cats; they meant the world to her. Why would someone do that? It's so cruel, she's going to be heart-broken." Elise searched frantically among the debris, desperately trying to find a cat that was still in one piece.

Angela put her arm around Elise. "Come on, Els, you're going to cut your hands on that stuff. I'm sure the cleaners wouldn't have done it. Look, come back inside, I'll make you another drink and we can ring your solicitor man; maybe he knows something about it."

Nursing a fresh cup of tea, Elise opened the door to her mother's study. Apart from the desk and chair, the room was completely empty and spotlessly clean.

"What's in there?" asked Angela, heading towards a small door.

"It's just a little storage room, and I've never looked inside."

Angela pulled on the doorknob.

"I can't open it, it's locked, check the desk drawers and see if there's a key."

Elise started checking the drawers, but they were empty. Elise shrugged her shoulders. "There's nothing in here," she said, but Angela wasn't about to give up and reaching up, she ran her hand along the top of the door frame.

"Got it!" she shouted, triumphantly and shoved the key in the lock.

Both girls stood back in amazement at the contents; Shelves lined the walls of the room and every one was stacked with carrier bags. Elise recognised some of the logos from high street fashion shops; other bags looked much more 'high end' with cord handles and raised lettering. Angela pounced on the bags and began opening them.

"Els, you've got to see these; everything is brand new, still got the price tags on."

They started opening the other bags, every one contained clothing, all complete with labels and price tags.

"Where do you think they came from?" asked Angela, who feeling exhausted, had plonked herself in the office chair.

"I'm more worried about how she paid for them," replied Elise. "There must be thousands of pounds' worth of stuff here. God knows where Mum got the money from!"

Elise sat silently on the floor, surrounded by the piles of clothing. After a few minutes, she turned to Angela. "You know, I think Mum has been doing this for years; she used to come in from time to time, loaded up with bags. Announcing that she had a new case and needed a new look.

"Grandmere never said anything, but a few days later, I would trail round the shops with her, returning everything. When I asked her, she just said that Mum had changed her mind."

Angela got off the chair and delved into some of the open bags.

"Well, she didn't steal anything, the receipts are in the bags, it looks like she bought all this stuff in the last couple of months, so you should be able to take some of it back and get a refund or a credit note."

"I'm going to ring Alex, I need to know what the hell has been going on."

Chapter Fifty-Three

"Alex is on his way over," Elise told Angela. "Come on, let's have something to eat and wait for him to come."

Half an hour later, there was a loud knock at the door, and Elise ran to open it. Alex and Jim were standing there and Elise beckoned them in.

"I'm really sorry, Elise, all those bags should have gone last week. I didn't want you to find them. Louise wanted to take them all with her, and when the nurses told her that there was not enough room and suggested that she picked her favourites, she started shouting and swept them all off the shelves. One of the girls managed to salvage a couple, but they just wanted to get her out of there as quickly as possible before it escalated into a full-blown meltdown. The doctor rang me and I asked the cleaners to get rid of the broken ones.

"They were supposed to have arranged to have everything picked up. I'll sort it out. I really am sorry, it was the last thing that I wanted you to see."

Elise nodded. "I should have guessed, I'm just more worried about all this shopping. How did she get the money to pay for it all?"

Alex poked his head around the office door. "She's always had a thing about shopping sprees," he said, shaking his head at the hoard. "She's always had her own bank account, and had an allowance each month, and sometimes she did go a bit overboard. Madame Giselle had a debit card, and had written the number down, Louise found it and emptied the account when your grandmother was bedridden."

Seeing Elise's stricken face, he quickly added:

"Don't worry, Elise, your grandmother gave me a large amount of money for safe-keeping. The bank got in touch with her when they realised large amounts of cash were being drawn out and I put a stop on the account. Unfortunately, there was very little left by then. But again, there is nothing for you to worry about. It's all been taken care of."

Angela, seemingly unfazed by the conversation, quickly interjected. "So, all this stuff is legit, and Elise can do what she likes with it."

"Absolutely," replied Alex.

"No worries, then Els, we can take back what we can and eBay the rest!"

"Perfect solution, Angela," said Jim. "You look like you might be in need of some new stuff soon."

Angela tugged at her t-shirt. "Yeah, I'm beginning to look like Winnie-the-pooh!"

Jim and Alex said their goodbyes after handing over the paperwork for grandma's car to Angela. "There you go, once it's insured, you'll be ready to go."

Elise couldn't face going out that evening, and they ended up sitting at the kitchen table munching on pizza, garlic bread and spicy wedges.

"You're all right, aren't you, Els? You must be feeling stressed out of your brain with all this shit."

Elise nodded. "I feel a bit shell-shocked, but I'm getting used to that," she said with a smile. "Come on you, it's getting late, and I've still got to make up the beds. You'll have to make do with my old room until we figure out how to get a bed into the attic."

After a late start and a lazy breakfast, Angela set herself the task of sorting out the shopping. "I'll make a start on taking this lot back to the shops, and see how much money we can raise, if you're sure you don't want any of it."

Elise shuddered in horror. "I don't want to ever see any of that ever again. You'll be doing me a favour, getting shut of it, and use the money to get yourself some new stuff. Could you drop me off at my flat, so I can start packing up my stuff? I've sorted out the insurance, so you're good to go!"

Angela obligingly drove Elise to her flat and insisted on coming in to help.

"There's still some room on the back seat of my car," she said proudly, tapping the steering wheel. "We'll be done in half the time."

Elise, unable to persuade her otherwise, grudgingly walked up the steep steps and opened the door.

"Jesus, what a shithole!" said Angela, as she turned herself sideways to escape from the tiny kitchen.

"How the hell could you stomach living here?"

Elise shook her head. "You know what, Angela, I have no bloody idea, so let's just get my clothes and bits out and get out."

Elise emptied the wardrobe and chest of drawers, piling everything on the back seat of Angela's car, then staggered back down the steps with her mirror and trunk. Everything else was unceremoniously dumped into the skip.

After an exhausting couple of hours, Elise carefully photographed the electricity meter reading and locked the door. Everything else could be done from the comfort of the cottage, and Elise couldn't wait to escape.

Angela gave her a hug. "Better make sure your car starts before I go," she said.

Elise had great faith in her trusty little car, and jumped in. The engine spluttered into life and Angela waved before pulling out of the tiny car park.

"We're going home," Elise announced to no one in particular and set off back to the cottage.

Elise didn't feel really free of the place until she had emailed her notice to the landlord and arranged to return the key.

She sat at the table with a fresh cup of coffee and for the first time in a while started to think about work; only a few days left before she had to face the horrors of Alice, and sort out whatever chaos Gerry had created in her absence.

Chapter Fifty-Four

Leaving Alice and Kate gaping after her, Elise glided out of the 'ladies', then scurried over to her desk. Her heart was pounding, and her stomach was again doing somersaults. She was furious with herself for letting Alice get under her skin in the space of about five minutes. She would have to man up, or failing that, take up Angie's offer to come and 'sort her'.

As Elise leant forward to switch on her computer, she heard the office door open. Thinking that Kelly had actually managed to learn the code whilst she had been away, she glanced back at the keyboard.

"Morning, Elise, I'm so glad that you came back!" Elise looked up to see Mike standing in front of her, behind was a very attractive woman, with perfect hair and head to toe couture. Elise couldn't help but be impressed.

"Mike, how lovely to see you," she said, jumping up from her chair.

"Allow me to introduce my sister, Miranda, she's usually the silent partner, but today she's made an exception."

"Is there somewhere a little more private to sit?" asked Miranda.

Elise nodded. "Well, we could sit in Gerry's office, he's not here yet, I'm sure he wouldn't mind."

"I don't think that's going to be a problem," said Mike, leading the way. At that moment, Alice and Kate burst out of the toilets.

Alice stopped in her tracks.

"Mum, Uncle Mike, I thought you were still up in Scotland, when did you get back?"

Miranda cast her eyes slowly over her daughter. "We got back two days ago. We both wanted to thank you personally for holding the fort whilst Elise has been away, and of course, for all your hard work. It must have been such a difficult decision for you, having to miss your grandmother's funeral."

Alice gave her mother a quick peck on the cheek. "Yes, it's been hell; I will probably need a few days off, now Elsie's back, just to recuperate."

Mike opened the office door and stood back as Elise and Miranda walked in.

"Are we having a meeting?" asked Alice.

"We are," said Miranda, "so off you go and carry on all your good work, we wouldn't want you to keep any of your clients waiting." She then firmly closed the door and sat down. Alice, however, was not giving up without a fight and barged into the room.

"If this is a management meeting, then shouldn't I be involved? I have been virtually running the place since Elsie went, and shouldn't Gerry be here too?"

"Alice, why don't you make yourself virtually useful? Go and get us all some coffee."

"What would you like, Elise?" asked Miranda, taking her daughter firmly by the arm and ushering her back out into the corridor.

"Cappuccino, please," said Elise in a barely audible whisper.

"Right, a cappuccino for Elise, and two lattes for me and Mike. Sugar, Elise?"

Elise shook her head. Alice was glaring at her with unconcealed fury.

"But it's Elsie's job to do the coffee run." She protested still resolutely hovering by the door.

"Not anymore," said Miranda, closing the door in Alice's face.

Alice flounced through the office. "Kate," she screamed, "go and get some bloody coffee."

Kate jumped up as if she had been shot.

"A fucking cappuccino for the scarecrow, and lattes for Mum and Uncle Mike. Get me a caramel latte, and hurry up. They're about to fire her, and I don't want to miss anything."

"What do you mean, why would they fire Elise?" Kate was beginning to feel more nervous, with every passing second.

"Don't be dumb! The office has been running fine without her, why would they keep her on? Gerry must know about it, that's why he isn't here. He's probably just giving them a chance to tell her in private. Anyway, I've proved that I'm more than capable of doing that silly cow's job. So, it's my time to move up the ladder."

Kate took twenty pounds from the petty cash tin and set off to the coffee shop. She felt the need for some fresh air! The thought of having Alice running the office was just too much to stomach. Alice had spent the last four weeks indulging in one long shopping expedition, showing up occasionally to drink coffee and have a chat with Gerry. He in turn had spent the last few weeks trying to hide from Arek, and had barely noticed Alice's absence.

Kate shuddered at the thought of Gerry's smirking face and floppy hair. The office without Elise had been unmitigated hell. Arek had been running around like a lunatic; pausing only to march into Gerry's office for daily shouting matches.

She and Arek had done their best to cope. It hadn't taken either of them very long to realise just how much work Elise did, and how completely useless Gerry had proved to be.

"Well, I'm glad she's back, and I know someone else who will be delighted as well!" Kate thought to herself, and entered the coffee shop, waving frantically at the young man standing behind the counter.

Chapter Fifty-Five

Elise's heart sank. Her trip to Paris had obviously not met with their approval; she sat quietly on the chair, awaiting her fate.

"I can't apologise enough for my daughter's rudeness, Elise; she is, I'm afraid, a perfect example of a spoiled brat, and I must take at least some of the blame for that." Miranda sat down, carefully smoothing out her skirt, and looked across at Mike.

"Firstly, please accept my abject apologies. Unfortunately, I, Miranda and my wife have all been up in the wilds of Scotland for the past month, taking care of my mother, and sadly for the last two weeks, dealing with her estate. There was no internet connection, and hardly any reception, so we've all been out of the loop. I only found out what had been going on, when we got to the airport and all the emails came flooding in." Mike stopped to draw breath, and Miranda took over.

"Arek arranged to meet us on Saturday and he certainly didn't hold back. To say we were appalled, is putting it very mildly; anyway, the upshot of it all is that we had a meeting yesterday with Gerry, and he decided that it was time for him to move on. He is going to start up his own company, so we decided that gardening leave was appropriate. Needless to say, he will not be coming back."

Elise was beginning to feel very light-headed and confused. She had no idea what gardening leave meant, and wasn't even sure that Gerry had a garden. If he had gone and she was about to be sacked, who was going to be running the place? Surely, they couldn't be putting Alice in charge?

A loud knock on the door stopped everyone in their tracks.

"Come in," said Mike, pleasantly surprised by his niece's sudden display of manners.

He was sadly disappointed to see Kate enter the office.

"That one's yours, Elise," said Kate, carefully putting the cup down on the desk. She handed the others to Mike and Miranda and rushed out of the office nearly tripping over Alice who was crouching behind the door.

Kate was about to say something, but changed her mind when she saw the furious look on Alice's face.

Alice's legs were beginning to ache; they all seemed to be whispering, and even with her ear pressed against the door, she could hardly make out a word.

"How fucking long does it take them to tell the bitch to take a hike?" she thought to herself. Her calves were beginning to cramp. But she managed to bunny hop round enough to wave at Kate.

Kate had sat herself at the far end of the office, she felt utterly miserable, and extremely nervous. She checked her watch for the umpteenth time. "Where on earth was everyone?" She knew Kelly had an appointment at the dentist, but Gerry, Arek and Dave should have been in ages ago. "Did they know?" she wondered. "Maybe Mike had emailed them and given them the 'heads up' about sacking Elise."

Kate noticed Alice waving her arms in her direction. Her heart sank. Was that it? Had they sacked Elise? Kate wanted to cry. She was suddenly overwhelmed by an intense feeling of hatred for Alice. The thought that Mike and Miranda actually believed all the crap Alice had fed them about running the office, made her blood run cold. Alice was possibly the laziest and most incompetent girl Kate had ever had the misfortune to work with, and the possibility that she might be about to be given Elise's job was too much to bear.

Alice didn't seem to have heard anything as she was making no effort to move away from the door.

"Coffee," she mouthed furiously at Kate.

Kate walked over to Alice's desk and casually picked up the cup. She headed towards the desk closest to Gerry's office, sat down and started poking around industriously in one of the empty drawers. She glanced through the glass; all that was visible was the back of Elise's bowed head, which was blocking out Mike. Kate took her chance and grabbing the cup, slid off the chair and on to her knees. She then shuffled towards Alice, holding the coffee aloft. Alice grabbed the cup and glared again at Kate.

"I've been cutting you some slack recently, Kate," she whispered. "But once I'm in charge, you'd better pull your finger out and watch your back, otherwise, you're going to find yourself out on your fat arse."

With that Alice turned her back and pressed her ear against the door.

"Alice," hissed Kate, "you can't do that, the others will be arriving any minute."

As if by magic, the familiar buzzer sounded as the office door opened. Kate in her haste to stand, lurched forward and toppled over the crouching Alice, who in turn went sprawling across the floor, and started screaming as the coffee pooled under her chest.

"Get off me! I can't fucking breathe," she shouted, managing at the same time to viciously elbow Kate in the ribs.

Arek and Dave momentarily transfixed, sprang into action and sprinted across the carpet. They quickly helped Kate to her feet and sat her in the nearest chair.

Mike in the meantime had opened Gerry's door and was staring with disgust at his still screaming niece. Without a word, he stepped over her and was quickly followed by his sister and Elise.

"Hi guys! Perfect timing," he announced with a grin.

"I'm sure you would all like to join me in congratulating Elise, as she has kindly agreed to take on the task of running this place."

Cheers erupted from Arek and Dave, and even Kate managed a teary smile. Alice, steaming with rage at being ignored, suddenly jumped to her feet.

"You can't be serious," she shrieked. "That's my fucking job, and where the hell is Gerry?"

Mike, averting his gaze from his coffee-stained niece, continued.

"Gerry has left to start up his own company, and we wish him the very best. Miranda and I have a meeting with a client, so we shall leave you all in the more than capable hands of Elise."

Miranda took Elise's hand and leaning forward, whispered in her ear. "The hiring and firing is all in your hands now, so if you feel that you have anyone here who might cause you problems, remember that you have my blessing, if you choose to dismiss them." With a wink, and a smile, she and Mike headed towards the door, leaving Alice squealing in the background.

Arek grabbed Elise's hand. "God, am I pleased to see you, this is going to be wonderful."

Dave, who had been kneeling by Kate's chair, stood up and added his enthusiastic congratulations. Elise walked over to Kate, who was crying quietly into Dave's once pristine handkerchief, and held out her hand.

"How about it, Kate, do you think you can cope with me as your boss?"

Kate looked up at her. "I can't imagine anything better." She managed with a strangled sob.

Elise, drawing herself up to her full height, turned to face Alice. Alice, incandescent with rage, found herself having to tilt her head back to look Elise in the eye.

"What about you, Alice?" said Elise, lowering her head towards Alice. "Do you think you would like to work with me?"

Alice cocked her head to one side, and raised a finger to her cheek.

"Really, Elsie, that's so kind of you, let me think about it for a minute."

Silence reigned as Alice tapped her manicured finger nail against her cheek.

"There, I've thought about it. No, go and fuck yourself. I'm going to call Gerry. I'm sure that he needs someone of my expertise to help him, and with you in charge, the firm will be bust in a week."

With that, Alice turned towards Kate. "Get your bag, Kate, I'm sure Gerry and I can find something for you too."

Kate shook her head. "Sorry, Alice, I'm staying here."

Alice was stunned for a moment. "Perhaps you're right, Kate, to be fair, you don't really have the right image for us; so, you're probably better off staying put with the rest of these losers."

Without a backward glance, Alice tottered across the office and slammed the door shut behind her.

"Ding Dong," shouted Dave, giving first Kate and then Elise a huge hug. The door buzzer sounded again. Everyone smiled with relief as Kelly wandered in.

"Hi everyone, sorry I'm a bit late. Did I miss anything?"

"No, Kelly, nothing to worry about. I'm treating everyone to coffee and cakes, I won't be long."

Elise took the stairs two at a time. Her head was buzzing, and a huge smile had appeared on her face. A strange sensation was coursing through her veins, and she had no idea what it was.

She walked into the coffee shop and heard the girl at the desk shout Freddie's name.

As Freddie bolted across the shop to greet her, Elise realised what the strange feeling was: pure unadulterated happiness!

The End